THE DRAGON'S GLARE

BOOK TWO

THE SURVIVAL TRILOGY

BY

T.J. & M.L. WOLF

WITHDRAWN

This is Book Two of THE SURVIVAL TRILOGY.

In Book One, *A Gleam of Light*, a surprise plea for help brought Una Waters back to the Hopi Reservation where she grew up, to help solve a mystery that threatened their traditional way of life.
With the help of friends, new and old, Una confronted her painful past, found proof to qualify an ancient site for protection under law, and stood up to a stiff-necked general, whose agenda was more concerned with retrieving a mysterious power source.

COPYRIGHT

Cover illustration
by Rebekah Sather

ISBN: 1981840877
ISBN-13: 978-1981840878

CONTENTS

CONTENTS

CONTENTS

PART ONE

THE UNEXPLAINED

---

*"Real knowledge is
to know the extent of one's ignorance."*

--Confucius

1

LIGHT THE LANTERNS

Confetti swirled through the cold night air, just after dark on February 5, 2019, as people gathered along Mott Street in Lower East Manhattan. It fell in their hair, on their clothes. Mostly first and second generation Asian immigrants, they eyed the spectacle of dancers and acrobats, drums, and music making its way through Chinatown.

Una Waters tightened a traditional Hopi shawl around her neck, trying to cope with 20 degree weather and 40 mph winds. This wasn't exactly her idea. But offers to attend anything remotely festive did not come along that often, and she needed a change of pace.

Political chaos in D.C. had taken its toll. She'd lost too many colleagues to budget cuts, leaving her Department short-handed. When a coworker contracted the flu just two days before, she jumped at the chance to take his place in New York. Sure, it was unfamiliar territory, but the Interior Secretary said she had "good instincts" and would get plenty of help from local police.

She only hoped it would save her sanity.

A stout, white-haired oriental, wrapped in a bright red scarf waved at one of the marchers. "*That's* my grandson," she said, eyeing an eight-year-old in a pink hooded jumpsuit with disc-like snout and swinish ears atop his head.

A ginger between them smiled, "It's the year of the--"

"*Pig*," said Una to her friend, "Yeah, I get that."

A colorful cardboard tube popped suddenly nearby, releasing more confetti. Una jerked away--and bit into one corner of her lip, causing it to bleed.

"Relax!" said Madelyn, offering a tissue from her *Coach* leather handbag, "What's the worst that could happen? It's a *parade*, for god's sake! Not the end of the world!"

Una shuddered, pressing the tissue to her lip. It clotted quickly in the cold. "There's...too much going on!"

She *thought* a trip to the Big Apple might break up a long winter. Everyone said it would be 'fun'. But with towering edifices at every turn and stifling crowds, she found it increasingly hard to breathe.

"I just...need some air," she said, stepping off the curb.

There she abruptly froze, face-to-face with the gaping maw of a Chinese dragon, with yellow fangs and piercing red eyes, carried by dancers using poles at regular intervals to simulate the undulating movements of the mythical beast.

Madelyn pulled her back. "Should've read your 'scope!"

"My whaaat?!!" Una replied.

She brought it up on her cell phone, reading out loud:

> "LIBRA: Today is a 5--this Full
> Moon you Are at a crossroads.
> One door closes as another opens.
> Consider the past as you envision
> the future. Adventure is inevitable.
> Live for today."

"So?"

Madelyn shook her head. "Forget about work...y'know?!"

"But I don't--"

"Believe in it? Maybe you *should*. Reading mine the first time, I was hooked. But I'm a Pisces. *Everything's* addictive to me. I know. I'm 30...with a degree. People say I should grow up...realize there's no outside force affecting me. *I'm* in charge of my life. But they're wrong--they just don't know it."

Una frowned. "Really? Ever notice how *gendered* astrology is? Women's sites all carry horoscopes, but you never see one aimed at men."

"Okay. So most of my girlfriends admit to at least a *creeping* interest. Men just laugh it off. It's different for them. They *feel* in control. Women need a way to make sense of an unfair universe. Why shouldn't we look to the stars?"

Oddly enough, her friend was right--but for reasons she couldn't possibly imagine. Una's own encounter with Hopi prophecy three years before had opened *her* eyes regarding otherworldly influence. The powerful artifact she brought back to D.C. remained safe--for now.

But how long would it be until someone came looking for it?

Madelyn made off toward a red and yellow food cart. "Too much coffee. You need to eat."

Una's eyes wandered--meeting up with a stranger's across the street, his face obscured by a hoodie and dark glasses, in black leather pants with chains around his waist--and turned away. It made her nervous. Was she being *watched?*

For months, she'd been restless, unable to sleep, wondering if there was *something* outside her apartment windows at night. At first, it made no sense. She thought she might be losing her mind, until she discovered a report on military robotic micro-drones, the size of insects. So...it was *possible.*

But why? Nightmare scenarios played out in her mind. Maybe a Defense geek finally deciphered their "take" from Tocho's mystery cave in Arizona--and realized what was missing. Could she be a suspect in their investigation?

She unconsciously felt her neck, touching the silver chain she'd worn nonstop for three years-- wanting to dial the general's private number, first out of curiosity then fear...wondering if *he* could put a stop to it.

"*Xīnnián hǎo!*" said Madelyn.

Una jumped.

"It *means* 'Happy New Year'. Relax. I come bearing gifts!"

She accepted a yellow *Lao-Chi* paper carton with its red circle logo, popping a warm, tasty morsel into her mouth. It brought a smile to her lips.

"Lucky Dumplings," said Madelyn. "From an authentic family diner, nearby. Owner's a friend of mine."

"But how...?"

"This is practically my old stomping ground. I grew up in Brooklyn, remember?"

Una nodded, as something bright caught her eye.

From a balcony, people released red Chinese lanterns--small, paper hot air balloons powered by candles. Rising silently, they glowed softly in the night sky, creating that "ahh" and "ooh" factor for crowds below. Wind carried them precariously close to buildings on every side.

"Aren't those...*dangerous*?" said Una.

"Oh no!" piped the oriental grandmother. "Tradition. They symbolize joy, and wisdom... mostly."

The sky seemed ablaze.

"Mostly?"

"Is said in ancient times...a beautiful bird, favored by Sky Emperor, flew down to Earth. A villager killed it by accident. Angry Emperor ordered village and its people burned on 15th day of the New Year. Out of fear, villagers hung red lanterns, shot fireworks--so village appeared to be *already* in flame. It...saved them."

"But--"

"The Lantern Festival," said Madelyn, "Coming up."

The old woman grinned. "Wait. You'll see. Most fly for a little while, go out and float back down."

On calmer days, Una thought. But these appeared to be swirling higher, out of sight, over rooftops. They resembled twinkling stars. From a distance, one might easily mistake one for a UFO.

For a moment, she detected a subtle *shift* in her surroundings. The world slowed to a halt. All external sound ceased. Standing perfectly still, a sense of calm flowed through her, like nothing she'd ever known.

Then a voice came...from afar.

"Yo! Space cadet!" Madelyn snapped her fingers.

Normal sight and sound returned.

A colorful float adorned with fresh flowers glided by, to the festive sound of gongs, lutes, and mandolins. Shaped like the Great Wall of China and painted in red, its center featured the Temple of

Heaven, surrounded by a Memorial Archway, Beacon Tower and Lion Guardian statue, traditionally placed at the entrance of an imperial palace. Employees waved beside the familiar logo of *Sunny-Side Inc.*

Pop! Pop! Pop! filled the air...

And people turned, with alarm. It wasn't fast and random, like firecrackers, but the distinct pattern of *gunshots.*

Heads dropped along the curb, to escape the line of fire. Fingers pointed up toward a flaming lantern as it descended like a wayward meteor.

Sparks flew as it crashed into the Great Wall.

Flames shot up from the Beacon Tower, as it toppled into the Temple. Black smoke filled the air. An attendant screamed in agony as scalding hot wax poured over his face. Onlookers stared in grief.

Firefighters who were in the parade and along its route quickly responded, and the blaze was soon under control.

An ambulance sped the victim away.

But in spite of everyone's best efforts, the float was destroyed. Police towed it away, allowing the parade to resume. They would impound it back at the station, to search for clues. In all the confusion, only Officer Shen spotted a peculiar white mark, spray-painted like graffiti on one side of the Wall.

Its three curved, pointed prongs struck *fear* in his heart.

7

"M-m-my god!" said Madelyn, clearly shaken, cigarette in hand. "W-what are the chances?"

She spun around in a circle.

"I'm sorry about all this. *My* horoscope said to simply 'let go'. I've always identified with my sign. Whenever I don't understand what's happening, *Pisces* seems to hold the answers."

Still no response.

"You're *lucky*. Libra's the only sign that doesn't have an animal or humanoid symbol. It's just scales, y'know? And I feel that about you in a weird way. You've never been just a 'cat person' or a 'dog person'. You're more...balanced."

Madelyn froze. She could not find Una.

"I don't understand. It's *supposed* to be the Year of the Pig--more friendly, less chaotic, attuned to cosmic energies. The Chinese version of 'Don't worry, be happy'."

Maybe it was all the pushing and shoving. Somehow, the two of them got separated.

They couldn't even make eye contact.

"Una? *Answer* me, for god's sake! Maybe this *wasn't* a good idea. I thought we'd have some 'fun' is all...take your mind off. We should split...you know? Find a nice quiet bar to settle our nerves. I could sure use a drink right now."

Something snagged one of her heels.

She looked down.

It was a half-empty carton from *Lao-Chi*.

***

Confetti flew once more as Madelyn drew slow, deep breaths, to ward off a panic attack. Breathing always helped. She carefully aligned herself along the edge of Mott Street, scanning in both directions.

The parade marched on, with lion dancers, magicians, and colorful, high-flying banners to welcome the Chinese New Year.

But Una was nowhere in sight.

2

VIOLATION

Madelyn followed the parade along most of its route down Grand, up Canal and finally to East Broadway, with no signs of Una. Repeated calls on her cell went unanswered. New York or not, it was still a school night, and by 10 PM most folks were on their way home.

Our motel, she thought. *Of course.* Una wasn't feeling well, and in all the confusion, must've gone back.

She decided to pick up the pace.

Aromas of chicken dumplings, steamed rice and beef noodles came from the half-open door at *Lao-Chi*. Voices carried. All in Chinese. Though she could not understand a word of it, their frenzied tone was clearly one of alarm.

What did it all mean?

Finally, she reached *The Yin-Yang Inn*, hoping for good news, only to find their room untouched, with two empty beds.

Something was wrong.

It was not like Una to just run off. Madelyn had no choice. She picked up the phone and dialed 9-1-1.

The dispatcher sighed. "Sorry, ma'am. Without more to go on there's nothing we can do. When people celebrate, they get a little crazy sometimes. If she doesn't show by morning, you can file a police report."

Great. That's just great.

The nightstand alarm clock read 11:59. Tomorrow was *supposed* to be their first day on the job. Not a good time to go missing. *No...stop it,* she thought. *Block the negative.* Maybe something came up, like an emergency.

She could only hope to find Una the next morning, waiting for her at the 5th Precinct--with a whopper of a tale to tell.

She'd try to sleep--with a light on, just in case.

***

Despite its century-old facade, with "1881" boldly displayed above its main entrance, the Station House at No. 19 Elizabeth Street proved to be spacious and modern inside. Ascending a beautifully carved oaken staircase with newel posts to the second floor, Madelyn tried to catch her breath.

The DETECTIVES OFFICE appeared empty and dark. A faded handwritten note taped above the doorknob read:

Have a seat --
Someone will be with you

Sitting alone, in the dark, staring at old black and white portraits on the wall reminded her of a conversation with Una, just before the parade:

Out of the blue, she turned to Madelyn, "It's so *weird*."

"What?"

"Well, it's just that I've been thinking of someone I knew back home, a dear old friend who passed away several months ago: Kuwanyauma. She was a spirit elder in Oraibi."

"How old?"

"A hundred, at least."

"So she died. *That's* no surprise."

Una shook her head. "That's not the weird part. I can't explain it, but... somehow it feels as if she's *here*, somewhere nearby. I know that's impossible."

"Maybe not. Could she be reaching *out* to you, from the grave?"

"I don't know. Why?"

"It...*happens*, that's all--or at least, so I've heard."

"You ever--?"

"N-n-no," said Madelyn, shaking, "Not me."

And that was it. *Spooky*. In spite of the NO SMOKING sign, she found herself reaching for a cigarette.

Forty minutes elapsed before she heard footsteps coming down the hall. Madelyn pitched her third smoke out a half-open window as a heavy-set man in rolled up sleeves with a faded blue tie came through the door, flipping a light switch.

She trembled as their eyes met.

"Sorry, ma'am," he said, reaching to shake hands. "Detective Stone. I was afraid this might...we're in the squad room, downstairs. You must be--"

She squeezed. Her firm grip surprised him.

"Madelyn Kramer...but everyone calls me *Maddie*. I guess...we...got our signals crossed. I'll be...fine. Just a little nervous. Last night, the parade was more than we...anyway, just need some coffee, is all. So...she's already here then, downstairs with you?"

He frowned, "She?"

"Una Waters, of course. We're from D.C. She's a real go-getter. Probably showed up the crack o' dawn. Only wish I--"

He shook his head. "No sign of her."

Maddie's heart leaped into her throat.

"We've gotta *do* something--fast!"

"What do you mean?"

"Last night, she *disappeared*. I can't explain it, but somehow, she gets these *vibes* and...the parade was a bad idea. She kept scanning the crowd before...before ...now she's *missing*--and it's all my fault!"

Stone patted her back, approaching the staircase.

"Don't blame yourself. It's Chinatown. *Anything* can happen. We'll get on this, right away."

***

Minutes later, Police Officer Burke stepped outside, tugging at something under his collar. "Bulletproof vest," he explained. "On patrol, I used to pause for tea, shake hands with young people. Not anymore. Now, they all carry *guns*--and know how to use 'em."

Madelyn eyed his heavy-trigger Smith & Wesson. Stone wanted her to wait at the Station. But she simply *had* to tag along.

"How long's it been?"

"Forty years, give or take. Through twelve commissioners and three different uniforms. Most retire with a pension after twenty. Me, I get restless."

"So now what?"

"We cover the beat, step-by-step."

"But--"

"Don't worry. We've got help. Six more, combing the streets."

"Like you?"

"Well, not exactly. Auxiliaries: men *and* women in uniform. They don't make arrests or carry weapons. They find trouble and call for help. All Chinese-American. They speak the language. It helps."

They soon found themselves wandering East on Canal Street, not far from the parade route. City workers were still picking up from the night before.

He met with several shopkeepers, including a florist, a baker, and the balding vendor of an open-air market. Fresh-caught salmon, displayed on ice, went for about $5 a pound--less than half the cost at stores in uptown Manhattan. Tuna steak, slightly darker and bruised, went for about $6.60.

"You like? I wrap for you!"

Madelyn grinned back at him politely, trying not to breathe.

From his vest pocket, Burke produced photos of Una and the spray-painted graffiti from the parade float.

Like the rest, the vendor denied all knowledge. But his shifting eyes told another story.

"You think they're all *lying?*" asked Burke, afterwards.

She frowned. "Not exactly. They're afraid."

"Can't say I blame 'em. My first beat in '69 was an all Jewish neighborhood, part of a team that swept drunks off the street. We stuffed 'em, twenty at a time, into a police van. Those days are gone. The 70's brought new immigrants, street gangs and drugs."

Between Lafayette and Broadway they crossed a small causeway covered in scaffolding. It was flanked by the rear of an office building and Chinese laundry, with a parking lot entrance halfway down.

Madelyn couldn't explain it, but she felt as if they were being followed.

A huge dryer exhaust vent exited from cement block, curving up toward the sky. Suddenly, the air smelled of fresh linen. From inside, through the wall came the rhythmic, steady sound of washing machines. It blocked the noise of people out on the street. And something else: as tension left her body, she found it weirdly *comforting*. It reminded her how laundry sounds once brought that safe, warm feeling to a tumultuous childhood. A small sign read *Bennie Lee's*.

"Don't see those much anymore," she said.

Burke grinned. "Bennie's third generation. In the 80s, every neighborhood had laundries. We keep losing 'em. But they're not going out of business. Their leases are denied, or hiked out of reach. They're being driven away."

"Why?"

"Greed. It's happening all over the city. Longtime owners remove low renters like laundry, deli and pet-care salons, then sell to developers who convert their buildings into high end properties."

A middle-aged Asian woman stuck her head out the door.

"You need help? Come inside."

"Excuse me," said Madelyn. "We're looking for a friend. Did you see the parade? Or anything strange overnight?"

Something stirred suddenly in the alley, beside a city dumpster. Papers flew. What at first appeared to be an oversized stray cat turned out to be the wild-eyed, bearded face of a homeless man.

"Lights!" he cried, "From sky...came down *here*!"

"Ignore him," the woman said, annoyed. "'*Professor*' sleep here at night. Won't stay in shelter. Deli feed him sometimes."

Officer Burke approached the man slowly, urging Madelyn to stay back. Though disheveled, the man wore Nikes, new-looking sweat pants, and a purple hoodie with the white flaming torch logo of NYU.

"All right, take it easy, friend. Maybe a stray lantern came down this way. It happens. You...got a name?"

"Chong...er...Harry. Light come down. No Lantern. *Bigger.* Take off chill. No sound. Then, disappear. Remind me of triple quasar at Keck Observatory, 2007. Only much brighter. Had to cover my eyes!"

A metal creaking sound from the dumpster turned everyone's gaze.

Burke reached for his gun, but then, thinking better of it, grasped an edge rail, and hopped up to look inside.

Madelyn gasped as the laundry door slammed. Chong, too, was long gone.

"Okay, hold it...right--"

Then he froze as *Una Waters* emerged, disoriented and dazed, pushing mussed hair back in the red morning light. She struggled at first to stand up. The dumpster was half full.

"How'd I...and who are...*Maddie*!" she said, looking down. "What the *hell's* going on?"

Burke helped Una down, slowly, onto the street. She seemed calm, almost drugged, with no apparent signs of injury.

"Thank god," said Madelyn, embracing her. "I was so worried!"

"Miss Waters? You...all right? In cases like this, we have...protocols. Do you feel...*violated*? Hospital's nearby. I'll take you there."

"Wait! The parade. What about the *fire*?"

"It's all over. That was hours ago."

Una frowned. "What? No, you're *wrong*. It just happened!"

The two women's eyes met.

"It's after 6 AM," said Madelyn. "Remember *anything*?"

"Just bright light...and then, you found me."

"Could be date rape," he whispered. "Confusion, amnesia. Listen to her closely. She may describe feelings of paralysis, or dissociation between mind and body. She needs...a doctor, right away."

***

By mid-morning, Una left the ER at *Beekman Downtown*, still angry. Otherwise, she checked out fine, enabling her to report for duty by noon.

Detective Stone did not know what to make of her mysterious delay, so he ignored it. She came highly recommended, even if the assignment was only temporary.

Besides, they had a lot of ground to cover.

He tossed a printout of the weird graffiti onto his desk.

"What's *that*?" she asked.

"We don't know, for sure. Some think it's a new gang--maybe the one responsible for that fire last night. Graffiti's used to mark territory, identify targets or simply scare people. And it *works*. No members ID'd, so far. Could be a corporate protest, but that's just a guess. We're looking into it."

"Okay, so why am *I* here? Any immigration violations? Threats to air-water quality?"

Stone shook his head.

"What, then?"

Rising from his seat, he quickly scanned the room, inviting her to follow him. "It's more...*complicated* than that."

They entered a private office, away from the squad room, behind glass.

Finally, he drew a deep breath.

"Something *else* happened last night, something we can't quite explain. Orders from top brass are to keep it hush-hush for now. No leaks to the press. We think the two may be related, but we can't prove it yet."

"Prove what?"

"Last night, about the same time as that parade fire, there was a *cyber breach* here at the precinct. Someone got into our computer. Personnel files. They got everything: names, addresses, contact numbers--including your transfer from the Interior Secretary. We don't know who or how, but the source appeared to be...far way."

"*How* far?"

"You wouldn't believe me if I --"

"Try me," she said.

He left a crumpled piece of paper, and walked away.

Unfolding it carefully, Una found a single word circled in red:

SHANGHAI

3

LOST

Una shivered, stepping outside as she left the Precinct Station House, still shaken, about half-past 1. She braced against a chill east wind.

"Any luck?" said Madelyn, trying to put on a smile.

She held up a composite sketch of the tattooed stranger. "Guess my memory's not so good. Looks like half the people in Chinatown."

"So?"

She paused. "You're right. It's *more* than that. Maybe I took a bump on the head, maybe not. But I still can't remember what happened."

"But the hospital...I thought--"

"Sure, sure, a clean bill of health. What do *they* know?"

Una broke into a brisk walk. Madelyn could see she was upset. Never mind the fact they were discussing police business on a public street. No one paid much attention. It was New York, after all.

"Too many questions, if you ask me! *Any history of depression, sleep disorders or STD's...alcohol abuse, painkillers ...family members who suffer from dementia?* They're trying to find a cause for my amnesia--which is probably only temporary. I get that. But I'm *not* losing my mind!"

"Of course not."

"And *another* thing. NYPD's got its own special 'task force'. Did you know that?"

Madelyn could see she was on a roll. No sense in breaking the momentum. "For what, exactly?"

"Drugs, gangs, prostitution--you *name* it!"

"Okay...your point being--"

"Why do they need us?

"The assignment was last minute. We're just fill-ins."

"I don't mean that. They *wanted* someone from the Department of Interior. Why? So far, I see no reason."

They had walked a couple blocks, and the streets were filling up fast. Soon it would be rush hour. Una's distraction wasn't helping. With no destination in mind, they could get lost in the shuffle.

"*That* I can answer. There's a file in the Director's office. Apparently, the Interior Department once had an Immigration Branch, dealing with Chinese regulation until about 1947. They made a few missteps...and more than a few enemies. Some people have *long* memories."

"You don't mean--"

She nodded. "My guess? If things go wrong, we're here to take the blame!"

Una stopped all at once, twirling with her head skyward, disoriented, like a child in the midst of tall trees. "Where are we?"

Madelyn reached for her cell phone.

"Forget it. Let's call a cab."

The Manhattan office for *Sunny-Side, Inc.* didn't exactly ring a bell for their Qwik-Ride cabbie, Mr. Hou, but once given the address, he promised to get them there "In no time!"

It seemed to take a bit longer.

"This traffic's a nightmare," said Una after twenty minutes, "How can you stand it?"

Mr. Hou grinned, "Ancient Chinese secret: the key to survival--let go of fear!"

Madelyn rolled her eyes, "Why *Sunny-Side*?"

"Okay, so maybe the attack was symbolic. But I've done some checking. They've been implicated before. All the usual complaints: poor working conditions, unequal pay, and threats to deport illegals. But I suspect it's *more* than that, maybe so well hidden that its victims never see the light of day."

The car abruptly swerved to avoid a bearded old man, with crazy long hair, standing in the road. He seemed to be in a daze, like a zombie staring *into* the cab...directly at Una.

Madelyn sighed, "What's *wrong* with him? He might've been--"

"Stop the car!" cried Una.

"Almost there," the driver said, "Two more minutes!"

"No! Stop NOW. My god! It was *him*!"

Their cab screeched to a halt. "Who?"

"The homeless man, you know...we saw him behind *Bennie Lee's*. Don't you remember? That woman, *what* did she call him?"

"The 'professor'!"

Una popped open her door, leaping out onto the curb. She read the distress in Maddie's eyes. This impulsiveness was getting to be a habit.

"Don't worry! It's...something I have to do. Go to *Sunny-Side*. Find out what you can. I'll catch up with you later!"

She had no time to spare. For an old man, he was light on his feet. Una saw him duck into an alley beside a parlor named TATTOO YOU. She made a mental note to check their selection...for three-pronged designs.

At least we're in broad daylight, she thought, racing to keep up. *I've learned my lesson. No more night walks.* She felt good. Maybe cycling at the 'Y' was finally paying off. Not like riding horseback, but still good for cardio.

She paused in the alley. Metal grating at its far end essentially left no way out. Yet their was no sign of him. She recalled her first impression the other day: like a cat--essentially invisible, until it moves.

But would he give himself away?

"So...what's a quasar got to do with UFO's?" she shouted.

There was a moment of silence, when she thought he might not show--or worse--that he had given her the slip and was already gone.

Then, she detected the slightest breath, and turned around.

The 'professor' appeared completely calm, hair pulled back neatly into a pony tail, hands at both sides, feet together, like a butler awaiting instruction. His deep blue eyes were completely clear.

"You'd be...*surprised*," he said.

Una was not afraid. She pulled a newspaper clipping from her pocket, provided by a friendly nurse who approached her for no apparent reason just before leaving the ER. Apparently, *someone* believed her.

She handed it to him. Dated January 2016, it read, in part:

ECONOMIC REALITY: TRAGIC LOSS
Dr. Harry Chong holds a doctorate in plasma physics, a masters in electrical engineering, and astronomy. Until recently, he was a respected, full-time professor at NYU. Now...thanks to cuts in government funding--plus an academic scandal that dismantled his life in less than six months...he's living on the street without a job.

"So, you know," he said.

"Some, but not all," she replied. "Enough to realize that you're not crazy, and *maybe* we share something in common. The other day, you spoke of bright light. You said it reminded you of a triple quasar."

"Only *brighter*. I was forced to cover my eyes."

"What else did you see? I...can't remember what happened. But I was there. It's...important for me to know."

For a moment he paused, to study her, like a chessmaster assessing his opponent--or a poker player. Was she bluffing? He wanted to trust her, more than anything. Because *trust* was so desperately missing from his life. After a year of homelessness, he nearly forgot how it felt. He wanted to feel it again.

"The scandal was a lie," he said. "They set me up, loaded false emails into my laptop, placed huge sums of money into my bank account. I never knew its source. I was disgraced. My papers destroyed. All that I own...is up *here*."

He pointed to his brain.

"I believe you," she said.

And suddenly, tears flowed from his eyes.

"To answer your first question," he said, trying to regain his composure, "My work dealt with *Field Resonance Propulsion*. It was unofficially sponsored by NASA. Officially, of course, they do not study UFOs. The goal was to design a spacecraft 'propulsion' system for galactic and inter-galactic travel without prohibitive 'travel times'. In other words--"

"From here to *there*...in no time."

He nodded. "The concept was developed utilizing research into the causes of solar flares, black holes, quasars...and unexplained phenomena. UFO studies imply an ability to cross large stretches of space in relatively short time frames. They are often observed to disappear *instantly*, then reappear at a nearby location. The high speed, right angle turns, abrupt stops or accelerations and the absence of sonic booms--despite calculated speeds of 22,000 mph or more--suggest that UFOs may generate *artificial gravity*. Radiative effects on the environment--such as burns, dehydration, stopping of car engines, TV and radio disruptions--suggest that UFO propulsion involves *electromagnetics* which we do not yet understand."

Una sighed, "So now you're homeless? Why not at least accept a warm bed in a public shelter? It's better than freezing to--"

"Because now, I'm off the grid. No records to keep track of my wherabouts. First, they destroyed my work--to keep it a secret. Now they're after *me*. Don't you see? It's my only way to survive."

"And the light you saw?"

"Was *real*. Advanced propulsion, no doubt."

"You mean like military prototypes?"

He shook his head. "*Someone* brought you back-- from where I cannot say. People see I'm homeless and automatically assume I drink or do drugs. They write me off, as a *lunatic*. My mind is still sharp. I sleep in a tent most nights, take vitamins and read in the public library. But mostly, I stay invisible. To keep my eye on *them*."

Una's heart ached. If such a brilliant mind could be cast aside, what hope remained for the rest of humanity?

Suddenly her cell chimed the chorus of "Uptown Girl" and she knew it was Maddie trying to call. Una turned away briefly to read the text:

NOTHING DOING AT MY END.
COMPLETE STONEWALL.
HOW ABOUT YOU?

She turned back to apologize--and gasped. Like an alley cat, Professor Chong had vanished into thin air.

4

LAO-CHI

Una returned to the 5th Precinct around 4 PM, hoping some hot coffee might clear her head. She found Madelyn in the squad room with Detective Stone and two of his fellow officers eyeing a blow-up of the peculiar three-pronged symbol from the parade attack, taped to a large dry erase board.

"Any luck?" she said, smiling.

The men all gave her dirty looks.

Maddie frowned, discreetly taking her aside. "Don't antagonize them."

"Why? What's wrong?"

Her head shook. "No match. They've searched online, scanned their graffiti database, even tried a Chinese translator--"

"What about tattoo parlors?"

Panic lit up in her eyes. "N-not so fast. Hold that thought. They're waiting for some kind of expert--"

A gangly kid in thick glasses with curly black hair, barely out of his teens came abruptly through the door, in an oversized t-shirt and faded jeans, with books under each arm.

"*Rufus!*" said Stone. "For god sake. What took you so long?"

"S-s-sorry, sir, I had to dig these out of my IT locker. Never thought they'd actually come in handy, but *now*--"

"All right already! Get on with it."

"Y-yes sir...right away, sir."

Pausing to gather his thoughts, the young man carefully spread out seven volumes on the floor in a semicircle, each precisely opened to a bookmark.

"So, I cross-referenced our *graffiti mark* with historic symbols from religion, folklore, and mythology. We *may* be looking at a cryptographic 'signature'...not unlike that of the Zodiac Killer, allegedly responsible for at least seven murders in California in the late 60s and early 70s. All investigated but never--"

"*Murder?*" said Madelyn, "But I--"

"The hot wax victim is *dead*," said Stone, "That makes it a homicide."

Rufus sighed. "Anyway, there may be a clue in its basic design: three curved prongs...or 'heads' emerging from the center. The power of *three* is universal. In Chinese it represents *Sanctity*, the auspicious *Number* for good luck, and *Magic*. Symbolized by the triangle. In Taoism, a philosophy from the sixth century, it stands for the *Great Triad*:

Heaven, Man, and Earth. It's also the number for *Time*: past, present, and future."

She nodded. "In astrology, triple planetary alignments are known as a *Triune Council*. One example: the Venus retrograde in which Scorpio joins up with Mercury and the Moon. Scorpio's the sign of the Sorceress, as well as death and rebirth."

There was a lingering moment of silence.

Rufus tried to smile. "Yes, well...we're looking for any connection to the past, like the Chinese Gold Bar Cipher of '33."

"The *what*?!" said Detective Stone.

"In 1933, seven gold bars covered in strange symbols were issued to a General Wang in Shanghai and deposited into a U.S. bank. Their meaning is still unknown. So far, all we can say is there's 'no identifiable threat'."

Stone stood up. Apparently, he'd heard enough. "Anything else?"

"Only this--there is an ancient saying:

*Events that come in three's
are worth noticing.*

"But we've only had one attack."

"So far," he replied.

Watching Rufus depart, Stone threw up his hands as a delivery arrived from *Lao-Chi* with tantalizing aromas of chicken, rice and vegetables. "That's it. I give up. Nobody knows."

Madelyn frowned. "What do you mean?"

"It's hopeless! Unless--"

"*I* know," blurted the delivery boy, squinting at the board.

"Jianyu?" she replied.

All eyes turned on him.

"Yes! So sorry! Not mean to interrupt."

Stone cringed.

"Or at least, I've *seen* it before--in a very old book...owned by my grandfather."

Una hopped suddenly to her feet.

Maddie grinned. "You thinkin' what *I'm*--"

"*Exactly*," she said, "I'm famished. Time for some lucky dumplings--if you know what I mean!"

***

Minutes later, the two women sat at a small bamboo table in *Lao-Chi*, one block away. Beyond its reinforced glass storefront, the remaining windowless walls featured a wrap-around mural of *Lhasa*, the capital of Tibet, including the red-and-white *Potala palace*, which dominated the skyline from every corner, *Norbulinka palace*, *Jokhang temple*, and the *Sera* and *Drepung monasteries*, all against a breathtaking backdrop of the Himalayas.

The mural, more detailed than any photograph, seemed incredibly life-like. Peering into it, one could almost *feel* the sky moving, leaves fluttering on trees, and the presence of native wildlife--an Imperial eagle, highland wolves, a wild yak, giant panda, snow leopard, golden-haired monkey, or river rhinoceros peeking out from the brush. They were not apparent at first to the casual eye. Only after several deep breaths and an effort to relax would these 'gifts' of Tibet come to light.

"Potala once served as the winter home of the Dalai Lama--before he went into exile," their waitress smiled, wearing the red circle logo. "Its living quarters, murals, chapels and tombs number a thousand rooms."

The red circle, in fact, appeared everywhere: on menus, walls and doors, in tiles on the floor, and even the restaurant ceiling.

Una recalled a partial quote on the reverse of a small portrait of the religious leader in Moki's bedroom in the First Mesa village of Walpi:

...one's enemy is the best teacher.

And she wondered what they might have yet to learn from perpetrators of the attack--including the secret of their three-pronged symbol.

A middle-aged oriental woman, hair neatly tied back, came out briefly to greet them, donned in black chef's attire from head to toe.

"Hongi!" said Madelyn, jumping up to embrace her. "This is my good friend, Una, here with me from D.C."

"*Tah-shi de-leh*! Hello!" the woman said, as they clasped hands. "You are Hopi...yes?"

She nodded.

Hongi smiled. "We are like sisters, long lost, from far sides of the globe. You are most welcome...any time!"

They barely sipped butter tea before food arrived. There were dumplings, of course, known as *momos*: freshly made with chicken, juicy and singing with flavors of ginger and Chinese celery, served with sweet chili and soy sauce. Then came *thali*, a shiny platter topped with a mound of rice ringed by radish pickles, daal, fried bitter melon and mustard greens. They also enjoyed *thentuk*, a hand-pulled noodle soup with beef. Finally, for dessert, there were *tsel roti*, gigantic nutty-tasting rice-flour donuts.

Una could not help feeling a sense of *deja vu.*

Beyond a fondness for turquoise, used by both cultures to ward off evil spirits, she noticed the abundant use of silver and coral, familiar colors and patterns in textiles, and long braided hair, worn by both men and women. But what caught her eye most: a cylindrical wheel on a metal spindle, near the door-- for its striking resemblance to the Hopi Rattle.

"The prayer wheel," their waitress observed. "At its core, a 'Life Tree' made of wood, with mantras wrapped around it. Spinning it has the effect of reciting many prayers--to bring wisdom and good karma. Some say it enhances spiritual power."

Maddie's eyes lit up. "You mean clairvoyance, precognition, mind-reading...*that* sort of thing?"

The waitress smiled. "The prayer wheel can transform one's surroundings, to make them peaceful, pleasant, and conducive to the mind. Touching it brings one closer to...*enlightenment!*"

Una sighed. For the moment, at least, she felt completely at peace--for the first time since arriving in Chinatown. Maybe Hongi was right.

A young man came out from the kitchen in black chiffon pants, sandals and a sleeveless tunic, also bearing the red logo. She recognized him as Jianyu, the delivery boy. He bowed humbly before them.

"Apologies, please! Grandfather not here. Every day, just before sundown, he goes to temple. It helps him to meditate and reflect, to seek purification and forgiveness, and develop a kind heart. He has tried to teach me, but I still lack discipline. Too many distractions. One day I hope to follow in his--"

"All right, already," said Madelyn, "We get that. What about the *book?*"

He froze.

"You know...'very old'? Can't we just take a peek? We don't have time to waste. Besides--"

"Greetings," said a remarkable voice, from behind.

They turned at once to see Mr. Lao, bald in half-moon wire rim glasses, long gray beard and Fu Machu moustache, standing quietly with hands folded before the mural of Tibet, as if he had just stepped out of it.

No one heard him enter the room.

"The book is *Bai Ze Tu*--considered lost, but not to all. Authored by Huang Di, legendary Yellow Emperor, in 2500 B.C.. While on patrol in the East, he first encountered the creature *Bai Ze*, who dictated to him a guide to the forms and habits of all 11,520 types of supernaturals in the world, from shapeshifters to mind-sifters--and how to fight them."

Una rose from her seat, entranced by his calming demeanor, the light in his eyes otherworldly. It almost reminded her of the Spirit Woman, Kuwanyauma. She had so many questions:

> *What did the mystery symbol mean?*
> *Who, exactly, was behind it?*
> *What was their purpose in America?*
> *Could they be stopped?*
> *And what did any of it have to do with her?*

She felt compelled to find answers. Mr. Lao appeared to hold the key. If only--

The restaurant door flew open as a giggling young couple stepped inside. Wind brought a sudden gust of snow, forcing Una to shield her eyes, as a shiver went through her spine.

She opened them to find herself standing face-to-face with the mural's majestic *Jokhang temple*. On its rooftop were iconic statues of golden deer flanking a Dharma wheel, victory flags and a monstrous fish.

She could *almost* hear chanting.

Finally, as they prepared to exit, she found a mantra displayed inside the main entrance:

The
sacred circle
directs us to the center of
our being-- where we remember
our relation to also the four footed,
those who swim, those who fly
and all that grows. Within
the circle we are
one.

5

SERENDIPITY

Una left *Lao-Chi* feeling content in the backseat of a Qwik-Ride taxicab, headed back to *The Yin-Yang*. They'd had enough excitement for one day. Even Madelyn, who was ordinarily more of a night owl, seemed to move in slow motion.

The soothing voice of an independent radio talk-show host was the only thing blocking out chaotic noise as they traversed dark, snow-covered streets lit up with neon signs through Chinatown.

"We were lucky to to get one so close to shift change," said Maddie, freshening her red lipstick in the reflection of a lighted compact. "Sometimes, people wait for--"

"Hey! I thought you were *bushed*," said Una.

"Oh, I *am*...or at least, I *was*. I mean, a girl can't let herself go, just because it's getting dark. Quite the opposite, in fact. Who knows? The night is still young. *Anything* could happen!"

"That's what I'm afraid of."

Ever since her 'vanishing act' during the New Year's parade, Una found it increasingly difficult to close her eyes. It was not the same anxiety that kept her awake nights in D.C., but it might as well be. How could she ever hope to concentrate without sleep? Ever focus on the task at hand?

So far, they could find no link between the mysterious attack on a *Sunny-Side* corporate float that resulted in one homicide--and a seemingly coincidental cyber breach at the Fifth Precinct Station House, still unknown to the public. Computer experts remained tight-lipped regarding their investigation.

Without any leads, it was all guess-work.

All signs pointed to the *possibility* of a new street gang, who apparently used graffiti to strike fear in the hearts of residents--if it existed at all. Even Stone wondered out loud if the 'gang' might be a 'red herring', intended to throw them off track. So far, not a *single* gang member--not even the hooded stranger in chains she'd seen with her own two eyes--could be identified.

And Una could not even account for her *own* whereabouts while both events were taking place! Was she kidnapped? Interrogated? Or did something *else* transpire, altogether?

Somehow, she just couldn't accept *not knowing*.

Besides herself, only a homeless man had admitted to being in the alley that night behind *Bennie Lee's*. But police had already checked every shelter and charity soup kitchen within five miles of Chinatown. Harry Chong was nowhere to be found.

Could she have been the victim of a military Black Op *mind sweep*--used to extract information pertaining to otherworldly contact? Did they ask about the Hopi Rattle? Did she cooperate, or put up a fight? And what, if any, would be the consequences?

Something told her deep down inside that her suspicions were all wrong--that it could *not* have happened that way.

Una had already examined herself thoroughly-- from head to toe--for any signs of invasive injury, such as scars from physical torture or needle marks from administration of "truth" serum. Plenty of rumors had floated around D.C. about "crossing the line" in places like *Guantanamo*. For the sake of National Security in the face of a terrorist threat, such measures *might* be justified when dealing with foreign spies--but a private U.S. citizen, with no history of protest or acts of anti patriotism?

NO. She could never believe that.

What, then?

Whatever transpired that night apparently had no effect upon her official role here, in New York. *Someone* still wanted her to see it through, find out who was responsible and who they might be working for. *Shanghai?* Sure. Maybe. But it seemed...too simple. Too obvious. Of course, it would be only natural to suspect the Chinese government, or a subversive group with international ties acting on their behalf. But it would be damn hard to prove.

She suddenly detected the smell of smoke.

Madelyn held a cigarette in one hand, discreetly trying to conceal it by extending her arm out the cab window.

"What are you *doing?*" said Una.

"Trying to calm my nerves," she said. "You're not the only one who's afraid. According to my 'scope, we should've been home by now. It feels *wrong*, somehow. Like it'll only get worse if we stay. I don't know, maybe it's just me. But lately, I'm feeling left out. What's going *on* with you? You seem so secretive, so withdrawn. Like there's something you don't want me to know. I thought we were in this together!"

"We *are*. It's just that, well, I'm still freaking out about what happened the other night. Maybe it was nothing. Maybe I had too much to drink and couldn't handle it, got caught up in the crowd and wound up two blocks away, sleeping it off until morning. And I could live with that--but right now, I just don't know what to think or believe. My *gut* tells me there was more to it--a *lot* more. And a part of me just can't rest--until I figure it out!"

The two women held hands.

And for some reason, the voice on the radio suddenly became louder, as if the driver was annoyed by their conversation, and trying to drown them out:

41

"There may be another principle at work here," said the talk show guest. "Are you familiar with...*serendipity*?"

"Of course," replied the host, "Happy accident--another word for 'luck'."

"Well, not exactly. That *is* the prevailing view, of course, but I refer to its more *precise* meaning: discovery of *that which is unsought*, seemingly by chance, though possibly by design of an outside force, beyond one's control. Sometimes referred to as fate, or destiny—operating beyond the ordinary 'forces of nature'."

"You mean *supernatural*?"

"That's one way of putting it. Another would be 'beyond human knowledge'. Otherworldly. Originating beyond the confines of this planet, and possibly the known universe. Another *dimension*, perhaps."

If only Jack was here, Una thought. With all his elaborate theories about missing persons and unexplained phenomena. He'd spent years collecting eyewitness reports from people with nothing to gain but a clear conscience. Out West, where earth and sky remained unchanged for centuries, people seemed to have better respect for legends, for mysteries connecting past and present.

She could almost hear his voice in her mind from the day they first met, in the Third Mesa graveyard:

> "I've heard a few tales that would
> knock your socks off. Scary shit,
> in the middle of the night. There
> are a few stories I'd *like* to write.
> Stuff I'd put in print--*if* I thought
> I could get away with it. But some
> things...you *can't* report, even if
> they're true."

Scary shit was right--the kind most people ignore, because it's their only way to cope. Why fret over the *unthinkable* in a world with so many pleasant distractions at one's fingertips?

She paused to study the throng of mostly twenty-something year-olds racing around them still, in taxicabs, on sidewalks, all so busy, preoccupied with 'modern life'. The world of *her* Hopi childhood, with all of its ancient tradition, belief in Sky People--beliefs that shaped her conception of man's place in the universe--was completely *unknown* to them. Could anyone under the age of thirty even imagine a world without cell phones?

Their taxicab turned the corner through a chaotic intersection with bright lights reflecting off heavy snow, when the glare in Una's eyes suddenly triggered a *flashback*:

> *The strange sensation of walking, alone,*
> *on a busy street at first, oblivious to sound*
> *and movement, as if suddenly everything*
> *around her remained frozen, complete peace*
> *of mind flowing through her, like a drug,*
> *and then...*

> *Not even awareness of hot or cold, light*
> *or dark, as if all her surroundings faded*
> *to neutral, like an endless fog, gently*
> *enveloping her body, so that she began to*
> *float, her feet no longer touching the ground,*
> *and then...*

> *Feeling a strong presence nearby, but unable*
> *to see anyone, then realizing that she was*
> *unable to move, except maybe her eyes, and*
> *fleeting, physical contact, like warmth on*
> *her skin from a curious source,*
> *and then...*

Madelyn squeezed her hand, and it was over.

Her eyes refocused--and she was still in the back seat of a Qwik-Ride taxicab, facing her best friend in the middle of traffic on a busy street in Chinatown, on a cold night in February, approaching their motel.

Any minute, they would stop and climb out.

And she noticed a beep from her phone which seemed odd because it was the first sound she could clearly identify above the din outside.

She reached into her pocket, pressed a small button to light up its screen, and there was a message:

MISSED CALL
FROM WINSLOW, ARIZONA

PART TWO

ANCIENT FEAR

"If you stand straight,
do not fear a crooked shadow."

--Chinese Proverb

6

THE OMEN

Una paid the cab fare as Madelyn climbed out of their Qwik-Ride to stand in a half empty parking lot beside the yellow bricked *Yin-Yang Inn*. It was already dark and getting colder by the minute.

As their driver pulled away, she paused in midstep, to consider the time difference between New York and Arizona. If Jack was three hours behind, 7 PM local time would make it around 4 in Winslow. No problem there. But would returning his call be such a good idea--or would it only distract her from the task at hand? *No*, she thought, *this is more than coincidence*. Not a peep from him since her return to D.C., three years ago. For Jack to be calling at all he *must* have a good reason.

"No, no, no, NOOOO!" shrieked Madelyn against the night air.

Una suddenly looked up.

She found Maddie trembling with their room key-card in one hand, newly lit cigarette in the other, pacing in high heels. But there were no clues to the source of her apparent distress--until she glanced at their red motel room door.

· There it was *again*, freshly spray-painted in white: that peculiar three-pronged symbol from the parade.

This time, it felt like an *omen*.

A brief scan of their surroundings revealed nothing but empty sidewalks. Una could not believe her eyes. Not a soul. Not *even* the motel manager, who surely must've heard Madelyn's scream.

Then again, maybe *that's* what kept him out of sight.

No doubt in Chinatown, this sort of thing happened all the time. But Una was not accustomed to gang intimidation.

"I wonder what it means," she said, trying to sound logical.

"What do you *think* it means?" said Madelyn, blowing smoke. "They're watching us. Can't you feel it? Like a set of invisible eyes, everywhere we go. *I* can! I should've known this would happen."

Now Una began to shake, and she couldn't tell for certain if it was the cold or her own fears beginning to rise. Suddenly *they* had become the target, and it was not a good feeling.

Maddie fiddled with her cell.

"What are you--"

"My scope!" she said, holding up the small screen:

PISCES : Today, haste and lack of
reflection can be at the root of difficult
situations, marked by wrong decisions.
Do not over indulge. Gloominess comes
in the form of danger and secret enemies.
Collaborations could be erratic. Beware!

"It's all there in black and white. What is *wrong*
with me? People born under my sign aren't ordinarily
susceptible to bad luck, but we *can* bring it upon
ourselves. I should've...given you a heads up!"

Una's first instinct was to dismiss the whole idea.
Madelyn had a tendency to over react. But there was
no denying the seriousness of this situation. Had this
"enemy" gained access to their room--and maybe her
laptop? Could it *still* be waiting for them...inside?

"We can't take any chances," she said, dialing
Detective Stone at the Precinct Station.

Madelyn popped a Valium to calm herself. She
always kept a few on hand.

***

Minutes later, police arrived. Stone rushed over
to greet them.

"You two all right?"

Maddie began to laugh uncontrollably. "All right?
Does it *look* like we're all right?" Running mascara
made her face resemble a Beyonce music video.

Like a true professional, he kept his cool.

"Er, that's not exactly what I meant, ma'am. That is, well...have you noticed any signs of foul play?"

She groaned. In the flashing lights of police cruisers, her teased up red hair appeared to flicker, in flames. "You mean, *besides* the 'death-mark' on our door?"

Using a police ram, two officers broke it down. A third followed closely behind with his weapon drawn.

Everyone seemed to brace for the worst. Madelyn covered both ears, as if anticipating an explosion.

A crowd of onlookers instinctively followed her example.

Una did not know whether to laugh or cry.

After a moment of silence, the officers reappeared, unscathed.

"All clear," said Stone, "Feel free to return. I'll post an officer outside if it'll--"

"Are you kiddin' me?" said Madelyn. "We can't stay here now. It's not safe. The *karma* is all wrong. We need to--"

And suddenly, she stopped, as if an alarm went off in her head. The look in Stone's eye gave her a chill. She sensed a lack of empathy, like one might encounter in the gaze of a great white shark, or at best, a total stranger. Her Pisces intuition told her *not* to trust him.

"We'll...be *fine*," she said, breathing slowly to convey a sense of relief.

And he bought it.

She traded glances with Una. Moments later, the women waved pleasantly, as police drove away with their photos and assorted bits of 'evidence' from the scene.

"Okay," she said at last, "Now can you tell me what just--"

"Remember what I said before...about taking blame?"

She nodded.

"Well, call it a *hunch*, but I got the feeling just now that this whole routine--with the door I mean--is part of a set-up."

"By the NYPD? No way. That's im--"

"Maybe not everyone, you're right. That's too big a scandal. I don't know. All I'm saying is--"

"Stone. His reaction was so...predictable. Almost like he *expected* this to happen. Think about it. We're both from D.C., which makes us unwelcome. Now it looks like the gang's against *us*. Get rid of us, end of--"

"Yes," she nodded. "But it's not that simple. So--"

"We need *proof*."

"And we can't find it here. We need--"

"To be 'off the grid'," said Una. "That means no credit cards, no security cams, away from the public eye. But *where*? Where can we go? We need a place that's nearby. A place we can find...peace."

Reaching into her purse, Maddie retrieved a crumpled napkin printed with the *Lao-Chi* red circle logo and phone number.

And suddenly, it all became clear: why immigrants from Tibet, with their music and food and philosophy, their familiar temperament, respect for nature and seemingly coincidental beliefs all made her feel at ease.

Hongi's kind words played over in her mind:

"You are most welcome...any time!"

And she realized the purpose of her trip to New York might go beyond this assignment. Privately, she had wondered why the boy, Moki, first touched by the *Gleam of Light* in the Mystery Cave kept a small portrait of the *Dalai Lama* among his things.

And what happened to his brain, enabling him to receive data from a spy satellite...in *Chinese?*

It was no secret that intelligence experts in D.C. had long feared *The Red Dragon's* growing sphere of influence, from military might to space exploration. Possessing 20 percent of the world's population and an ever growing economy--predicted by some to surpass the U.S. as early as 2029--its place on the world stage was simply too big to ignore.

Perhaps these events were all *meant* to lead her on a personal journey as well, not only to uncover the mystery behind the three-pronged symbol in a very old, old book, but also to explain why *she* had to come.

Kuwanyauma, the Spirit Woman in Oraibi, had once encouraged Una to "follow her heart". And then, somehow, she experienced *deja vu* upon her arrival here--sensing the old woman nearby. Was it part of a dream she'd forgotten...or one yet to come?

"There are *other* ways of knowing," Madelyn once said.

At the time, Una did not understand. "What do you mean? A seance?"

"Of *course* not. Give me some credit. I'm more down to earth than that. You might consider trying...*hypnosis*!"

But she wasn't ready for *that*. It seemed too 'far out'. Besides, who could she ever trust?

New York was beginning to feel a lot like D.C., only *bigger*. Like the Amazon rain forest compared to Lincoln Park--full of predators, ready to pounce.

And Chinatown was a world unto itself.

It was a wonder so many managed to survive. Statistics from the Department of Interior *proved* it. Chinese-Americans suffered higher rates of poverty than the general public.

She recalled her first day on the street in Manhattan, hailing a cab beside a poor woman exhausted from a difficult day of job hunting:

"I thought America would be heaven," she said, "But all it is is *cold*!"

With bags packed, they finally left *The Yin-Yang* around 7 PM, closing their door, now taped over with cardboard--apparently the manager's attempt to deflect negative publicity.

Too late, she thought.

Was it an *omen*? Perhaps, but not the kind one might expect. People in ancient times believed that signs from the gods could foretell the future, good or bad.

Many, like her friend Maddie, still found answers in the stars.

As a child in Hopiland, Una believed that the Sky People were ever present, watching from above, helping her find her *place* in the universe.

Perhaps they were leading her still.

7

HAUNTED

Hongi graciously received Una and Madelyn at the rear entrance to *Lao-Chi*, just after dark. A narrow stairway led to the family's modest second floor apartment. Though still full from their meal, earlier, the women did accept freshly brewed butter tea--to chase off the winter chill.

"We haven't much to spare," she said, refilling their cups from an old silver pot, "But you are welcome as long as need be."

Madelyn's description of their ordeal at *The Yin-Yang* left out no detail. Regardless of their suspicions pertaining to Detective Stone, they had to assume the threat *might* be real. "We were scared shitless," she said. "And couldn't bare to stay another night. Do you *know* how that feels?"

Up to this point, Hongi sipped thoughtfully from her teacup. But now, her hand seemed to tremble. Una detected a tear in one eye.

"We seldom speak of it," she began, drawing a deep breath, "My father says it is best to forget the past, live in the present. But in my youth, I knew many fears living in Fujian, on the coast of mainland China.

"Like many before us, we fell under the strict one-child policy that went into effect in 1980. I was pregnant with my second son when we left in '89--otherwise, he would not be here today. Sometimes I still have nightmares about them trying to take away my baby. A mother never forgets."

"*Second* son?" asked Madelyn.

"Yes, our first, *Ming*, only two when we came to New York, fell in with the wrong crowd as a teenager, and disappeared. That was eight years ago. We fear he may be dead...or worse."

"*Worse?*" said Una. "I don't--"

"Chinese believe we're surrounded by spirits of the dead. Ghosts are everywhere. Ancestor worship involves communion with them. But when people die violently, failure to offer proper sacrifice can make them return as a *hungry ghost*, to torment family members still alive."

Una frowned.

Hongi caressed her hands in return.

"For those who leave to live *outside*, in places like Taiwan, there is an even greater fear--of the *future*. They are afraid that one day, Red China will attack and destroy everything."

"What do *you* believe?" said Una.

Hongi sighed. "In America, we'd hoped to leave fear behind. The modern world, far removed from ancient ways, is less guided by superstition..."

Madelyn unconsciously felt for her silvertone Pisces charm bracelet. Ruled by the water element, its two fish were accompanied by green emeralds, playful dolphins and Neptune's three-pronged trident, all meant to bring her *luck*.

"...But now, it seems, the old fears have returned."

***

In spite of their comfortable surroundings, Una found it hard to sleep. Maybe it was all the *'ghost'* talk. The thought of restless spirits roaming about seemed to make more sense in a place like *Hopiland*, with its sacred landscapes and ancient petroglyphs. But not here, in New York City.

She almost felt guilty for intruding on this poor family, striving so hard to survive in a place fraught with danger at every turn.

Preparing for this trip, she learned that most Chinese restaurants were family owned, staffed by immigrants looking for work as busboys, waiters, or cooks. Their biggest problem: securing *citizenship*, which began with a high-priced asylum lawyer, followed by application for a Green card. The process often took years to complete.

They could not hide here for long. Stone and his officers would find them. Under the circumstances, their need to "escape the spotlight" might be understood, but they could not flee responsibility. There was a mystery here to be solved, and people in D.C. were expecting results.

One thing the two big cities seemed to share: *night sounds.* Stand near an open window at any hour and one could hear an endless stream of voices, music, traffic, police sirens, people shouting, and dogs barking...sometimes nearby, but mostly far away.

Suddenly, she felt the need to breathe and found herself stepping through an open door that led to a graveled rooftop.

Here, above the din of city lights rose a star-filled sky.

Una sighed with relief, comforted by the thought, at least, that somewhere out there, the Sky People might be watching over her.

Alone, for the first time it seemed, since entering the big city, she paused to glance at her cell, and felt an urge to call Jack. If anyone would understand her conflicting emotions in the face of danger and uncertainty, it would be him.

Harry Chong seemed to think her disappearance and memory loss *might* be part of some high-tech, clandestine operation--so high that even *he* could not identify its source.

Jack was *good* at that sort of thing, digging for answers where most people simply gave up, daring to explore the *unthinkable* because he knew anything was possible, and he wasn't afraid of the truth.

If only, she thought.

Feeling perplexed, with a cool breeze sifting through her long dark hair, she suddenly gasped--as a shadow stirred nearby.

It was grandfather Lao.

"The stars," he said. "Do they speak to you?'"

She paused only briefly. "Oh, no--that's Maddie's thing, not mine. She's a Pisces and *says* I'm a Libra, but I don't really know what that means."

"Too bad," he replied.

She wondered how long he'd been standing there, invisible, until the moment he chose to speak-- just like in the restaurant.

"So, umm...what're you...I mean--"

He grinned. "We are not so different, you and I. So many questions. I come up here at night, seeking answers. Over 3,000 years ago, my people discovered the 10 Heavenly Stems and 12 Earthly Branches, used as a way of counting time, for generations.

"My people have drawn *star maps* since the seventh century. Astrologers make celestial globes, to show the position of stars in time. They watch the sky for heavenly omens...to predict the future."

Una sighed. "If only there was something to it. Something *real*, I mean."

The rooftop on one side was partly snow covered. From within his robes, Mr. Lao produced a walking stick, handmade, covered in symbols and strange writing.

"I know why you are here," he said.

Reaching down, in the snow, he carefully reproduced the curvy three-pronged symbol from their motel room door.

Una began to tremble.

"I'm...not here to pry. It's just that, we... don't know where else to turn. The boy said--"

His eyes brightened.

"In China, there's a prophecy, recorded in the 5th century A.D., known as *The Divine Incantations*. Few people living in the world today know of its existence. Even fewer know how to read it."

She found herself backing away from him slowly, toward the door. She wanted to know the truth, and felt certain this would be her only chance to speak with him one-on-one.

But she *also* felt the need for 'backup'. If only she could crack it open, enough for Madelyn to overhear the conversation. It might prevent her from feeling like a fool later, trying to repeat it, word-for-word.

Gently she turned the knob from behind, pulling it out enough to barely wedge the heal of her boot against it. But its metal surface was ice cold, her fingers went numb and she lost her grip.

The door closed again.

As a last resort, she dialed Madelyn on her cell phone. Faintly, there was a muffled response of surprise as she answered.

"The prophecy says, 'One day, a *divine figure* will come to Earth...gather the chosen, and then...destroy the world'."

She could not believe her ears.

"Una?" she could hear Maddie's voice, "Where are you? What the *hell's* going--"

"*Some* say this 'destruction' is symbolic, that it will only be 'destroyed' for those who do not believe. Unlike here in the West, Chinese view 'the end of days' as part of a cycle. For them, the word *apocalypse* describes a shift in power...the birth of new government."

She frowned. "But you said *divine*. I don't understand. How much do we really *know*?"

"Very little, I'm afraid. Most often, *'divine'* means 'from or like a god'. As in 'divine hero', or 'divine messenger', like an Angel--something that goes far *beyond* the range of normal human experience. We might say...'Supernatural'."

Una's spine shivered.

Just the *thought* of it was enough to freak her out. Her mind returned to her *flashback* in the taxicab with Madelyn:

Complete 'peace of mind'...surrounded by 'fog', then...a 'presence' she could not explain...

Was it part of a dream, or something more?
So far, she could find no words to describe it.

"I *can* tell you this," he said, after a pause, "These people you're dealing with are part of a *chain* that goes way back. They've been waiting a long time for this prophecy to come true. *They* believe this 'figure' has often shaped human history, and its return will bring about CHANGE unlike any we've ever faced before. They *also* believe it has a name, represented by your symbol: SAN-TOU-LONG."

At *last*, the answer she'd been waiting for.

"Which means?"

"THREE...HEADED...DRAGON!"

***

Safely inside, beneath a warm blanket, Una thought she might finally get some rest. At least Maddie knew she was not losing her mind. The rise of Ancient Evil in the modern world was not *exactly* what she expected.

This assignment was getting out of hand. Any threat to Chinatown seemed like a trial run...for something *bigger*.

But where? And when?

Maybe soon.

Closing her eyes, she had no idea what to expect. But somehow, she knew the *next* attack would be linked to New York, that it would affect many more lives, and...like it or not, she would find herself at the *heart* of it.

She only hoped it could wait until morning.

8

CONTAGIOUS

Una woke the next day just after 7 AM to hot green tea with fresh, steamed 'basket buns', both salty and sweet; stuffed with eggplant and chives, or sugar and sesame seeds. Because nearly everything served at *Lao-Chi* was made by hand, from scratch, Hongi was already in the restaurant kitchen, downstairs, with half of her family doing prep work.

She glanced over at Madelyn, still asleep, and sighed.

It seemed wrong to impose on these poor people. What was she *doing* here, anyway? Trying to hide from police? As if no one would figure out where they had gone to stay. She felt guilty, to say the least.

Fear could be *contagious*, spreading from person to person. She sensed it within herself from the moment they arrived in Chinatown: fear of strange customs or beliefs. Fear of people she did not know or understand--before they had even met. And she wanted to run away.

For once in her life, it made her realize how most Americans probably felt about entering Hopiland.

Last night, surrounded by cops at *The Yin-Yang*, she succumbed to fear, feeling threatened by unknown assailants--or conspiracy theories that could send her and Maddie shuffling back to D.C., defeated and empty-handed.

But that was no way to be.

This family survived--by *facing* their fears every day. She could picture them, cleaning countertops, chopping meat and vegetables, pouring oil to fill metal wok drums, cracking eggs to separate them, making XO sauce from dried shrimp, scallops, chillies and garlic--all to be ready for meal service, by 11 AM.

We must go, she thought, nudging Madelyn. Time to get back *up* on the horse. Gang or no gang. It was the only way to solve anything.

***

As they neared the Fifth Precinct Station House, Madelyn was in complete agreement, *almost*. "Whatever you do, try not to mention our lodgings-- for now," she said, "Too many cops can be bad for business!"

Una sighed, opening the door.

They found the place more chaotic than usual. Aside from standard police work--issuing a copy of an accident report, or helping someone fill out a complaint form--FBI agents in dark suits seemed to be everywhere, seizing computers, cell phones and case files.

It almost looked like a *raid.*

Madelyn snagged Rufus, the computer geek, walking by. "What the hell's going--"

"Justice Department oversight," he said, "Cyber Shield Division. *Supposed* to be only temporary. Let's hope. Detective Stone is fit to be tied, along with everyone else. We can't wipe our *ass* without permission. Really sucks."

"Why?" said Una.

"Something about 'glitches' reported with surveillance cameras, in places all the way from New York to D.C."

"So--"

"It seems they all happened at exactly the same time: 1:11 AM. So far, no explanation."

"In numerology, 1 is the number of *creation,*" said Madelyn, "The primal force from which all other numbers spring forth. It is *said* that when you truly understand the function of 1, you will know all there is to know, and *enlightenment* is yours."

Rufus tried to keep a straight face, wondering if she was for real.

He preferred to look for a synchronous event, to give the incident meaning. Computer hacks, even those wrongly motivated, generally commanded respect from average users, who had no clue regarding the way things actually worked. The selection of 1:11 was *probably* intended to convey meaning. If only they could figure it out.

"No more *excuses!*" shouted an angry voice across the room. "If we can't function, that puts the people of this city at *risk*. By noon. Do you HEAR me? Up and running!"

Both women subconsciously stepped away, toward the exit.

A group of IT experts came shuffling out of Stone's private office with blood apparently drained from their faces.

Rufus grinned. "That's *another* thing. Police communications are down not just in New York, but between us and the Feds. We can't reach the FBI, or Capitol Hill or the Pentagon. It's like we're *cut off* from the world."

Una's ears perked up. "Why military?"

He shrugged. "Somehow, it's all tied to *satellites*. First report cited one used for climate and terrain monitoring by NASA. They notified the Department of Defense, which is responsible for investigating any attempted interference with U.S. satellite operations."

It didn't take long for that angry voice to find them.

"You two," said Stone appearing suddenly, red-necked and huffing like a locomotive. "In my office-- NOW."

Madelyn couldn't help but feel like a school girl, caught smoking in the boys' locker room. She found no sympathy in Una's eyes. Apparently such things didn't *happen* growing up on a reservation.

Still, it all seemed a bit over the top.

By the time they stepped inside a glass enclosure known as 'the fishbowl', Stone's demeanor had changed. He even managed a smile.

"Okay, ladies," he said, clearing his throat, "Out there, you'll hear plenty of rumors, half-truths and denials, mainly to keep the public at bay. In here, there's *no bull*. The National Oceanic and Atmospheric Administration, which includes the National Weather Service, took its Satellite Data Information System offline approximately ten hours ago after an *unexplained* incident, which keeps weather agencies around the world from receiving forecast data. According to their statement, 'It's not clear who the perpetrators are.'

"Well, that's not *exactly* true. The NOAA's director told *me* it was a hack-- and it was *China*. We don't know yet if it was the Chinese government or if criminal elements were involved. This by itself is nothing new. Cyber-attacks by hackers over the past three decades have included data like background checks and security clearance codes, targeting U.S. industry.

"But this time, it *appears* to be highly specific: aimed at Defense Companies with weapons-system information."

Madelyn shook her head. "I don't get it. My interview with company heads for the *first* target came up--"

"*Sunny-Side*? Believe me, it may *look* like a department store outlet here in the states, but that's just for show. In markets across the globe, including places like Southeast Asia, they rank high as a major purveyor of stealth technologies...like surveillance and wiretapping. This helps oppressive regimes to control dissidents, by eliminating privacy, and freedom of speech."

"I don't understand," said Una. "How do you *know* all this?"

Stone grinned, leaning back in his chair, hands behind his head.

"Are you kiddin' me? I'm an old Army dog, with plenty of connections. They *need* people like me in the private sector, just in case."

"Of *what*?"

"Well, you know...*invasion*!"

"But I don't--"

"Sure you do, sure you do. You just don't want to admit it, that's all. People like me keep tabs on suspicious characters who threaten the fabric of this fine nation. Mostly from places we've never heard of, with names we can't even pronounce. They don't understand American values. How *can* they? My last tour of duty was in Japan. How do you think I got assigned to Chinatown?"

Una could feel her temper rising. What a bigot. What an *idiot*! With no basic understanding of the people he was policing.

"But Japan and China are two completely different countries. You can't just lump them to--""

"Same difference!" he said, "Anyway, we're not here to debate. Feds are calling the shots now. The FBI has its own set of protocols. In fact, your presence here may no longer be required--but that's not my decision."

"Whose is it?"

"Intelligence bigwig, headed our way. That's all I know. When he arrives, we'll see action. No more sittin' around, with our hands tied. *You'll* see."

He opened the door to his office, at last.

Both women shared a singular thought: *Find Rufus.*

***

With dark suits from wall to wall, curiously enough, the computer geek found himself in low demand. While others pointed fingers, Rufus ran a slew of tests on one PC the others seemed to have missed, trying to solve the mystery of what had happened to communications.

He knew that specific counter measures would be taken, to upgrade security.

When hackers breached the weather satellite, overnight it forced cyber security teams to seal off data vital to disaster planning, aviation, shipping and more--all potentially crippling users for days to come.

Even before this, personal privacy laws were being violated every day. It was a big problem for police departments across the country. Most systems were simply outdated, with little or no thought given to security. That's how people like Stone got away with abusing the system, conducting searches without proper authority or even bothering to log in a user's name when accessing a Federal Database.

They found him with the PC's tower opened, attaching a kind of wired bypass, to create an unusual readout on the screen of his laptop consisting mainly of numbers, in computer code once referred to as DOS. Una read it once in a manual, she thought. Beyond that, it was meaningless.

"We...need your help," she said.

He grinned, without looking up. "Glad to hear it. I think I've isolated the root of our problem. The perps behind our recent cyber breach did more than steal data. They *probably* planted a virus! What can I do for you?"

"Tell us the truth," said Madelyn. "This whole mess, it's bad, but it can be *fixed*, right?"

"No doubt," he replied, "But we've got to do better. China's been testing space warfare systems for a decade. Sooner or later, they're bound to get it right. The *last* thing you want is cyber attacks on satellites. Even if you just switch them off, they're essentially space debris--which can cause a whole *new* set of problems. Everybody knows that!"

"One more thing," said Una.

She got down on hands and knees right beside him, hoping no one else would overhear. With so many Feds in the building, and *fear* at an all time high, it felt like an epidemic, growing worse by the minute. Leaning close, with lips to his ear, she whispered, "We can't trust Stone...and we don't know where to turn. Any ideas?"

9

OBLIVION

Rufus could only think of one person off the top of his head, not because of special rank or sphere of influence, but rather, a particular low key way of doing things.

"Officer *Shen*," he said. "Likable, with no real enemies--at least, as far as I know. He's--"

Then a sudden commotion in the hallway caught them all by surprise. A stampede of moving bodies made it seem like a fire drill.

"What the--?" said Madelyn, sticking her head out.

"*He's here*! *He's here*!" cried voices without explanation.

"S-sorry!" said Una as they raced to catch up.

***

Nearing the squad room, she could hear Stone briefing other detectives:

"Another minute, he'll come through that door."

"But I don't get it, sir," one objected, "What makes him--"

"*Qualified?* Try consecutive tours of duty in places like Pakistan with U.S. Army Air Cav Brigades in '06, "Operation New Dawn" in Iraq and an American rescue mission in Syria, for starters. He's served with distinction at *Fort Dix*, New Jersey, *Yakima Training Center* in Washington State, and more recently, *Camp Navajo*, Arizona. Something called "Operation Underhill". Black Ops. Specialty: *cyber-espionage*. A true blue American--with security clearance so high they don't even have a name for it. Suffice it to say, we're all below his pay grade."

Una shook her head. There was too much noise. Did he say...*Camp Navajo*? *Arizona*? No, of course not. Impossible. She tried deep breaths. Even a careful listener could make mistakes.

People converged toward a rear entrance used mostly for prisoner transfers and deliveries to the Station House.

Glancing through a rear window she could see a black armored Humvee pulling into the parking lot, coming to a slow stop right *outside* the door. A shiver went through her spine as she recalled its intimidating size, with distinctive plating and bullet-resistant glass.

Just like the ones that came to Hopiland.

She told herself it was all coincidence. The Army used those vehicles all over the world. Especially since 9-1-1, New Yorkers, perhaps better than anyone, understood the need for security.

New laws allowed the use of armed forces to "restore public order" as needed in cases of natural disaster, epidemic, or terrorist attacks. *Some* people said it only made sense to accept help from the military, working hand-in-hand with police to provide checkpoints and patrol public events, like the Boston Marathon or the Kentucky Derby.

But these moves were not without controversy. When officials spoke of "responding to civil unrest" with measures like crowd control, others feared the loss of personal freedoms, like the right to free speech. The *last thing* anyone wanted was a protest march outside the police station.

No *wonder* they used the back door.

Police and FBI had gathered outside. Three men left the Humvee in Black Ops uniforms to enter the Station House, but she couldn't see any of their faces. One wore a red beret. That *had* to be him--the "big-wig" they were so worried about. The SOB who'd turn them all on their heads.

Suddenly, her heart fluttered.

It would be an impossible coincidence, of course, but she couldn't deny the possibility. What if it *was* Ashcroft? Nearly three years had elapsed between them, without a word. What would happen if they came face-to-face?

Where to begin?

Sure enough, the chaos outside found its way into the station. People poured through the narrow doorway, spilling to either side, in waves. First came a handful of cops, who quickly gave way to dark-suited FBI, followed by supervisors in neck ties, until finally, with escorts, emerged the man in the red beret.

Then, before she had time to react, the procession made an unexpected turn. Una cringed as her and the General nearly *collided*.

He paused, looked her right in the eye, and grinned.

She gasped.

But he seemed at a loss for words, and turned away.

Wait! she wanted to say, but then stopped in her tracks. Maybe the timing was all wrong here, in the midst of a crisis. Maybe he was distracted, with too much on his mind, too much responsibility, no time for personal reunions.

Or, *maybe* he was just being an ass!

Una would *not* let him slip by so easily--not after years of wondering what *might* have been, tossing and turning at night, fretting over imaginary spies outside her window, afraid she might never see him again.

No way.

Their paths had crossed for a *reason*. What did the radio guy call it? *Serendipity: discovery of that which is unsought.* Well, she never expected to find *him* here. Besides, it was part of her job to avail herself of any and all possible resources to help solve the mystery at hand. These attacks in Chinatown, her "lost time" episode, and now, Ashcroft's return...were all *connected*, somehow.

People might call her crazy. But not Maddie. She'd probably find it somewhere in her horoscope.

So be it. Una marched right up behind him.

"Excuse me, General. Agent Waters, here as special liaison from--"

He abruptly spun around to face her, grasping her by the sleeve, pulling her aside. Blood rushed all at once to her head.

"Yes," he whispered, "I'm quite sure you have every right to be here. But why *now*? Why after all this time?"

So, he noticed.

"Well, I just happen to be...*hey*! What's *with* you? We're on the same side."

"Are we?" he said, with eyes narrowed, "I wonder."

What was *wrong* with him? How'd he ever get so...so...

"Colin! I don't under--"

"Yeah, well, I never heard from you, so I figured-_"

"Figured what? *What exactly*?"

And their voices suddenly carried, above every one else in the room.

All eyes turned.

"We need...all the...*help* we can get, Miss Waters," he said thoughtfully, lowering his voice with a smile, to diffuse the tension. He patted her shoulder, like a comrade. "Glad to have you on board!"

Two dark suits came forward.

"Transmissions," he said, "We may be dealing with a hijacked satellite connection. The attacker first infects a targeted computer with malware. Your dish. Where is it, exactly?"

They pointed upward, and soon the general's entourage split up, between the elevator and the stairs. A minute later, they were gone.

Madelyn breathed a sigh of relief. "Out of sight, out of--"

"*Don't!!!*" said Una with fire in her eyes.

***

In the momentary silence, the two women came to realize they'd been completely shut out.

"For a moment, I felt...*forgotten*," she said.

Maddie laughed. "Like *that* could ever happen! Honey, that man is Sagittarius, through and through--"

"But don't you have to know his--"

"Birth date? *Please*. Sometimes, I can just *feel* it. Not all who wander are lost. He's a vagabond, and an eternal traveler. He has the flair and confidence of a born leader. A clear thinker, with a big picture approach--and a thirst for adventure. That also happens to make him a *perfect* match for Libra. Believe me, the two of you will never be bored!"

Una rolled her eyes. It all sounded a *bit* too much like a pep talk.

A woman dispatcher appeared, quietly roving about the station, from the reception desk to each computer screen, inspecting them one by one.

"Where's Rufus?" she said.

They pointed upward.

"It *figures*. Every one disappears at the same time, and now there's no one to ask!"

"What do you mean?" said Una.

"My network just went down. I can't reach a single squad car anywhere in the entire city. And they can't reach me either. I...can't explain it. It's never happened before, and I...well, I..."

"What?'

"Well, I'm no computer genius, but I'm *pretty* sure there's an icon here that doesn't belong. See it there? Triangular shaped, in the bottom left-hand corner. I don't know where it came from."

"So?"

"So you click on it, and nothing happens. Well, that's not right. Icons don't do that--just *appear*, for no reason. Normally, they--"

And suddenly, the screens turned dark red, every one of them at once. The weird, little icon suddenly enlarged itself, until it revealed *another* white shape inside it: three curved prongs, each of them becoming thicker until they grew scales, and a snout, opened wide with sharp teeth--from the maw of a *dragon*!

Then, the screens went dark, as lights flickered.

A scream came, from outside, loud enough to make you cringe--not on the street, as one might expect. Crime in Chinatown, like everywhere else in New York, knew no boundaries. Shooting victims often showed up on their doorstep.

This voice came from *above*, on the roof.

The women instinctively looked up, then exchanged troubled glances. What could possibly go wrong?

Moments later, someone came racing down the nearest stairwell. They could hear him gasping for breath.

Detective Stone appeared, one hand clutching his chest, the other bracing a wall for support as he came stumbling toward them. By the look on his face they thought at first he might be having a heart attack.

But then, they noticed his white shirt and tie, stained in blood--apparently, not his own.

"Wh-what happened?" the dispatcher cried.

Stone struggled for words. "Satellite dish...rigged...high voltage. It...was a trap! We've got...casualties. Ambulance...on its way!"

With that, he collapsed.

None of them said a word. They could already hear sirens.

As seconds ticked by on the station clock, the three women could do nothing but hold hands, and pray.

Una shuddered, fearing the worst.

10

FATE BOUND

According to Stone's report, a single fatality had resulted from the electrocution of an FBI agent, apparently grasping a "live wire". But there was more to the story. If not for swift action, taken by Rufus, others might have died.

Unfortunately, this also earned him a trip to the ER.

Roof returnees appeared speechless, still in shock, all except for Officer Shen. "I found *this*," he said privately to Una, presenting a broken chain with a pewter dragon belt buckle. "No one else knows. I thought you--"

"Thanks," she started to say, but seemed torn. The trail on any lead might not last for long.

"I've *got* this," said Madelyn, racing toward the front door, "Riding with Burke to the hospital. Don't worry. I'll call you."

She nodded. The chain *seemed* to match one on her suspect, at the parade. Turning it over in her hand, the buckle showed "TY" engraved on one side. *But what did it mean?*

The dispatcher eyed Una's thoughtful manner. While others seemed to run in circles, she sat quietly at an empty desk, eyes closed, trying to picture something in her mind.

She touched a lifeless keyboard. "I don't suppose...?"

"Not a chance," the dispatcher replied. "Still down."

"It's okay," she said softly, almost at a whisper. Mentally, she retraced her steps, trying to keep up with Professor Chong, that day she leaped from her cab, to run after him. He slipped into an alley beneath a snow covered sign.

Suddenly, she smiled.

"What is it?"

Una rose, abruptly to her feet. "Just a hunch."

Outside, with flakes coming down, she hailed a Qwik-Ride. People shuffled along the sidewalk. Few would ever realize that their police force was completely shut down. Better for them not to know.

"Where to?" the driver said.

"*Tattoo You*," she replied.

***

Like most tattoo shops in New York, it wasn't much to look at, from outside, at least. Inside, licenses appeared on display, with vintage flash art, custom jewelry and an autoclave. All appeared to be in order. Still, she feared the people might be scary or mean.

It was small, with one tattoo artist and one piercer, situated about three feet apart, no walls between them. Much to her surprise, there was no 'doctors office' or 'hospital' smell; more like stale cigarettes.

Since both were preoccupied, she took a seat.

SpottieOttieDopaliscious by Outkast played on shop speakers.

"First time?" a woman said beside her with short, spiked pink hair. She seemed awfully young to be covered in so much 'body art'.

"Well, I..."

"Don't be shy, honey. Most don't know what to expect. It's not like you see on TV, where the artist is free the minute you walk in, talks to you for hours, listens to your problems, holds your hand and you leave best friends. But if you want a quality *tat*, this is the place."

She flashed her name, *LOLA*, inked on her thigh.

"First time I came was my 20th birthday. Man, was I scared! I picked out a picture, then, within an hour or so, I got it. *Loved it.* Hurts, but doesn't kill you. That was two and a half years ago--the first of 8 and many piercings. I now have 25 holes I wasn't born with."

Una began to have second thoughts.

"Help you?" said the owner, stepping out from the back. A small Asian woman with cropped gray hair and big loop earrings, she grinned through black lipstick, in a tank top with the motto:

Look Better
NAKED
Get A Tattoo

She smiled. "Your artwork is...*striking*."

"Original," she said. "Not mere copies, like other shops. I started with blackwork and tribals. Very popular in the '80s. Explored native cultures of the world. Now inspired by *Organic Geometry*; the structure of leaves and shells, repeating patterns that fascinate mystics, philosophers and shamans. Help make sense of the universe. You...*like*?"

"Yes, very much," she said. "But I'm--"

"Take your time. Flip through the book. We do mostly Japanese, Chinese and American. All our own design."

In her absence, Una decided to play along. Incredible works of art jumped out from every page-- supernatural and horrific--sending shivers through her spine, but nothing came close to what she had in mind.

Lola grinned. "Wondering *why* you came here?"

Her hood shook.

"Let me tell you. The reasons change over time. Most of us get inked at first to pay *tribute* to a loved one. So, the tattoo has special meaning. Some do it to express *creativity*, like a story they're trying to tell. An artist can help them with that. Others do it for a sense of *control* over their own bodies. It makes them feel whole. And those are all *good* reasons, right? The ones that make sense."

She nodded.

"But then, there's the *dark* side, the ones we don't talk about, like...the pain. *It hurts so bad, it feels good,* right? When you've reached the point of no turning back. When you can't wait to get another, and another. That's when you know: you're *hooked*."

Una finally gave up on the book. Then she noticed a series of framed photos, with happy customers. *One* of them, slightly blurred, featured a man with a tat on his shoulder--clearly *three-pronged*.

"Excuse me," she said, reaching for her purse. It was time to get answers--or get out of there.

The owner reappeared.

"'I was wondering...this belt buckle, was it made *here*?'"

Her eyes narrowed, as she snatched the book away. She seemed anxious, glancing back, toward an empty doorway. "Where? Where did you find this?"

"On a rooftop. It's...hard to explain."

"I *bet*," her voice changed, turning mean. "You...some kind of cop? Bet you think I tell you who bought it. *Impossible!* We take cash only. No receipts. You... go now! And don't come back!"

Outside, Una spied the owner through storefront glass, marching, book in hand, toward the back. Hopefully, no one noticed the small "bug" she'd attached to its spine. Rounding the corner, she tossed an empty frame, tucking the folded picture in her pocket, and donned ear buds. At first there was only static, but then, she heard voices, the owner first:

> "It was *her*."
> "So?" another replied. "Big whoop."
> "Your photo's gone. She must've
> taken it."
> "Okay. I'll get it *back*!"

She ripped off her buds, scanning all around.

When an armored Humvee pulled up, out of nowhere, with the U.S. Army logo, she sighed with relief. She recognized its two young men in uniform, from the Station House.

"Good day, Ma'am," one said. "Please get in."

"Hey, wait a minute. What's the big idea?"

"We're not at liberty to say, Ma'am, except...it's a matter of National Security."

It seemed like the lesser of two evils. So, she complied.

***

Within minutes, they arrived at the entrance to an exclusive restaurant in an alleyway off East First Street.

The sign read simply: *KO*.

Both officers escorted her inside to a private dining room, past the main, which was curiously empty for this time of day. Offered pliant leather seating at a rectangular table constructed out of black walnut, she suddenly recognized her dinner host as he stood to greet her, formally.

"Miss Waters," said Ashcroft, "Glad you could make it."

She huffed and puffed, shifting her gaze from side to side, "It seems I have no choice! By the way, where *is* everyone? It's so...so...quiet."

"Privatized, for the evening. Courtesy of U.S. Army."

Ordinarily, reservations here started at $250 per person, without special arrangements. Few people ever dined here in private. Few could afford it.

His men stepped away from the table, saluting him.

"Thank you, gentlemen. *Dismissed*!"

The table was immaculate, beginning with fine wine, in uncannily delicate glasses. A variety of serving trays gave off steaming aromas of barely seared, gently smoked lobster tale and spaghetti squash, rice and vegetable medleys, all seasoned to perfection. For dessert, there was bittersweet tart shell filled with pastry cream and dark chocolate mousse, and hearty, well-rounded barley tea.

"*American Nouveau*," he observed, "Guided by the Japanese *Kaiseki* tradition--or so I am told. Food that is unexpected, but extraordinarily delicious. The menu is twelve course. Founded by a remarkable chef who is rarely seen, with other equally impressive establishments in Toronto and Sydney. Rumor has it that he lurks in an underground lair, staring at a wall map with pins, marking his dominion."

Una tried to appear angry. "You...you can't just *hijack* people off the--"

"It's not like that," he said, "You're free to go anytime, although..."

He paused, suddenly taken aback. The room's chandelier lighting reflected off her silver Corn Maiden amulet.

"You still--?"

"I never stopped," she replied.

His eyes moistened. "My apologies, Miss--"

"*Una*," she corrected him.

"Yes, of course. Well, something you should know: the 'incident' we encountered earlier today, might've gone far worse, if not for--"

"What, exactly?"

"Your boy...*Rufus*! He sensed...*danger*, somehow. His quick thinking saved many lives--including my own. He *insisted* on being there. Told me it was...*your* idea. I...well...I owe you an apology...and a debt of gratitude. It seems that fate has brought us together. We...*need* each other."

Her heart fluttered.

And the smile on her lips conveyed many things to him in that moment-- cherished memories and girlish dreams and hopes for the future--things she could barely express. But it did not seem to matter.

Somehow, he *knew*.

There was no need for words.

Two hearts beat as one.

11

UNBELIEVABLE

Beneath a city street light, Una's breath appeared in the cold night air, as she spoke to Madelyn on her cell.

"I need to go slow," she said.

"Newsflash! You're not *gettin'* any younger. Don't let him slip away this time. It may be your last chance!"

She rolled her eyes, hailing a cab. "So...how's Rufus?"

"He *seems* okay, but it's the strangest thing. Doctors say he got a *flash burn*--caused by electrical arcs that pass over the skin. Intense heat and light can cause severe burns in a fraction of a second. Skin damage is largely superficial. Tissues below are unaffected."

"That's *good* news, right?"

"Except for one thing. They *say* it shouldn't be possible. The FBI guy died from high voltage, with most of the damage *beneath* the skin. Just the opposite!"

"What are you saying?"

"It's a mystery, that's all. And *another* thing: according to Rufus, it wasn't just a power surge. Something weird happened. There were lights in the sky, moving a hundred feet overhead. High voltage lines produced a shower of sparks. Everything dimmed, and then...KABOOM! He had only a split second to pull others away from the dish. Afterward, people said they felt a sensation of being *anesthetized*! He called it...a UFO."

Una did not know what to say.

"Hello?" said Maddie, "You still there? So anyway, like I said, life is short. Don't let fear stand in your way."

Una shrugged. "I have no idea what you're--"

"Are you freakin' kiddin' me? You're *afraid*...afraid of love!"

"No, no, no--you've got it all wrong. Afraid to let my guard down, maybe, afraid of distraction, certainly, but--"

"Okay, so explain to me how you forgot."

"Forgot what?

"What day it is! You just *happen* to have a romantic dinner with the man of your dreams, and you forget that it's Valentine's Day? *Plleeeaasse*!"

"All right," she smiled. "Maybe you've got a point. Anyway, it's late, my Qwik-Ride is here, and I've gotta go. See ya!"

Una nearly slipped on ice as she reached for the cab door. From a crowd of strangers on the sidewalk, someone leaped forward, suddenly.

She felt afraid to turn, gripping her purse.

People said New York was a rude city. True enough. But most people here had high-pressure jobs. Their time was precious.

It was also a place where tons of people had to walk or use public transportation--with its own unwritten code of conduct.

At peak hours, there could be a hundred and fifty walking on a given block, trying to get to work, a thousand more on a subway train, fifty trying to get off a bus, a hundred trying to go up or down a staircase.

And yet, every day, unthinking tourists paused in the middle of busy sidewalks, held up trains by trying to force the doors open, blocked stairwells or tried to board a subway car without letting others off.

The frantic pace could not be stopped.

To interfere with it, was simply being *rude*. New Yorkers had learned to curse at *anyone* who got in their way.

It was part of survival here.

So, in a city where everyone acted so rude to her, Una found herself asking only one question: *What am I doing wrong?*

She tried to let go, but then, with each of their hands pulling on the cab door, it opened.

From the radio, music played, "*Take it eeeaassyyy...*"

"Hear *that?*" the man said, "They're playing our song!"

Una turned. She could not believe her eyes.

It was *Jack Howser*--in the flesh--from Winslow, Arizona. Jack the newspaperman. Jack the conspiracy buff, collector of strange tales and ancient folklore. Jack, the only one three years ago who believed in her no matter what, because he was *there*, on Flight 564, back in 1995. Jack, who was not afraid to seek the truth, because it mattered. Jack, her *compadre* and friend.

He slid in the back seat beside her.

"Sorry for just 'showing up' like this, but you never returned my call. With all the buzz from MUFON about the latest sighting over New York, I just *had* to--"

"Wait," she said, "What are you talking about?"

"Nine days ago. That would make it the night of--"

"February 5th."

"*Exactly.*"

"Where to?" the driver said.

Una's face went completely blank.

Jack grinned. "Hope you don't mind. I...just got into town and...there's a great all-night diner not far from here. How about some coffee?"

She nodded.

"*Moonlight Cafe.*"

They wound up on Brighton Beach Avenue, seated at a booth with an ocean view. It took three cups for Una to get her bearings. Maybe it was too much info to process all at once--first dinner with Ashcroft, then running into Jack.

Maybe she just needed time.

"Quite extraordinary, really," he said, talking non-stop. "Last time anything like *this* happened was in New Zealand, December 1978."

"What do you mean?"

"Pilots first noticed strange lights above the town of Kaikoura, near the coast. They were seen by hundreds of people. Above 2000 feet, aircraft encountered a gigantic lighted orb, but at low altitude, it moved more like a helicopter, remaining airborne but completely motionless."

"So?"

"Then, like now, Defense officials came up with a variety of explanations, stating causes such as lights from squid boats reflected off clouds, unburned meteors and sightings of the planet Venus. No surprise--the New York Port Authority attributes *this* event to Chinese lanterns and fireworks!"

Una gazed at the moon's reflection off the Atlantic Ocean. Tears welled up in her eyes.

"I can't...talk about this right now!"

"It's late," he said, "Forgive me. I shouldn't have dragged you out here. Not when you have a job to do. I'm sorry. It's just...I don't know, *something* told me to ...anyway--"

She wiped away her tears.

"No, don't say that. You were *right* to come. I've been thinking of you. In fact, there's something about that night, my first day in New York. Something *happened* that I can't explain. I know it sounds foolish, but I can't even trust my own mind."

Jack suddenly perked up. He was almost ready to call it a night. Reaching into his pocket, he pulled out a mini tape recorder.

"I hope you don't think I'm crazy, but--"

Una laughed. "Crazy? You? Not at all. You're one of the sanest people I know. It's *me* that's going crazy! Trying to keep it all inside, trying to focus on my job--following leads that get stranger by the minute--and all the time, afraid that if I drop my guard for even an instant, they'll--"

"They'll what?"

"I don't know. Figure out my *secret*, I guess--the one that gnaws at my brain, keeps me on edge...a blank spot that I'm simply unable to fill."

"*Amnesia?*" he asked. "Why didn't you say so? There are ways around that. Have you tried hypnosis?"

"God, no! That scares me even more. I'm afraid of what I'll--"

"Find out?"

She nodded.

Jack switched off his recorder.

"Maybe you're right," he said. "I *thought* I came to follow a story, but this may be the *real* reason I'm here!"

Una's demeanor seemed to shift.

Sitting up straight, she poured a fresh cup of coffee and signaled the waitress for food. She pulled out her cell.

"What are you *doing*?"

"Sending Maddie a text, telling her not to wait up."

"What about your job? Don't you have--"

"Responsibilities? Of course. But right now, they'll have to wait. We're onto something. Maybe bigger than both of us. Anyway, I've got a gut feeling that you're on the right track. One mystery leads to another. I already know the next step."

"You do?"

She grinned. "It came to me just now. You remind me of someone I just met. He's young and bright and full of questions. His name is Rufus. And right now, he's sitting in a hospital bed--because of something he saw. Something no one else wants to talk about--because they're afraid. It's connected, somehow, to this whole crime wave in Chinatown-- and *I* believe it's connected to me. Sounds crazy, right?"

Jack raised his cup. "You said it!"

Eating breakfast with Jack at 3 AM at the *Moonlight Cafe*, overlooking the Atlantic Ocean, wasn't exactly what Una had in mind. But then, maybe it was exactly where she needed to be.

Jack waited for her to finish her pancakes before saying another word. His mind raced back to Arizona and the Mystery Cave, to their secret recording of Ashcroft at Camp Navajo, spilling his guts about UFO legends, satellite anomalies, China and Area 51.

He had a few connections of his own in New York, thanks to the *Arizona Journal*, and MUFON.

She might not be prepared to face the answers. If *only* she had the courage to follow through. Not everyone did. Of course, he couldn't say for sure because he didn't know the particulars. At this point, he could only guess.

But he thought he knew where to look.

"Okay," said Una. "The wheels are turning. What's up?"

"Do you trust me?" he said.

She smiled at him with big brown eyes.

"That's all I need to know."

12

INTELLIGENCE

Jack and Una sat together on a bench along the waterfront, greeting the New York sunrise. Bounded by Coney Island at Ocean Parkway to the west, the beauty of Brighton Beach was not marred in the least by ice along the shore.

"Are you *sure* about this?" he said. "We haven't slept a wink. My friend has agreed to let us sit in--but just so you know--even for me, we're talkin' uncharted territory."

"Jack," she smiled, "Cold feet?"

He grinned back. "Not exactly, more like a *shiver*--in me bones. Like your first time in the ocean, going underwater. You know how to swim, but you still *feel* unprepared."

"I'm ready if you are."

"Okay, so now what?"

"The first step."

***

The hospital duty nurse could not explain why Rufus had been moved from his semiprivate room. There were apparently no doctor's orders. When Una flashed her "Special Consultant" badge for the NYPD, they were cautioned against trying to enter the 11th floor "Security Corridor", allegedly reserved for patients at "high risk"--without further explanation.

Despite its apparent absence from any hospital diagrams, they found it, completely isolated, with two FBI agents stationed outside the door.

Jack seemed confused. "I thought you said he was--"

"Okay," she nodded. "He *is*--or was, according to Maddie. In fact, he was soon to be released. I don't know--"

"It doesn't matter. Right now, we've gotta get *in* there, which should be no problem except...wait, do you recognize them?"

"From the station? No, I don't *think* so, but--"

"Good," he said. "Maybe it works both ways. Let's see. We'll need a quick change of...*there*," he pointed to a door marked STAFF ONLY.

Una read his mind. "You've gotta be--"

"Ever play doctor? You know, as a--"

She frowned with disapproval.

"No, I suppose *not*. Well, follow me!"

Minutes later, she adjusted the buttons on her nursing scrub top. She didn't feel particularly good about the deceit, but had to admit, she couldn't come up with a better plan.

Jack met her in the hallway, decked out in surgical scrubs and cap.

"Hey, that's not fair!" she whispered. "What makes me a nurse and you a freakin'--"

"Luck o' the draw, my dear."

She spied an agent leaving his post. "It's now or never!"

"One more thing," he said undoing her top two buttons. "A little cleavage, if you don't mind? We *need* a distraction!"

Una rolled her eyes.

Handing her a clipboard, Jack began to spout medical-sounding gibberish from old reruns of *Doogie Howser*, without the slightest notion of what it meant, hoping to waltz right in.

"I'm sorry," the agent said, refusing entry. "But your ID tag is missing. This patient is under Federal protection."

"Yes, yes of course," he replied, coolly, "I can wait. A colleague of mine is en route with it, from the OR. But *surely* you can let the nurse check his vitals? We need to monitor him at all times."

Una sensed an opening here, and slipped inside. The empty bed did not alarm her at first, assuming Rufus must be in the bathroom.

But it was empty too.

Her only clue: a discarded paperclip on the tile floor.

That was just like him! Too resourceful to wait around, he'd picked the lock to an adjoining room-- and already escaped.

Water was still moving in the toilet from a recent flush, so it must've happened just moments ago.

She'd have to pretend, to buy him some time.

"Oh...*nurse*!" sounded Jack's voice, distressed. "That's enough for now...we *do* have rounds to keep!"

And she knew he was in trouble.

"*There now*," she said out loud, trying to play the part as she stepped back into the hallway. "I'll be back to--"

"Hey! Just a damn minute!" an agent shouted as Jack split--past the *real nurse*, now approaching.

On cue, Una dashed in the opposite direction.

Sprinting down the nearest stairwell, she took an elevator on the next floor, all the way down to the main lobby.

Moments later, she stepped outside.

A blue and white bubble-shaped hospital SECURITY vehicle with orange lights swerved up suddenly to greet her at the nearest curb, the driver quite happy with himself.

"*Rufus*!" she exclaimed. "B-b-but where's--"

"Right *here*!" squealed Jack, popping his head up from the back seat. "Hop in already!"

They drove away, nice and easy.

***

"We'll have to ditch the car," said Jack.

"Way ahead of you!" cried Rufus, entering a Greyhound station.

Slipping a stolen credit card into the nearest kiosk, he produced three one way tickets to Hoboken. "*This* should keep'em confused!"

Jack and Una followed him, to a boarding counter.

She huffed with dismay as they ducked into the nearest Men's Room and climbed out through an open window.

"*Now* what?" she groaned, outside again at last.

"Food," said Rufus. "I'm starving!"

And so they wound up drinking beer at *Tony's Pizza Palace*, a hole-in-the-wall on West 47th street.

Rufus ordered them all another round.

"I don't get it," said Una, "How'd you--"

"Know you were coming? Same way I scored us some wheels and free tickets. Computers, security cams and electronic starters...they're all the same to me. Like a puzzle to be solved. Ever try *Rubik's cube*?"

Jack and Una shook their heads.

"Anyway, what's next?"

"Next?" she said. "You can't go home right now, for one thing. None of us can. What *happened* back there?"

"Feds are tryin' to pin me is all," said Rufus. "They don't have a clue what's going on, so naturally, they--"

"On the *roof* I mean! Maddie says you saw *lights*...in the sky?"

He seemed a bit hesitant, in front of Jack.

"Look, it's okay. Jack's an old friend of mine, a reporter from Winslow. Sort of an expert on the paranormal--missing persons, ghost towns, UFOs--you name it!"

Rufus sighed with relief.

"Okay, well, it's like she said. The power surge was no accident. I had a feeling it was happening on purpose. Like some *intelligence* at work. That's when I saw the lights...a hundred feet overhead!"

Jack looked him square in the eye.

In that moment, they exchanged a bond of trust, from geek-to-geek--like discovering a kindred soul who truly appreciates *Fire in the Sky*, or believes in *Ancient Aliens*.

Una sensed a team forming. As they rose to their feet, it became clear that Rufus would be with them from now on.

Jack sighed. "Time for step two!"

***

The drive took just over two hours, by rental car. Upstate New York featured expansive snowscapes and open roads, a welcome change of pace from the big city. In the Catskill Mountains, they came to a nine room Bed & Breakfast with plenty of hot coffee and a big, cozy fireplace where people gathered at night to chase off the winter chill.

"A great place to hibernate," said Una.

A sign near the reception desk read:

WELCOME
EXPERIENCERS

"The facilitator is a certified hypnotherapist," said Jack, directing them to a small table. Rufus brought over three cups. "We first met in Long Island a few years back, following the case of a huge cylinder that appeared in the night sky. According to eyewitnesses, it was even more visible than the moon--bright, with flashing lights--but completely silent. She interviewed half a dozen, including two police officers."

Slowly, a few people trickled in, apparently guests of the Inn, taking coffee to their seats, as well.

"What are we *doing* here?" said Una.

Jack drew a long sip.

"This is *awesome*," said Rufus, reading from a brochure, "'Support for those who believe they've had contact with UFO's.'"

She didn't know what to say.

Finally, an older woman appeared in glasses and gray hair, wearing a simple sweater and blue jeans, with a kind face. She greeted several people by name, and waved briefly at Jack, before sitting atop a swiveled seat at the center.

"Welcome," she said. "We come together here about once a month, to remember that we are not alone. It's a time to reflect and offer one another encouragement, as we strive to...accept post-contact trauma, and other phenomena associated with...*close encounters.*

"I see a few new faces. Rest assured that we are a caring community, with open minds. You will not face ridicule of any kind. We are here for you, but also for the people in your life who don't understand the isolation, and pain that you, as an *Experiencer*, cope with every day. Would anyone like to begin?"

A construction worker, in his mid thirties, raised a hand.

"We all know the classic signs that lead to awareness...feeling disturbed about odd events, spans of 'missing time', mysterious nosebleeds or fear of certain places. For me, it began around age five...a bright light would come into my room and the door would open, and there would be a kind of fog, just shining through the whole house. Figures would appear, with big eyes. A lot of times I'd wake up the next morning in tears saying, 'Why me? Why me?'"

Una began to fidget--not because she was bored, or feeling a lack of compassion. She understood what Jack was trying to do, make her feel less stigmatized by her own sense of loss and confusion about the night of the parade...help her make *sense* of it somehow.

But why? Why *couldn't* she remember?

"I'm not necessarily fearful," said a single working mother and college graduate. "I'm just nervous about how others may react. Marks would show up on my body. One time I woke up with three red diagonal lines."

Rufus seemed to perk up at the pivotal word: "three".

Two young women, sisters, raised hands together.

"Our first encounter came during childhood," one said. "But it didn't stop there. A few times, as adults, we've been abducted together."

"The greys--or whatever you call them--are good at erasing your mind," said the other. "They'll leave you with *bits and pieces*."

Una's mouth fell open.

The next speaker recalled vivid memories on board alien spacecraft, including contact with children, described as "alien-human hybrids".

Una began to feel faint. Maybe it was the subject matter...or too much heat from the fireplace. Suddenly, her sense of uneasiness about the whole thing became *unbearable*.

"I...need...air," she whispered to Jack.

Pretending to get up for coffee, the three of them stepped outside.

"What gives?" said Rufus. "That was *awesome*!"

"All I can tell you is this: those people in there are sincere, and I have no reason not to believe them," she said, "But...*that's NOT what happened to me!*"

Driving back, with Rufus sound asleep in the back seat, Jack turned to Una with a look of unease on his face.

"By the way, you might not want to hear this, but I uncovered something. That UFO on the night of February 5th--DOD knew all about it."

"Defense?" she said, shaking her head. "No. That's impossible. You must be--"

"Radar tracking, video surveillance, the whole shabang! Dropped out of orbit, on cue, about the same time as a cyber breach at NYPD."

"But Jack, that information is classified. How do you *know* that?"

He grinned.

"Are you *kiddin'* me? Darlin', *that's* what I do!"

13

STARLIGHT

Heading south, to New York City, Jack offered to share his hotel room overnight. They all needed time to process their encounter with "Experiencers" upstate, and to catch up on their sleep.

Una jumped, sensing vibration from her cell. She held it up, relieved to hear a familiar voice.

"*Maddie*! Thank god! You wouldn't believe what I...well, that is, I'm not even sure I believe it myself, but, anyway...I'll have to explain it all...later. Look, I need to ask you something. But first, promise me you won't think I've gone off the deep end!"

"Okay," she said slowly, "I'm...all ears."

Una paused to glance at her two male companions. Jack seemed preoccupied with the road, searching for landmarks. Rufus held a pocket-sized guidebook to his face, reading with the aid of a small flashlight.

"I'm wondering if you can offer...some *advice*. I've never been good with this whole...*astrology* thing. You know that. Call me a skeptic."

"Or a fool."

"That, too," she grinned. "Anyway, lately, I'm beginning to wonder if there might be something to it--more than intuition, I mean. Maybe I should be more... *open*...to what the stars have to say."

Madelyn seemed hesitant. "Girl? Are you okay?"

"Yes, of course. Perfectly safe, for now. It's just, that well, suddenly my mind is filled with so many questions."

"No *wonder*. As a Libra, part of your life's goal is balance, the highest form of which can only be described as...*inner peace*. The only way to reach it may be through conflict. It can be scary, even unbearable, but you *will* endure--to make things right. It can also be a fatal flaw. Sometimes, Libras refuse to be happy and live a full life--waiting for perfect harmony."

"What about...my *destiny*?"

Madelyn sighed. The whole conversation seemed a bit too *cosmic*. "It all stems from what's happening, inside you. By thinking good or bad, you continually project and create your own reality. To change your destiny, you must first change your state of mind. By the way, wh-where *are* you?" she asked.

"Heading for the Hyatt. It's just for one--"

"Oh my god. In Queens? You...c-can't do that."

"Why not?"

"The FBI. They I.D.'d Jack off security cams at the hospital and...and--"

"What?"

"They're *waiting* for you. Turn around. C-call me later!"

***

Still shaking beside the NYPD squad car with red sirens flashing, Madelyn watched police move in and out of the Hyatt's main entrance. Reluctantly, she had agreed to participate in the stakeout, just in case anyone showed up.

Cold cigarette in hand, she rummaged anxiously through her purse, trying to stay calm, hoping to play along, wishing more than anything that she could just slip away, but knowing that was impossible. *Damn! If only--*

"Need a light?" said Detective Stone, proferring a Bic flame.

She tried to smile, taking a puff, blowing a fresh cloud of smoke.

His creepy grin reminded her of a *Cheshire cat*.

Together, they watched and waited. Madelyn hoped he would not ask too many questions, or get too close.

She prayed for the night to end.

***

"Change in plans!" said Una, abruptly.

Jack pulled off the freeway, screeching to a halt with both hands on the wheel. He wasn't mad exactly, just confused.

"What's up?" said Rufus, leaning forward.

"Forget the Hyatt...FBI's waiting. If only--"

"There's a place I know, in Owls Head...back a few miles, off the beaten path. Hunter's camp. Cabins are mostly empty this time of year. We may find water and nonperishables, like peanut butter, canned veggies or pasta."

"Sounds perfect," Jack said. "Tucked away, out of sight, beneath a blanket of snow."

He turned the car around. With any luck, they'd still make it in plenty of time to catch a few winks.

Soon, they had left the open road, crossing hilly terrain. Jack slowed. The headlights of his four-wheeler reflected off steep embankments with fallen trees. A white-tailed deer ran for cover.

"Are you sure about this?" said Una.

Rufus nodded. "I used to come here as a kid. Not to hunt so much, although my Uncle tried. I used to bring my camera."

"No kiddin'?" said Jack, "Ever see--"

Something streaked downward across the night sky, producing a short-lived trail of light.

All conversation stopped as they met a fork in the road.

"Ever wish upon a star?" said Jack.

Una recalled her "heart-to-heart" that night at Camp Navajo with Colin, three years ago, when he spoke of star constellations as if they had personalities, like *Orion*, the Hunter, and *Pleiades*, the Seven Sisters.

She remembered wishing that night for love that would last...forever.

"Of course, it's not really a 'falling star'," said Rufus, "but tiny bits of dust and rock, falling into the Earth's atmosphere and burning up. The 'trail of light' is actually called a *meteor*."

"Of *course* it is," she sighed.

Rufus guided them sure enough, and in no time, Jack pulled up beside a rustic cabin in the foothills, with an outhouse around back.

"No permits. No locks," he said.

Inside, they found a wood stove, a generator, shotgun-shell Christmas lights, duck decoys and a stuffed coyote.

Jack spied a rack near the fireplace with two rifles, a box of ammo, radio with batteries, and a deck of cards.

"We're in luck," said Una, opening a small pantry. There were jugs of drinking water, bags of *Doritos*, breakfast cereal, mac & cheese, a jar of pickles, and even a box of *Bisquick*.

Rufus grinned. "All the comforts of home."

She wanted to give him a hug. *Most* kids his age would complain.

They shared a simple meal before preparing to turn in. It almost reminded her of lean years, growing up on the reservation. They had just enough food to survive--with nothing to spare.

After a few minutes outside, the men returned with plenty of fire wood to last until morning. An adjoining room held two simple cots.

"I'll take first watch," said Rufus. "Technically, of course, I *am* younger with better stamina, and I actually require less sleep. But if you--"

"Okay," Jack nodded, "But wake me in three to four hours. If you hear anything--anything at all--the least bit out of the ordinary, get me at once. And don't step outside. Got that?"

Rufus winked at Una. They both knew Jack was nowhere near as brave as he pretended to be.

She found it surprisingly easy to fall asleep. But in her *dream*, the 'falling star' did not simply fade away:

It came down suddenly,
beneath the trees, to land, not far
from their cabin, enlarged,
like a giant pearl.

And she ventured out
--in spite of Jack's warning--
approaching the light.
It gave off
no heat or sound.

From its center, came
white...blinding...
silvery light.

She felt compelled to enter,
by a voice--from her youth.
And Una was not afraid.

The dream ended abruptly. She sat up, with her cell phone vibrating, in one hand. It was nearly 3 AM.

"I got tired of waiting," said Madelyn.

"It's okay. Tell me. The *you-know-what.* Is it safe?"

"As far as I know. Why ask?"

"It's complicated. Anyway, I--"

"Girl, you worry too much. To even find it, any thief would have to be a magician, or psychic, or--"

"A *mind reader?*"

And suddenly she recalled Mr. Lao, speaking of his book, *Bai Ze Tu:*

"...a guide to the forms and habits
of supernaturals in the world,
from shapeshifters to mind-sifters
--and how to fight them."

Maddie sighed. "Well, yeah, *maybe.* But honestly, who could...do...uch a thing?"

Their connection was failing.

Una moved closer to a window. "Okay, listen, about that..."

"You..ant me...to...*wha-wha-wha*..."

There *seemed* to be interference, like a chopper overhead.

"Maddie? Can you hear me? *Yes.* I'm sorry. Do you *mind*?"

"Funny thing...*wha-wha-wha*....I *knew* this... ould ...appen!"

"When--er I mean, *how*?"

"Just...this...orning!"

Fresh snow began to fall, only making it worse. Una felt tempted to race outside, but remembered Jack's warning.

"Maddie? Hello?!? Maddie! You're breaking up..."

"It *came* to me...ike always...in my 'scope!"

And then the signal died. Una tried three times to reconnect, but it was no use.

Munching sounds caught her ear. Peeking out to check on Rufus, she spied him with a bag of *Doritos*, near the fireplace. He seemed to be engrossed in his pocket guide.

"What are you reading, anyway?" she asked.

"*Far East Folklore.* Filled with facts and trivia, history, customs, and more. I'll bet you didn't know *this*," he said, reading out loud:

> *In ancient China,*
> *if a meteor fell from the sky,*
> *it was considered a SIGN*
> *that something important*

would soon happen on Earth
--like a major battle.

Una cringed. *NO NO NO*. That's NOT what she needed to hear. They came here to escape, but they might as well be lost.

No signal meant no GPS and no way to communicate with the outside world. What if something happened? There was no way to call for help.

She reached into both pockets of her hoodie, staring up at the moon. One held a left over napkin from *Lao-Chi*, the other, a small packet. It crinkled to the touch, individually wrapped, like a piece of candy, or--

A fortune cookie! she thought. *Good thing Jack's asleep. He'd just love to watch me open this, see the look on my face, and laugh.*

She turned away from Rufus, hoping he would not see.

Ordinarily not superstitious, she felt an irresistible urge to open it. It played on her mind. Of *course* it was silly. Maybe even *foolish*. But no worse than reading your horoscope.

What if there's a message, meant just for me?

Finally, when she could stand it no longer, Una undid the wrapper, held the cookie in both hands and snapped it, to reveal a small paper ribbon. She held it up to the window:

LIGHT FALL FROM HEAVEN
MEANS SKY GODS ARE
WATCHING.YOUR LIFE WILL
SOON CHANGE--FOREVER

PART THREE

TRANSLATION

*"There are many paths to
the top of the mountain, but the view
is always the same."*

--Ancient Chinese

14

HEADLINES

The story was not treated as front page news. In fact, buried in the back pages of *The New York Times*, it might have easily been missed by the casual reader, and was, in fact, ignored by media outlets in Chinatown for several days.

But Jack was more observant than most. It caught his eye as they stopped for coffee at a small diner, en route to Chinatown:

> BREACH INVESTIGATED
>
> According to an unidentified source: a recent cyber breach at the NYPD Fifth Precinct has resulted in stolen personnel records and protected dept. data, considered vital to city security. The attack, linked to Shanghai, China, is currently under investigation by the Counter Terrorism Unit, and the FBI.

There was no need to tell the others. They would find out soon enough. Una could not bear to stay in hiding. Come hell or high water, she was determined to see it through. That meant returning to the Station House on Elizabeth Street. Rufus had complete support from Stone and his comrades on the force. They trusted him. If the FBI had questions, so be it. He'd rather face them surrounded by allies than alone in some isolated hospital ward.

Jack, on the other hand, considered himself a *wildcard*, not bound by police protocols. He had no plans to step inside. Experience had taught him to stay free of entanglements. Instincts also told him that the real story here was as much about Una as the mysterious events swirling around her. It all began with her arrival in New York.

But why?

He could not help but connect her "missing time" episode with the Hopi Rattle artifact they found in the Arizona mystery cave. What if its creators had returned? Could this somehow be the *next step* in their plan for humanity?

***

Traffic slowed to a crawl as they approached the Station House. In spite of the cold, Asian Americans, from young people in blue jeans to Chinatown elders in print dresses and overcoats, including seamstresses, waiters, cooks, and vendors, had apparently come out in force to make their voices heard.

Una pressed her face to the glass. "What's going on?"

"Some kind of protest," said Jack.

"Check it out," said Rufus, reading slogans like "Equal Protection", "Justice For All" and a banner in bold letters: "END THE CRIME WAVE!"

Looking around, she realized that shops and businesses of every kind were *dark*--an eerie sight on a normal weekday--with handwritten signs hung in the windows that read: "Closed for Police Protest".

"Something's happened. We must get inside right away."

Jack slowed long enough for them to jump out, waving as they marched through the crowd. "I'll...be in touch!" he said.

Two officers guarding the Station entrance nodded, one patting Rufus on the back as they went in.

Una sighed, searching for a familiar face. No longer crawling with FBI, the tension was still thick nonetheless. People looked up briefly and turned away, as if afraid to acknowledge them. The dispatcher was nowhere in sight.

"Over here!" said uniformed Officer Burke, shuffling them away from the squad room, where shadows paced, back and forth.

With a finger to his lips, he led them upstairs. Rufus grinned at first as they entered his darkened workroom, then frowned as Burke closed the door behind them and switched on the lights.

It was stripped, completely bare.

Except for a few scraps of wire left on the floor, everything else--his computer, filing cabinets and reference bookshelf (once overflowing with tech manuals and assorted texts on computer programming)--was gone.

"We can talk here," said Burke. "But it better be quick."

Una shook her head. "I don't under--"

"Press leak! You haven't *heard?* It's a PR nightmare, but there's nothin' we can do!"

"Who--?"

"Don't know! First we got slammed with calls, then people showed up in droves. No one's seen anything like it--except maybe Fisher. His retirement's a few weeks away, says it happened once in '95...sixteen-year-old shot and killed by cops in Brooklyn for carrying a pellet gun. Large protests afterward."

Shouts drew Una to the nearest frost-covered window. A fight had broken out between police and protesters. Paramedics rushed a bloodied, middle-aged Chinese man away from the scene.

"Our response," said Rufus, "Who's in charge?"

"Ashcroft. Went right over Stone."

"He's...here, *now?*" asked Una.

Burke nodded. "Wants security checkpoints around the perimeter, with street closures, parking restrictions...and a nightly curfew. Not everyone agrees."

"What do you mean?"

"Police auxiliaries, mostly Chinese-American, say it's a bad idea. Too many immigrants still remember how it feels to be 'occupied' with armed troops on street corners. The loss of freedom only stirs resentment--leading to more violence."

Una could not believe her ears. Everything was changing so quickly. She felt the urge to see Ashcroft, but could not find a good excuse to do so.

She only hoped the violence here did not find its way to Madelyn. By now, she'd be on a train to D.C.-- a little slower perhaps, but way safer. Traffic could be horrendous, and tolls super high. The Delaware Turnpike was considered the most expensive in the U.S. With any luck, she'd accomplish her task and make a return trip in 24 hours.

Officer Shen came out of the squad room to get a coffee refill.

"What's...the assessment?" she asked.

He tried to smile. "Cat's out of the bag! All this talk about Shanghai makes people nervous. Ask any Asian on the street. Their greatest fear: *U.S.-China War*. *How* it begins matters little compared to the consequences. The resulting *backlash* could make their lives in America pretty unbearable."

Suddenly, she had a terrible thought. What if the followers of SAN-TOU-LONG, the Three-Headed-Dragon, *wanted* war--in the hopes that they could trigger a set of events, to *make* their prophecy come true? They wouldn't be the first to seek radical world change. But, like the enemies of America responsible for 9-1-1, they couldn't *possibly* anticipate the consequences of their actions.

No matter how imbalanced the world might seem, war was not the answer. Only madmen believed in such things, people bent on world domination, like Julius Caesar, Genghis Khan, Napoleon and Adolf Hitler. Every one had their own idealistic version of the *perfect world* that would result from their actions, and all were doomed to fail.

No *wonder* so many people were afraid in Chinatown, fearing not only for their lives, but for the futures of their children. What kind of future might they live in? A world full of hate--or love, and mutual acceptance? One of free choice--or conformity and servitude? Enlightenment...or deception?

Above all, the pursuit of truth and understanding must remain high on the list of human endeavor. *Truth* could not be ignored or forgotten. Her quest to find the truth had opened doors to the past for her people three years ago, and opened her mind to another dimension, to ways of knowing beyond human experience. Only by *embracing* the truth could humanity survive.

***

Una left the Station House through its rear exit. She would confront Colin later, when it was safe to speak her own mind, safe to find common ground and work together--away from public eyes.

But first, she had to escape the turmoil, and find a path to understanding. Where did that path lie? She could only think of one place, a place to purge herself of emotion, and refocus.

Snow fell softly before her. Big flakes came down on her hair and eyelashes, clinging to her clothes, and sparkling as they touched the ground.

It reminded her of the the *Snow Kachina*, a favorite character during the winter months. Because he lived on top of the Sacred Peaks he was credited with bringing the cold and snows to Hopiland. This winter moisture was absolutely essential for the growth of crops. He appeared in many winter ceremonies, the Soyal, Powamu, Palolokongti and the Mixed Dances of early spring.

Finally, Una reached her destination, pulled the door open, and entered *Lao-Chi*. Here she sighed with relief, as if entering a sanctuary. The silence felt very old, as if it came from another place and time. Its magic mural at once captivated her heart, enabling her to breathe more easily.

"Tea?" said Hongi, with a gracious smile.

She nodded and took a seat.

The feeling here was unmistakable. Not only did she feel welcome, but *expected*, as if they knew she would come.

The boy, Jianyu, appeared in black pants and sleeveless white tunic, hair braided down his back. Bowing humbly, he presented her with two gigantic rice-flour donuts.

"You read my mind," she said.

He grinned.

After several moments of peace and contentment, she began to wonder about Madelyn. The table seemed lonely without her.

Hongi returned with two small glasses.

"*Chang* wine," she said, "Very mild, slightly sweet and sour, not containing much alcohol. Considered ideal in winter to give a feeling of warmth and comfort, especially for nomads, who roam. Many say it has...*healing* properties."

Una sighed, raising her glass. Every word of it was true.

Another customer came in, ranting in Chinese, apparently distraught, waving a copy of *The New York Times*.

"More tea!" called Hongi to the kitchen. "Bring *oolong*!"

He handed her the newspaper, still shaking, trying to calm his nerves as she placed it on the table.

Una could not believe her eyes.

There on the editorial page, a small item jumped out, not only for its content, but its byline:

AMBASSADOR COMING
China's Ambassador to the U.S.,
Xiong Woo, is slated to pay a
working visit to New York City
within the next few days. Mr.
Woo hopes to promote bilateral
cooperation in the fields of
science, technology, culture and
trade. Recent unfortunate events
in Chinatown have spawned
rumors of espionage. He hopes
to diffuse any tension between
the two nations.

Contributor: Jack Howser, *Arizona Journal*

15

THE TEMPLE

A young woman in a black apron emerged from the kitchen, hair pulled back from her eyes with a simple barrette, bearing a bamboo tea tray. Hongi directed her to the distraught man's table.

"I am Liling," she said to him, smiling as she poured a nice hot cup from a small clay pot. "Mind and body are inseparable. *Oolong* is a special brew...to relieve stress and give you peace of mind!"

The Chinese teacup was low, shallow and wide, like a tiny bowl--just large enough for one or two sips.

Its complex aroma seemed to entrance him.

"Use both hands. Your fingers will not burn. Savor it in small amounts, and you will be...rejuvenated."

He nodded. Liling was soon out of sight.

Una held up the *Times*. "What's it mean? *Ambassador?*"

Hongi hadn't looked closely, up to now. Suddenly a black and white photo beside the story caught her eye, and she flinched, turning away.

Tears welled up as she abruptly rose from her seat, dashing into the kitchen, where stifled voices erupted all at once, up and down, sounding like:

"*ching-chong-wow-bow-wu-shi-wo-xi-hao*"

to the untrained ear--which, of course, had no meaning to Una--followed by clanging pots and pans.

She could not help but notice subtle changes in the wall mural wrapped around them. *Lhasa*, with its palaces, temple and monasteries, appeared dark with an angry sky above the Himalayas. Clouds moved in, casting shadows, and trees swayed, with leaves turned up. The animals had dropped out of sight.

Everyone traded whispers, except for a city worker in overalls, who apparently couldn't stand the suspense. "What's wrong?" he said, biting into an eggroll. "Did somebody...*die?* Maybe we--"

The young man, Jianyu, rushed out.

All eyes turned.

"Apologies! Very Sorry! We must...close for now. No charge!"

Liling accompanied him, providing small styrofoam containers.

"Please!" he said, "You...take home! No charge! Come, another day. Go home now. Thank you. Thank you...*very much*! Goodbye!"

***

Una found herself standing alone outside, in the snow, styrofoam in hand. She could not go back inside, or upstairs through the back.

Where to now?

She glanced at the time, and remembered: Grandfather Lao went to temple this time of day. In fact, it was not far away.

Tucked between a mini-mart and a fish market on Broome Street, *Zen Temple* displayed large gilded lions near its entrance, shrouded in mysterious chants and clouds of incense. Passing a donation box, she found two women in white robes, short haired, chatting beyond a large goldfish tank. There were plastic bottles of canola oil for sale, stacked in yellow pyramids.

"Are you from...*Immigration*?" said the younger, with big brown eyes. She seemed almost afraid.

"Not exactly," Una replied. "More like a friend of the family. I'm looking for ...Mr. Lao?"

The older one, in wire rim glasses, simply pointed.

She entered the shrine to find a 16-foot gold Buddha, resting on a lotus flower, with an ethereal blue halo, flanked by symbolic offerings. There were oranges, green curlicues of bamboo, fragrant lilies and silver coins.

"Welcome," said a new voice. "I am Zhang."

A buddhist monk appeared with his head shaved, in a saffron triple robe covering both shoulders, through which protruded his right arm. He wore sandals, in spite of the cold.

Una kept her distance. Placing palms together in "prayer" mode, at the center of her forehead, she bent her upper body at a slight angle, then returned to her standing position.

He grinned. "You seek answer? Consult 'moonstones'. First, kneel and clasp them together. In your mind, state name and date of birth. Pray for guidance, raise to your forehead, and toss onto floor."

Una sighed. Divination was not *exactly* what she had in mind.

She picked them up, both red, crescent shaped and made of bamboo, one side bulged, the other flat-- and obeyed.

All she could think of was Hongi's reaction. What did it *mean*? Would the Ambassador's arrival be a good thing or a bad thing? What difference did it make to the inhabitants of Chinatown?

The 'moonstones' fell with a thud.

He leaned over.

Both bulged surfaces were facing upward.

"*Yin yin,*" he said, "The Crying answer. When both fall flat, it means 'No'. The gods show...displeasure."

She wanted to run away. It felt too much like gambling, and that was no way to solve a problem.

Turning, the monk beckoned her to follow.

"Many seek divine guidance in love, career, or finance. They come half-hearted about their own decision, hoping the gods will agree. It is, therefore, not surprising that a 'No' reply is sometimes not taken very seriously. But you seek something...*more*."

Through a narrow arch he entered a sunlit arboretum beneath a glass dome.

Trees and flowers glistened from freshly applied water mist. Butterflies flittered and birds chirped. They sat together on a bench beside a small fountain.

"In Tibet, ancient books refer to flying machines as 'pearls in the sky'. As a young man, I traveled there with my family in 1948. One night, seated by a fire, I saw a great luminous pearl rise up from the mountains. The object drew a low, silent arc through the sky, dipping towards the ground before ascending out of sight. What it was, I cannot say."

Una squirmed in her seat.

"I'm sorry," she said, "What do you mean by 'pearl'?"

"It was round, with a gold-colored ring. From a distance it enlarged and came down suddenly, to the ground. A glow at its center appeared...white... and silvery ...so intense I was forced to close my eyes. Its light reached trees at *least* three miles away, casting shadows. Finally, it rose up...at breathtaking speed...and was gone."

Her mouth dropped--*just like her dream!*

"I knew you would come."

"How?" she asked.

"It's...hard to explain. We sometimes speak...of the *Akashic record*, a compendium of all human thought, words, emotions and intent in the past, present or future. Few know how to reach it through the etheric plane. Well...last night I went into a trance, and this is what I saw:

First, that war would begin.

From over Alaska will come rockets
with bombs from Communist
Russia, causing great devastation in
the United States and Canada.
Then...both will retaliate.

The Russians will have big satellites
in space. The Chinese will also.
There shall be a great rivalry, and
they will fight between themselves
in space. On Earth, people will
huddle in deep shelters.

And many shall be saved..."

"And *then?*" said Una,"What then?"

"That is all," he replied. "I cannot see beyond. Not yet. Perhaps, in time, more will be revealed."

Finally, Mr. Lao appeared through the trees of the arboretum, smiling like a man who had just returned from a long desert journey.

Una brought him a ladle of cool water from the fountain.

"Just like the old days," he said, drawing a sip. "A man's thirst can lead him far and wide. It is easy to get lost. The trick is finding your way home."

Returning the ladle to its perch, she searched the worn path nearby, but the monk was gone.

She frowned in dismay. "But I thought--"

He grinned. "You misunderstand. I *dwell* with my daughter. But my home, where my heart finds tranquility is *here*--in the temple. Like you."

"Me? No. I came--"

"Like so many, seeking answers...did you *not?*"

"Well, yes, but--""

"And what did you find? I know what happened at the restaurant."

Relief came over her face. "Hongi. I've never seen her so--"

"Angry? With good reason. Some wounds never heal. The man you call 'Ambassador' was once a Chinese border guard. In '89, before he knew my daughter was pregnant with a second child, my son-in-law, Jiang, worked in Bhutan, processing timber, near the border.

"He saw many flee to Nepal, hoping for safe passage to India, where the Dalai Lama had established his government-in-exile, with thousands of Tibetan refugees. It's a dangerous thing. Asylum seekers have lost limbs to frostbite, perished in blizzards, and been arrested by border patrols.

"Jiang wanted to help. So, he became a guide.

"That year, a group of unarmed refugees attempted to flee Tibet via the Nangpa La pass, a commonly used trade route. They were fired upon by Chinese border guards. The victims--including Jiang-- were shot from a distance as they moved slowly through chest-deep snow."

Una sighed. "I...didn't know."

He smiled. "Now, you see. The temple provides a gateway to answers...to hopes, and dreams and sorrows...of those who survive."

16

ODYSSEY

Una left *Zen Temple* still wondering if Hongi would forgive her ignorance, waving a newspaper photo of the man who killed her husband. *What a mean thing to do!* There was no way to know, of course--but somehow, it *felt* like a lame excuse.

Mr. Lao walked humbly beside her, hands tucked inside his button-down wool coat, eyes set straight ahead at all times. Pushing seventy at least, he never seemed out of breath. The journey to *Lao Chi* on snow-covered city sidewalks would take about twenty minutes.

He seemed immune to the cold.

A beep from her cell brought a smile to Una's face as she read a text message:

> HEY GIRL! GOT IT. SORRY FOR
> DELAY. FOUND H-CHARTER TO
> FLY BACK IN HALF THE TIME.
> DEPART DULLES TOMORROW
> 8AM. CALL YOU FROM LGA.

"Good news?" he asked.

"Sort of. Madelyn's on her way back from D.C. soon, by helicopter. Should land at LaGuardia tomorrow. Thank god! I was beginning to worry."

"You do that a lot."

She smiled. "Of course! What *else* can I do? This whole town is on edge. Not just Hongi. I can feel it in the way people act. Even at the temple! The monk, Zhang, had great insight, with astounding tales from Tibet, but even *he* described visions of world war. Nothing's been right since I got here. Is that all we have to look forward to?"

"You know better than that. My people and yours are linked together, for all time. We share hope that others do not understand. All this strife serves a purpose, to reveal true colors...and open one's eyes. Peace will come to those who accept the truth, no matter how strange it may seem. Our world view is changing. You are on the right path."

"What about the Ambassador? Aren't you--"

"Concerned? Yes, of course," he nodded. "I pray for my daughter, and her family. Awareness guides me, but I do not fear him or his kind. Tyrants come and go. They wear many masks. But their reign is short-lived. One day, he shall be forgotten, like all the rest. Until then, we must stay out of his way. He does not control *anyone's* fate...but his own."

Liling met them at the rear entrance to *Lao Chi*. She seemed reluctant to open the door.

"I'm...sorry to intrude," said Una. "Your family has been so kind, and they have suffered enough. We should leave you alone--and we will. Tomorrow. When Maddie gets back, we'll find another place to stay. I...*promise*!"

"But...where is grandfather?" she asked.

Una spun around, searching the alley. "What? He was right *here*, a minute ago, I--"

"Oww...*ow*! Jees! Not so hard--or I'll *scream*!"

Mr. Lao emerged quickly from around a corner nearby, dragging a young girl in spiked pink hair, leather jacket, destructed skinny jeans and high-heel boots, one arm twisted behind her back. The face seemed familiar.

"*Lola*? What are you--"

"Just mindin' my own business, until *grandpa* here decides to grab me--for no good reason!"

He did not have to say a word.

"Spying on us? So...you're *part* of it!" said Una, reaching for her cell. "Someone *else* was there, at *Tattoo You*. In the back. I could hear his voice, but never saw the face. I'll have to take you in for questioning."

"Oh, no you don't."

Lola jumped, swinging her boot high, kicking the phone from Una's hands. It flipped into the air and came crashing down, into a heap of snow.

Then, headlights appeared.

Una tried to pick it up, and Lola kicked again, knocking her flat. With a few more moves, she twisted free, ran and hopped into the open door of a black Jaguar, revving its engine. A cloud of exhaust filled the alley.

Suddenly, it came swerving toward them. Mr. Lao offered a hand, pulling Una to safety. As it passed, the driver's face rang a bell.

"Oh my god! That was *him*!" It was her suspect, from that night at the parade.

***

Inside at last, a soothing hot cup of *oolong* tea helped her relax enough to fall asleep. Hours later, in the wee of the morning it seemed, her phone beeped again, with a text, but she was too tired to read it:

> NO CAN DO. BAD KARMA--
> CHARTER PILOT'S 3-PRONG
> TATTOO! TAKING AMTRAK.
> HOPE TO GET THERE BY
> NOON. WISH ME LUCK!!!

And so Madelyn received no response, alone on a bench at *Washington Union Station*, in its food court, watching other passengers come and go. Still freaked out over the pilot, she vowed not to reveal herself--to anyone.

Thus another plan came to mind.

138

Fifty minutes had passed before a young, red-haired girl, apparently traveling alone, approached her with trusting eyes, "So sorry. Can you watch my bags? I need to, well--"

"Absolutely," she replied.

When the poor thing tried to emerge from the Ladies Room, minutes later, she found the door *locked* from outside. Pounding and screaming, she finally got someone to let her out.

But it was too late. Her bags--and Maddie--were gone.

***

Another impulse I may live to regret, thought Madelyn, sitting on the train. Considering what happened the *last* time, she decided not to text or call Una. Just in case *someone* was listening.

But she already knew the answer to that.

Every day in America, the government intercepted and stored nearly 2 billion emails and phone calls. Nothing was private. It was part of the NSA's job. They could target a specific communicator, using a phone number, address or name. It was all part of the government's plan, just like a nationwide network of smart cameras, deployed on every street corner in every city, to keep America safe--sending back data every few seconds to a central processing center, where it was analyzed.

So why didn't she *feel* safe?

Maybe because she knew computer hacking was also on the rise. Anything the government could track from the airwaves could also be hacked by an enemy with sophisticated technology. Maybe even *SAN-TOU-LONG*. More and more they were coming to realize, the events in Chinatown did not stem from a "gang" at all--but something much bigger.

She glanced at the time. Three hours to go. Three hours and she could hand off the *you-know-what* to Una. She'd only handled it twice now, without actually seeing it. Tucked inside a hollow, cast metal bust of the *Duke*, John Wayne--supposedly a gift for Ashcroft in case their paths should ever cross. A *mysterious artifact recovered from the Arizona desert* was all she'd been told. Valuable beyond compare.

Oddly enough, that description reminded her of the *Golden Fleece*, from Greek mythology: a symbol of authority and kingship. According to some, it had magical properties, bestowing unlimited knowledge or perfect health, or forgiveness from the gods.

And Madelyn believed *anything* was possible.

It was tied to Una's discovery in Hopiland, and her personal transformation since returning from there, three years ago--more self-aware, with greater empathy, less rigid in her thinking, more open to the spirit realm--and *maybe* her disappearance the night of the parade. She felt honored to carry it, honored to be part of whatever role it might play in solving the mystery surrounding Chinatown, and New York. Perhaps its value could *not* be put into words.

It certainly seemed *heavy enough* to be made of gold.

The trip proceeded without incident for two and a half hours, long enough to doze off a few times, always clasping her purse with both hands.

Then, about twenty minutes before arrival, the train slowed to a stop.

"Something down on the track," she heard someone say. "Tree probably. Heavy snows'll do that. It's not Amtrak's fault. Happened to me once before. Stranded six hours with no running water. Couldn't use the toilet. Good times."

A small boy peering out his window seat began to jump up and down. "Look! We're in luck. People...on *horseback*!"

Madelyn could see them, too. Approaching the train from one side. But they weren't exactly the U.S. Cavalry. No State Trooper uniforms or official insignia of any kind. They had rifles strapped to their saddles and...and...they were unmistakably *Chinese*.

Surely the train's engineer would call for help, or at least alert the station to their predicament. But how long would *that* take?

Her *Pisces paranoia* kicked into high gear. She felt doomed, like a passenger on a sinking ship.

She had to get off the train. *Now*.

***

An hour and forty minutes later, Una's smile turned to a frown at the *New York Penn Station* in Manhattan, as she watched everyone disembark, except for Madelyn.

"Thank goodness for those lumberjacks," a woman said. "Out of nowhere, clearing the tracks and all. Imagine! If they hadn't come along, we might still be stranded!"

That was it. Una *had* to insist on a search.

"It's happened before," said an attendant. "Someone on medication is confused or disoriented, getting off at the wrong stop--or even worse, mistakes an emergency exit for another compartment. But there'd be an alarm."

They *did* find an empty seat with three bags registered to one *R. Dawson*, of Ithaca, New York, but nothing else--except for a scribble in lipstick on the window.

"Looks like...a *fish*," the conductor said.

Una waited, pacing outside the train, staring at her phone. From the corner of one eye, she barely noticed a dark, bearded stranger, approaching from behind. When he came within three feet, suddenly two Military Police in camo appeared, leaping from the crowd. They wrestled him forcefully to the ground. People gasped in astonishment.

"Homeland Security," one said, cuffing the stranger's hands behind his back. "You're under arrest for criminal trespass, blocking a federal railway, and reckless endangerment of civilians."

"You all right?" said Ashcroft, standing beside her. "Silent alarm came in about twenty minutes ago. Apparently, one hitched a ride. We got here as fast as we could."

She began to shake, nearly fainting in his arms.

"I...I can't reach Madelyn. She was *on board*!"

"We know. Drone video picked up a lone figure on horseback fleeing the scene. My men are searching for her, now."

"But...how...*why*?"

"They're...more sophisticated than we thought. This whole thing's getting out of hand. We need to talk."

Una shook her head. "Not until--"

"Of *course*," he grinned, facing her, eye to eye. "I understand. She can't be far. First things first."

Just then, her phone beeped, and Una sighed with relief:

SORRY ABOUT THE MIXUP. HAD
TO IMPROVISE. SEE YOU SOON.

17

OBJECTIVE

Escorted by MP's to a black Homeland Security Van, the bearded suspect clearly understood instructions being given to him, but remained silent, with his head down.

Una could not help but wonder about the secrets he concealed within his mind: his worldview, its roots and rationalization. What occult beliefs guided him? And how much did he know about the cult's 'master plan'?

No doubt he felt compelled by some vision of a better world--one promised, perhaps, by *The Divine Incantations*? What was his role? To 'prepare the way' for SAN-TOU-LONG?

How does one prepare the way...*for invasion?*

He might consider himself insignificant, like so many who commit themselves to such an extreme cause, willing to make *any* sacrifice.

That made him even more dangerous.

"Don't trouble yourself," said Ashcroft.

"What do you mean?"

"I see it in your eyes...trying to put yourself in his shoes...wondering if there's any way you could *possibly* begin to understand. Well, forget it."

"Why?"

"Because *that* requires common ground. We have none. He'd might as well be from another planet."

She sighed. It was a normal response. Us versus *them*. But her life as a Hopi had taught her how it *feels* to be on the other side, to be misunderstood. People were often quick to judge or reject a worldview they did not understand. But living in Chinatown, even for such a short time, made her wonder what Americans could actually *learn* from people in the East. From a culture at least 5,000 years old. She'd already begun to explore the links between Hopiland and Tibet. Maybe that's why she *had* to be the one sent from D.C.--and maybe, in time, she'd bring Colin around, to open his mind.

"Where to now?" she said.

"Command Post," he replied, moving toward an armored Humvee.

"To interrogate him?"

"Amongst other things...*yes*! To learn all that we can about this cult...or *whatever* you want to call them. They're organized, in greater numbers than we ever anticipated. These acts of violence are not random. They seem to have a clear objective--that *must* be discovered. It's the only way to defeat them. I'll grant you one thing: such tactics, like inciting fear among the target populace, are nothing new. Ever hear of...*The Art of War*?"

"Not exactly."

"It was required reading at West Point Academy. A Chinese military treatise from the 5th century, BC, attributed to strategist Sun Tzu. Thirteen chapters, each devoted to one aspect of war. Hailed as an inspiration to great military leaders, like General Douglas MacArthur. The last chapter deals with espionage and intelligence."

"So?"

"Its wisdom cannot be disputed. Centuries of warfare bear out the truth it contains. As students, we were each required to commit certain passages to memory. One I have never forgotten:

'All warfare is
based on deception.
Hence, when able to attack,
we must seem unable;
when using our forces,
we must appear inactive;
when we are near,
we must make the enemy
believe we are far away;
when far away, we
must make him believe
we are near.'

Suddenly, there was a commotion nearby. With hands cuffed behind his back, the suspect apparently pushed an escorting officer to the ground, and ran off. They gave pursuit. Surveillance cameras showed them racing behind him along the nearest platform.

Everyone stood by, helplessly watching the chase unfold.

"Too bad they can't hang onto him," someone said.

"What's *really* sad," sighed another, "Police didn't even get to fingerprint him before he bolted. So, they can't confirm his identity."

Ashcroft immediately spoke into the 2-way radio strapped to his uniform. "Hold your fire. We will not endanger civilians. Copy?"

This was followed at first by only static, then a voice, seemingly out of breath, "Say again?"

"No guns. Physical force *only*. Got that?"

"Wilco," came the reply.

Cries of alarm rose from weary travelers, caught by surprise, along the chase route. The train platform was more crowded than usual, thanks to recent travel delays.

A station employee shook his head.

"Bad timing. Since December, we've had three train derailments. The latest: a New Jersey Transit the other night. No injuries reported, but first responders had to evacuate nearly a hundred people. Every time we lose a key section of track, it means more delays for repairs. Right now, we've got two tracks offline. That drops the number of trains per day from 1300 down to 1190. Makes a difference."

Ashcroft began to pace as his radio went silent.

Uh-oh, thought Una, *he's given them the slip.*

Additional troops arrived to join in the search. As they moved methodically through Penn Station, more trains were suspended, making a bad situation even worse for thousands of stranded commuters.

At the Station Control Center, housed in a nondescript office building about a block away, dispatchers braced for another "day from hell". On a 57-foot-wide curved black panel that took up an entire wall, a lighted map of tracks glowed red and green. Streaking through the heart of its network were blue lights, indicating tracks offline.

Another one lit up. More bad news for the busiest train hub in the Western Hemisphere.

Una came up close, to whisper in his ear. "What if there's more to this... than meets the eye?"

Ashcroft frowned. "I thought I just *said* that.

"I'm not talking tactics. I mean worldview. You said it yourself, 'He'd might as well be from another planet.'"

"I don't follow."

"*The Art of War.* It proves that the ancients knew all about warfare, enough that we're still learning from them, to this day. What if they knew *other* things ... things we don't like to talk about, because they don't jive with our view of reality? Things like...people from other worlds."

He grinned reluctantly. "*Aliens?* Is *that* what you're getting at? Look, I'm no fool. Anyone with sufficient military background knows about our dealings with ETs and techno-recovery. We don't discuss it with civilians. But that's not what we're facing here."

"*Isn't it?* We're always so obsessed with acquiring *their* technology, to give us an advantage over our adversaries. What if we're not the only ones?"

His eyes lit up. "Come again?"

"Well, it just occurred to me. All the conspiracy buffs who write books and such say we've been 'visited' throughout history. Some say the Nazi's had help in WWII, that recovered UFO technology has been reverse engineered for decades, kept secret from the public, but ready to use--when needed.

"What if it's all *true?* And what if one or more of these 'visitors' are now competing the same way--for technology? Suppose one is trying to acquire the secrets of another...and *we* hold the key?"

He was about to answer, when a his 2-way came abruptly to life.

"Sir? We have a situation...suspect cornered on platform, but resisting arrest...other units on site...we have him surrounded..."

The radio seemed to go out again.

"Dammit," said Ashcroft, "They *know* what to do."

"Switching...now," said a surveillance-officer(SO) nearby, streaming video from a mini-drone to a small monitor.

They could see the suspect from above, alone on the wrong side of the platform, one foot out, threatening to jump. The fall would not be fatal, but an oncoming train *could* easily mow him down.

Suddenly, one came zooming by, not slowing in the least.

It left no body behind. He had apparently jumped on board.

An MP tried to follow but fell, and was killed instantly.

"There!" cried the SO, pointing.

Fifty feet down from his entry point, the suspect exited the train from the other side, between tracks. Holding a knife to his throat, he slashed it. Blood ran onto his chest, and he collapsed, to the ground.

"Why?" said Una, in disbelief. "He didn't...*have* to die!"

"To...protect his secrets," said Ashcroft.

Moments later, as they neared his Humvee, everyone stopped and turned, at the sight of a horse, galloping toward them.

"Reinforcement?" quipped Ashcroft, "A little late."

Pushing Una behind him, he pulled out his weapon, a dual powered, mini machine gun, with laser sight. Its red dot moved up the horse as it approached, to its mysterious rider, centered between the eyes.

Two of his men quickly responded, doing likewise.

Hands reached up to remove the hood, half-covered in snow.

"Whoa! Guys! It's *me*, Maddie, for god sake!"

"At ease!" he commanded.

Una sighed with relief.

Her friend slid off a bit awkwardly, to one side.

"Not exactly my thing," said Madelyn, holding one hand to her back. She handed over her heavy purse. "At least I got the *you-know*--"

"I'm so *glad*," said Una, making eyes as she abruptly changed the subject. "We'll talk about...*shopping*...later."

"Of...course," she replied, gently stroking the horse's long, black mane. "Magnificent animal. He...saved my life."

Ashcroft frowned. "I thought you were a--"

"City slicker? I am. That's what's so remarkable."

"I don't understand."

"Neither do *I*, really, except..."

"What?" said Una.

"*Perhaps* we share something in common. I've read about Pisces dogs... incredibly sensitive, able to understand people without spoken words. A detector of friends and enemies, they say. Well, maybe horses are the same!"

An officer appeared abruptly before Ashcroft, out of breath.

"Suspicion confirmed, sir!" he said.

"Good work, Lieutenant," he replied. "Transport the body to our Command Post, for a complete autopsy."

"Yes, sir. Right away, sir!"

Una waited until the officer was out of sight.

"What was *that* all about?" she said.

He held up a current image from the surveillance drone. "Your friend, Madelyn, was right. It wasn't her imagination at LaGuardia, or on the train. The members of this cult all seem to share one thing in common."

Looking down, it took her eyes a moment to focus. There was the suspect's bare arm, with his clothing removed. Just below the shoulder, in black and red ink, was clearly a tattoo--of a *three-headed dragon.*

18

ONE FOR ALL

As they departed Penn Station by Humvee, the driver made a few unexpected turns through snowy Manhattan.

"Where are you taking us?" said Una.

"Special accomodations," said Ashcroft. "Courtesy of U.S. government. You need a safe place to stay, and I need *you*."

She liked the sound of that.

Within minutes, they entered *New Heights*, an old industrial park, and pulled into a cement parking deck. Outside, it appeared to be an abandoned warehouse, but inside it had all the trappings of a fine, upscale hotel.

"What gives?" said Madelyn.

"Out of sight, out of mind. Codename: CATBRIER. For Homeland Security, Special Ops, Secret Service, you name it. Off limits to the public. How else do you think we manage to stay so close without being seen? Okay ladies, two things: first, you can't tell anyone about this facility, because second, if you do, we'll have to *kill* you."

He wasn't smiling.

"What about--"

"We'll send for your things, tomorrow," he said, escorting them to a second floor suite with two double beds.

The women's eyes opened wide as he opened a heavy-duty, steel door. Their room had everything; a fully stocked refrigerator, complete bath accessories including fluffy white robes, night clothes and temporary daywear like unisex jumpsuits and even winter gear, all loose-fitting, and seemingly quite comfortable.

"There's a universal charger for your phones and complete internet access. But...*just so you know*, all communications are monitored 24/7."

"Home, sweet home," Una sighed.

After her train debacle and horseback ride, Madelyn needed time to unwind with a nice, hot shower.

Una had other plans.

"Colin," she said, taking him aside, away from his men, "All this talk of *war* is making me a nervous wreck."

"Fear and war go hand in hand," he replied.

"On the reservation, growing up, we had a few run-ins with 'federal peacekeepers'. Somehow, even with good intentions, innocent people always get caught in the crossfire. Just for today, could we take it *down* a notch? There's something I need you to see."

They ventured out again, just the two of them this time, to a major intersection at the confluence of eight streets: the Bowery, Doyers Street, East Broadway, St. James Place, Mott Street, Oliver Street, Worth Street and Park Row. Known as Chatham Square, at its center lay a small park.

Exiting the Humvee, Una led him by the hand.

"I *know* you're under incredible pressure to hunt down the bad guys and save the day," she said. "I respect and appreciate that. I'm *so* glad you're here. We *all* are."

He frowned, "*But--*"

She gazed upward as they approached a high, square, triumphant stone arch, eighteen feet nine inches in height and sixteen feet wide. Inscribed on it was a dedication in both English and Chinese:

> "In Memory of the Americans
> of Chinese Ancestry who lost
> their lives in Defense of
> Freedom and Democracy."

Searching, he also found a small bronze plaque, corroded green long ago:

> KIM LAU MEMORIAL ARCH
> Erected by American Legion Post 1291
> in 1961. Named after 26-yr-old 2nd
> Lt. Benjamin Ralph Kimlau, an air

craft commander in the 380th
Bombardment Group who was shot
down during WWII on a mission over
Los Negros Island on March 5, 1944.

"The people here speak many languages," she said, "Chinese, Japanese, Vietnamese, and more...BUT Chinatown is not Southeast Asia or Vietnam, it's not a war zone...and it's *not* the "native population"--it's *New York*, USA, plain and simple-- with "liberty, and justice for all". For every one of these immigrants, *that's* what it means to live here. Please...don't lose sight of that."

"I...won't," he promised.

***

As they reentered *New Heights*, a message came in for Ashcroft on his two-way. She managed to catch only two words: "black" and "sky", without any clue to their context.

"Understood," he replied, "I'm...on my way."

"Anything from--?"

"The autopsy?" he said. "Not yet. I'll let you know."

As he pulled away from CATBRIER, Una's phone began to vibrate and she *wanted* to take the call, but then realized the caller was unknown, which seemed really strange, since she had everyone's numbers in there. She thought it might be best to *wait* before answering, since monitors inside would hear every word. So, on a hunch, she decided to take a walk.

Finally, when she was half a block away, near the park entrance, she glanced at her screen to find a single worded text:

COMPADRE

So it *had* to be Jack.

Just then, a midnight blue Corvette pulled up with darkened glass, and it made her extremely nervous, fearing the door might open and Lola would jump out to grab her--or worse--and she felt ready to run, when the automatic window came down and there was *Take It Easy*, playing from the dash.

"I heard the news from Penn Station," said Jack. "You all right? How's Madelyn?"

She sighed. "Resting. I saw your byline in the paper. Where the hell have you *been*?"

He grinned. "Funny you should mention *that*. It's...complicated. C'mon. Let's take a drive."

"I've been...'sleuthing'," he said, "Above and below."

"What?"

"You know, investigating scandalous info, from a *news* point of view. They used to call it *muckraking*."

"And?"

"The Chinese have a name for Hell. They call it *Diyu*, the Realm of the Dead, depicted as a subterranean maze of various levels and chambers, to which souls are taken to atone for their sins. Depending on which interpretation you read, the "Courts of Hell" can number as few as four, or as many as eighteen. Each deals with different punishments, subjecting sinners to gruesome torture. It's all a kind of *purgatory* that prepares souls for reincarnation. Tortures include boiling oil, dismemberment, being frozen in ice, cast into a pool of blood or thrown off the mountain of knives."

"Jack!"

"Anyway, it turns out that Chinatown, like many older cities in America--including D.C.--has a mysterious underground. Once a labyrinth of tunnels were used to transport illegal goods for opium dens, prostitution rings and organized gangs. There's even a modern day mall beneath Doyers Street with dead-end hallways and locked doors, leading, well...leading..."

"Where? Where to?"

"I don't know, exactly. But I started thinking, *Why here? Why now?* And then I recalled some mystery lore about New York."

"Lore?"

They drove away from Chinatown, through crowded city streets, past the shopping district, until they reached Central Park. A fresh layer of snow frosted the benches and carpeted the ground. There was a special hush in the air and something magical in the Park's glinting whiteness.

Jack climbed out first, leading the way beneath snow-covered trees.

"Every so often, an odd story appears in publication that doesn't jive with people's expectations, and so it's soon forgotten. But if you put them together, they point to a pattern. Take Manhattan, for instance.

"In the Fall, 1981 issue of *Shavertron Magazine*, an article reported that Con Edison, while drilling a test hole in the north end of East River Park, broke through to open space about 200 feet below, suggesting the existence of a large cavern. The *Phoenix Liberator* in '89 reported that the Episcopal Church of St. John the Divine at 103rd St. and Amsterdam concealed the entrance to an underground cavern once used by an 'occult lodge', thought to be left over from former inhabitants of the eastern seaboard during antediluvian times. And the *Encyclopedia of Occultism & Parapsychology* reported in '97 that a man and his wife, traveling through winter snow, parked their car in the Lincoln Tunnel to wipe the snow off their car--and vanished without a trace!"

"What are you saying?"

"They might all be related. Why? Because New York is *also* considered a UFO hotspot. And one cannot help but wonder if sightings occur because the mysterious craft are originating from somewhere nearby."

"Like an underground base! But Jack, that's too *fantastic*. No one will ever believe it."

He grinned. "That *doesn't* make it less true."

"Okay...so where'd you get the scoop?"

His face went blank.

"About the Chinese Ambassador, I mean. Coming to New York? Some people are pretty shook up about that. Bad vibes, I guess. They say he's got a shady past."

"Wouldn't surprise me. It came into the *Times*, on a news wire. *I'd* worry less about him, and more about his wife."

"Why's that?" she asked.

"Nothing specific. Call it a hunch. The way she prances around beside him, I guess. Less like the spouse of a dignitary, more like a *queen*! Anyway, they'll be here in three days. Sure wish we could solve this whole mess before then. It'd mean less security headaches, for one thing."

"For some reason, New York's always a focal point."

"*Exactly*. And somehow, instinctively, people know that. What happens here affects the rest of the nation, and the world. Look at 9-1-1. It changed everything. Well, I've got this feeling, and...I don't know exactly how to say it, but I'm afraid the world is about to change again. In a way that's *bigger* this time. Bigger than any of us can imagine. And it's not just about the future of everyone we know, but future generations. It...scares me."

"Are you expecting more violence?"

He shivered, and suddenly realized that neither one of them was wearing an overcoat. Together, they turned, retracing their steps to the car.

"I'm not sure *what* to expect, exactly," he said.

Una tried to tell herself that it was just another conspiracy theory. If one paid attention, of course, there were too many to count, from psychics and talk show hosts and politicians and just plain ordinary people. Somehow though, she could not shake the notion that *this* time around, events unfolding were beyond human influence, almost supernatural--akin to the way ancient Greeks viewed their fates in the hands of gods on Mount Olympus.

Even if one accepted the idea of Sky People watching over mankind, and even though she had no personal knowledge regarding fright-filled encounters like those described by the "Experiencers" in upstate New York, she was beginning to believe, more and more, that *both* sides of the spectrum were possible.

Which made the truth *too terrible* for most people to think about. No one liked the idea of being manipulated by forces beyond his or her control. Self-delusion was infinitely more preferable to surrender--unless, of course, humanity actually had a *choice*.

Perhaps Mr. Lao had it right. The path to enlightenment and self awareness was no doubt fraught with sacrifice at every step, requiring one to "let go" of so many prejudices and egocentric ideas that it was impossible for many, if not most of the human race.

Only time would tell how many could stay on that path.

In the end, the survivors of this "test" might arrive together at a *new* understanding of what it means to be human.

Maybe *that's* what they feared--most of all.

19

WHISPERS

Una woke up, feeling uneasy, still trying to shake off Jack's newfound paranoia from the night before. Apparently, he had switched his rental car and cell phone in an effort to throw "suspicious characters" off his trail.

"Who?" she'd even asked, but he couldn't say, for sure. They might be anyone, from FBI to competitors for a rival media outlet to subversive agents for SAN-TOU-LONG.

Or maybe no one at all.

She didn't *mean* to insinuate that he was delusional. Jack was as solid as they come. But considering all that had happened since her arrival, the chaos in Chinatown was enough to stress out anyone.

As her eyes came into focus, there was Madelyn asleep on the--*wait a minute*--not her comfy full sized bed in the safety of CATBRIER, but a small sofa in the cramped guest room they shared--in the Lao family apartment!

What are we doing here? she thought.

Did she *imagine* it all...the KIM LAU ARCH visit with Ashcroft...his strange phone call about something called "Black Sky"...the eerie drive out to *New Heights* Industrial Park? If she hopped in a car and drove out there, right now, would she find an abandoned warehouse?

And what about Jack? Did they *really* take a walk in Central Park, to talk about New York mystery lore and UFOs?

She seemed to be losing her grip.

A toilet flush came from the hallway, a light flickered, and Liling's eleven-year-old daughter, Mia, passed briefly, exiting the upstairs bathroom.

Mia never said much.

Maybe it was because she was an only child. Maybe she felt neglected by her parents, always working so many hours in the restaurant. And *maybe* that's why she spent so much time alone, pouring through old family photos, gazing at smiling faces of people she'd never met.

At least she still had her grandfather.

Una felt unable to breathe. She needed fresh air.

Throwing on some shoes and an overcoat, she hiked a nearby flight of steps to the rooftop, hoping against hope that Grandfather Lao might be there, smiling, pipe in hand, facing the stars--ready to calm her fears with a few gentle words of wisdom.

Sliding a deadbolt, she opened the heavy outside door.

Alas, in the cold of night she encountered a scene that *did not* make sense. Snowflakes fell softly onto a long-haired male figure in blue jeans, seated at a wooden desk--face hidden because of the way he was turned--using a laptop computer and fluorescent lamp.

On the roof? In the winter time?

She closed it once more, stepping back.

Taking deep breaths, she took a cue from Madelyn, trying to psych herself up. Perhaps in the moonlight, snowdrifts had created a trick of light and shadow, enough to fool her temporarily and deceive her tired, troubled mind, to remind her of *something* familiar but clearly impossible.

He could not be there--now or ever.

Was she *dreaming?*

Finally, she pushed again. As the door opened, *this* time, the desk was turned somehow, as if the rooftop had swiveled in her absence, and the laptop's glow reflected from his eager, boyish expression, windswept hair and black-rimmed glasses.

"What's up?" said Rufus.

This can't be happening, she thought.

Half a dozen *other* thoughts came to mind as well; thoughts she'd rather avoid but could not escape as she tried desperately to make sense of it, somehow-- wondering if they were both *dead,* or if some unknown calamity, like a terrorist attack or alien invasion had put her in a state of shock, blocking her memory, rendering her unconscious, in a drug- induced coma or some out-of-body limbo, or maybe something *else,* altogether--an explanation that she could not even imagine.

Rufus grinned. "Cat got your tongue?"

"Well, no, not exactly, it's just that...how did you *get* here?"

"Beats the hell outta me!"

Was he *brought* there, by some unknown force, without his knowledge--or were they together in *his* dream because something had happened which made it important for them to meet, but impossible to achieve any other way?

God forbid.

"What are you *doing?*"

"Research," he said. "Ever since the train incident, I've been working on a theory. It was really Jack's idea. This whole 'subversive element' thing. It can't just be confined to Chinatown. Remember the communications *glitch* that shut down everything at the Precinct--*before* we all went up top, before I saw lights in the sky, and the power surge that killed three people? It stretched all the way back to D.C.! So...there's *no way* they found Madelyn by chance, just before reaching Penn Station."

"Which means?"

"They were tracking her, the whole time."

"But why? What were they--"

Rufus sighed. "Really? I think you know the answer to that. But hey, it's *your* delusion. I'm just a visitor. The point is not that they failed, but they *got* to you. It was a test to see how you'd react. Let's face it. They know where you are at all times. The CATBRIER makes you feel safe? Good. But don't count on that. They won't give up, ever."

Gloom and doom, she thought. *Thanks, but no thanks.*

"Are you here to help me, or not?"

"Of course...*and* me...and everyone else I know. You're getting closer to the truth, day by day. But it's *not* what you expect."

"How do you *know* that?"

"Because I *found* something...the proof that ties them together. It was here the whole time, right under our nose."

Una felt afraid at first to come closer, but then realized this might be her only chance. What if Rufus lay dying somewhere in a snowstorm or a car wreck, and this was a last ditch effort from his spirit, reaching out? Even Madelyn once said it was *possible*, the first time she sensed the presence of Kuwanyauma, in New York:

> "Could she be reaching *out* to you,
> from the grave? It...happens, that's
> all--or at least, so I've heard."

Images appeared on his computer screen, familiar at first: the corporate parade float that burned, overalls worn by Fifth Precinct civilian employees, and finally, scenes from a local TV news report about the Chinese Ambassador's upcoming visit.

Each time the image, when blown up, revealed remarkable hidden details ...and among them, the familiar, three-headed symbol of SAN-TOU-LONG: inside the corporate logo for *Sunny-Side*, stitched onto overalls worn by the Fifth Precinct clean-up crew, and even in a video close-up of the Ambassador's wife-- concealed within an ornately designed, ceremonial robe.

Una gasped.

"B-b-but that's impossible!" she said. "They can't be *everywhere*. It would mean...the battle is *over*. They've already won."

He shrugged.

Suddenly, a circular shadow descended from above, spreading out from Rufus to encompass the entire rooftop. No longer did snowflakes fall directly, but around them, beyond the edge.

Its source made no sound, whatsoever.

And she could not help but look up, sensing a kind of *deja-vu*, like she did in her dream that night at the hunting lodge with Jack and Rufus.

There it was: a giant, glistening pearl-shaped UFO, perfectly round, hovering like some kind of balloon. But she knew it was more than that by the intricate patterns of light that danced across its surface, the sense of intelligence emanating from it, like thought waves probing her mind.

She blinked, and more figures appeared.

The entire Lao family; Grandfather and Hongi, Jianyu, Liling and Mia were gathered around her, in a circle, holding hands.

And stepping forward to join them, a shadowy hooded figure emerged from thin air, with no face, making no prints in the snow.

And this creeped her out, even more.

Could it be the *hungry ghost* of Hongi's long lost son, returning now--not to torment them, but rejoin the family?

It *had* to be a dream. But how to escape?

She could run and jump off the roof. It used to work when she was a kid. Every time she found herself reliving a nightmare, she'd look for a place to jump, like the edge of a cliff surrounding Third Mesa, or a mountain top. But she'd always wake up *before* hitting bottom, afraid she might die. She could almost hear *Madelyn's* interpretation:

> "*Falling* in a dream may represent
> feelings of vulnerability and fear.
> As a Libra, your biggest fears would
> be: living out of balance with life
> and love, the disapproval of
> someone close to you, or the ugly
> consequence of conflict. You fear
> making the wrong decision."

No shit. But how could any of that help her now?

Maybe there was no *need* to escape. What if the 'pearl' represented something else, besides fear?

What if its 'intelligence' had come to offer help--a way out of danger and doubt? A way to find answers?

What if the Sky People were waiting for her *right now* inside?

***

Una sat up, all at once, shivering in cold sweat. A quick scan of her surroundings revealed two full beds, with Madelyn sound asleep nearby. The first rays of morning light came in through reinforced security glass. They were back in CATBRIER, safe and sound.

But before she climbed out of bed, before she was willing to risk another disappointment, falling like *Alice through the Looking Glass* into a whole *new* set of illusions, she had to pinch herself.

"Ow!" she exclaimed, with relief.

The nightmare was over.

But she could not let it end there.

Too many questions came to mind.

She could not rest until she went to visit the Lao family one more time, to make sure they were safe.

And one *more* thing--she had to find Rufus.

20

POINT OF VIEW

Madelyn slid in beside Una as they boarded a Qwik-Ride near the entrance to *New Heights* Industrial Park.

"You should be more careful," the Chinese driver said. "No one comes out here at night...except for troublemakers."

"Oh yeah?" quipped Madelyn, "Well, maybe that's why we came--to raise some hell!"

He smiled in his rearview. "You real comedian. Where to?"

"Elizabeth Street," said Una flashing her government ID, "Fifth Precinct."

"Okay...okay! No more funny business!"

Early morning snow fell in big flakes, touching softly to the ground. City streets seemed empty. They could not help but wonder why.

American flags in front of the Post Office and local library were flying at half-staff.

"Some tragedy, I'll bet," said Madelyn. "Could be a hometown resident killed overseas or something closer. My cousin fought in *Desert Storm* over in

Iraq...and almost didn't return. *He* once told me the flag is lowered to make room for an 'invisible flag of death' flying above. Used to happen in Brooklyn all the time."

Una's anxiety level jumped a notch. First, she dreams about a dead man's return, then...*this*! She told herself it was just a coincidence, but also decided *not* to tell Maddie. No sense in starting off the day with an *omen* or worse, hanging over their heads!

As they pulled up in front of the Police Station, something told her not to go inside.

"On second thought, take us to Lao-Chi," she said.

Madelyn grinned. "Good idea. No sense in facing them on an empty stomach. I could really go for some pick-me-up. Nice, hot tea with milk, salt and plenty of butter! Ever try *balep*? It's hot, greasy fried quick bread, cooked in a frying pan. Crusty, round and quite thin, sometimes made with potatoes, or apple sauce. *Yum*!"

***

As they stepped inside the restaurant, Una began to shake.

"You go ahead," she said to Madelyn, "I'll catch up."

It took only a few minutes for Hongi to appear, beckoning her to come back. They passed through the kitchen and went upstairs.

"I am sorry for your loss," she said, once they had entered the apartment.

She pointed to a copy of the *Times*, with a front page obituary for Officer Burke, apparently killed in the line of duty.

Una froze at first, then sighed.

Why did she have no idea?

"Please forgive my outburst the other day," said Hongi, as they sat together briefly, on a small couch. "It was not my--"

"You had *every* right," she replied. "I...didn't know about your past, with ...the Ambassador, I mean. This must be a difficult time."

Suddenly, eleven-year-old Mia appeared.

"*Una-luna!* I think of you every night, when I see the moon! Sometimes, I think you came from there, down to Chinatown."

As they embraced, she noticed a piece of wrinkled paper in the little girl's hand. It seemed familiar.

"What's *this?*" she asked.

"I wanted to tell you, before, but it was too late, you were gone. And then I didn't know if I should, because it seemed so--"

"*Mia,*" said Hongi, with a stern look of disapproval.

"No...no, I won't be quiet, and I won't go to my room. Not *this* time. I know this face. Uncle...Uncle Ming! I know you say it's impossible, but I've compared it to all the old photographs. The face is older, of course, but it's him...even if *you* can't accept it!"

Hongi leaped from the couch, seizing her by the arm. "Enough! Stop it, young lady! I've told you before--no more lies!"

But Mia resisted, pulling away, digging her feet into the carpet, twisting herself desperately toward Una, tears flowing from her eyes.

"Here!" she cried, "Take it! Take it! It's no lie! Pleeeaassee! You've got to *believe* me!"

The paper fell from her hand as Hongi dragged her away, kicking and screaming, her face full of tears.

Una did not know what to say.

Reaching down, she retrieved it, trying to straighten it out, and suddenly realized why it seemed so familiar.

It was a printed copy of the police sketch made of her suspect, from the night of the parade. She must have left it behind, when packing her things--unless Mia took it on purpose.

Why? Why would she lie?

They'd already been over this. According to Hongi, the restaurant was *open* that night. No one had gone to the parade.

She never shared the sketch, for that reason.

"Please forgive!" said Hongi, returning. "Mia is very young and... impressionable. This isn't the first time. She spends too much time alone, imagining all *sorts* of things, longing for things that can...*never be*! It comes from being an only child. The other children sometimes poke fun at her. She makes up stories about ghosts, to frighten them. We've tried to make her stop."

Una understood. As an only child herself, she knew that sometimes, the loneliness could be unbearable. She sometimes wondered if *that's* why she took such an interest in Hopi Kachinas, wanting them to come down from the sky and be her friends. Childhood made it easier to believe in such things, easier to hope for help from above, when all the adults around her had already given up.

It was part of the reason she left Hopiland after high school, afraid that disillusionment would set in, afraid that despair might crush all her dreams, like it had for her best friend, Chu'si.

She could not blame Mia for wanting to *believe* in something outside herself--even if that made her look crazy to other people.

Since arriving in Chinatown, she'd begun again to question some of her *own* beliefs, wondering if her sanity was being put to the test. Ever since the parade, she'd not been able to shake this incredible sense of *déjà vu* that kept coming to her, over and over again-- in the restaurant, at the temple, and more recently, just gazing up at the stars.

In her heart, she held a special place for Mia, feeling misunderstood in a world full of doubters. Adults tried to help by telling her to accept *reality*--but what if they were *wrong*, limited by their own ignorance?

Mia might be closer to the truth than any of them could ever realize.

"Think nothing of it," she said, tucking the folded sketch away in her pocket. "Kids have active imaginations. Don't be too hard on her. She's only trying to help."

Una sensed a tingle in the back of her neck as another door opened, bringing a wisp of cold air from outside, on the roof.

It was Mr. Lao, pipe in hand, brushing snow from his robes, smiling through fogged up half-moon glasses. "I knew you would come," he said. "I dreamed it."

Her mouth fell open.

Against Hongi's better judgement, he retrieved Mia and brought her out to sit beside him, on the living room floor. "GG!" she heard the child whisper with delight, apparently a nickname for Great-Grandfather. For a moment, they all sat together in silence, closing their eyes.

Una sensed this was a familiar ritual.

"This family has been living in fear," he said, "Far too long! What my daughter has told you is true. Since we lost Ming, eight years ago, we have feared the worst. He ran with the wrong crowd, doing unspeakable things, before he disappeared. And...according to our beliefs, to perform the lowest degree of evil deed, to steal or kill--motivated by desire, anger, or greed--can cause a soul to become a *hungry ghost*.

"But we are also guided by the actions of our ancestors, including those who sought to overcome fear. Una has come to us for a purpose that goes far beyond recent turmoil in Chinatown, beyond the designs of SAN-TOU-LONG. She reminds me of a tale that will benefit us all, to hear out loud. It points out the values of humility, selflessness, intelligence, and bravery displayed by a young maiden, long ago:

THE LEGEND OF CHI LI

Once upon a time, a monstrous dragon
set up his home in the Yung Mountains
of the ancient Chinese kingdom of
Yueh, and demanded that a young
maiden be sacrificed to him "on the
"appointed day" each year. The
people were forced to obey, for none
of the men that they sent were able to
defeat it. This went on for nine years,
but on the tenth year, a brave maiden
volunteered to be the next sacrifice.
Her name was Chi Li, the
youngest of six daughters.

Determined to do some good,
Chi Li asked her parents' permission
to become the next sacrifice. When
that failed, she offered herself to
officials of the village, respectfully
asking for help. They provided her
with a serpent-hound on a leash, a
sharp-pointed, sheathed sword

and freedom to make use of them.
Before battle, she prepared a sack of
rice balls, sweetened by malt sugar.

When the dragon appeared, she used
the rice balls to lure him from his lair.
The monster was so tempted by their
sweet scent, that she was able to unleash
her serpent-hound to attack. She drove
her trusty sword through the back of the
creature's head and neck--and it was
fatally wounded. She then recovered
the skulls of its nine victims, and
returned them to her village.

For outsmarting the evil creature, Chi
Li was judged by all to be "a worthy
wife for the king of Yueh"
and became its queen.

Mia found herself laughing with glee. "Chi Li was
very brave. I only wish I had her courage!"

"But you do," he said, "It's already there, inside
you, waiting to emerge. No enemy is so great that it
cannot be defeated. One must only discover its
weakness, to bring it down. The same may be said of
any dragon, whether it has one head, or three."

Una rose from her seat, and went to the door.

Mia ran up to her once more, with a big embrace,
and whispered, so no one else could hear, "I saw him,
I swear--*with my own two eyes!*"

***

Escorted by Hongi back to the restaurant, she found Madelyn enjoying dessert, sweetened cheese cake, topped with whipped cream.

"I thought you'd never return," she said. "Did I miss anything?"

Una winked at their host, "Just an ancient tale...about a young girl who slayed a dragon."

"Sounds right up your alley. Paper says Burke died from injuries caused by a hit-and-run. Plenty of eyewitnesses, but no descriptions of the car--or its driver. *Hard to believe.*"

"Maybe in New York," she replied, "But not in Chinatown!"

21

ANOMALY

Holding Mia by the hand, Madelyn escorted the young Chinese girl and her father, Jianyu, across the busy lobby of the Fifth Precinct Station House, after greeting them at the door.

"Una-luna!" the girl cried, letting go to embrace her Hopi friend.

"We're so happy you came," she replied. "I want you to meet Officer Shen. He'll be asking you a few questions. But first, let's find a snack machine and a quiet place to sit."

It was just after 9 AM. A huge red digital counter read:

HOURS TO GO : 36

"Countdown to the Ambassador's visit," Maddie explained.

Jianyu hesitantly nodded.

Moments later, he sat in silence, watching through a two-way mirror as Mia responded to questions from Shen with Una at her side:

"When did you *see* your Uncle?" he asked.

"Well," she replied, "I didn't *know* it was him, at first."

"What do you mean?"

"He didn't smile at me, or anything."

"Okay. So what happened next?"

"He was kind of lurking...around the market, I mean."

"Where was that?"

"About halfway between my home and my school."

"Near Mott Street?"

"Uh-huh. Sometimes it gets pretty crowded."

"Even in winter time?"

"Sure! People sell all *kinds* of things...year round!"

The open market between Lao-Chi and Mia's school sold everything from dried fish to frozen lobster to winter mushrooms. Usually crowded with vendors, hagglers and sight-seers, it was the perfect place to hide in plain sight.

Una gave Mia another hug, while her father spoke privately with Shen, who stepped away for a moment, returning with an application. The two men briefly shook hands.

"Jianyu tells me a lot of people in Chinatown are afraid of what might happen. They wish to be left alone, but know that's impossible. He feels that, rather than fear the consequences, it is better to *prepare* for the Ambassador's arrival. And so--"

"I've decided to help, by joining the Police Auxiliary!"

"That's wonderful," said Una.

He sighed. "My older brother, Ming, and I did not see eye-to-eye. He was a bully. Even chose the *black tiger* as his animal totem early on, symbolizing ferocity and courage, calling himself Protector of the Dead. I chose to side with the living."

"Really?" said Madelyn. "*I* know a little Chinese astrology. People born in the Year of the Tiger are thought to be brave, strong, stubborn and sympathetic. Your brother must've lost that *last* quality, somewhere along the way."

A young man came stumbling through the narrow hallway, steering a dolly full of computer equipment, with someone else, trailing behind.

"Rufus!" said Una. "How *are* you?"

"Okay, I guess. Getting back in the swing of things, since the FBI finally backed off. Jack's giving me a hand. My work room's a mess."

Holding a stack of computer books, Jack tried to smile.

"Say...*you're* into wildlife," said Madelyn, "Know anything about black tigers?"

Rufus paused to think.

"The black tiger is...*rare* in nature; non-striped, pure black. The number of verified sightings in the past century? Maybe three. It's American counterpart, with all the typical markings, hidden by excess pigment, is the *black jaguar*."

"No kidding!"

This rang a bell for Una. Just before their arrival, Shen provided her with a few details regarding the hit-and-run death of Officer Burke. A single image from a traffic security camera had given them the make and model of the car that apparently killed him.

It was a Jaguar.

And *that* was enough for her to realize that it must be the *same guy* with Lola that night in the alley behind Lao-Chi. Her creepy suspect was behind the wheel, and it *had* to be the long-lost brother: Ming.

"We'll put out an APB," said Shen,"See what comes in."

She needed to speak with Ashcroft. According to the Station front desk, he could be found at the *Mulberry Hotel*.

***

Una and Madelyn arrived at the Mulberry twenty minutes later, a thirteen story building on the Lower East Side of downtown Manhattan, near Little Italy. Right away, she noticed a peculiar row of trees surrounding it.

Madelyn began to sing, "Here we go round the mulberry bush, the mulberry bush, the mulberry--"

"What are you *doing*?" said Una.

"The...old nursery rhyme. Didn't you ever--"

She shook her head.

"Okay. Forget it!" she sighed.

Getting inside was a bit intimidating. First, they had to wade through concrete barriers, double-parked police cars, metal fencing, and surveillance teams in street clothes, just to reach the front door. Then, it took a standard magnetometer and x-ray screening to enter the lobby.

They soon met up with Ashcroft, reviewing hotel security plans with a special agent from the FBI.

"Guards on-duty 24/7 in the lobby by elevators?" he asked.

"Check," the agent replied.

"Both entrances/exits monitored by surveillance cams?"

"Check."

"Bomb-sniffing canine on the premises at all times?"

"Check."

"And the *concierge*...fluent in *both* English and Chinese?"

"Check and double-check."

"Very well," the general nodded, "That'll do...for now."

"So...why here?" Una asked, the moment he was free.

"Symbolic importance," he replied. "The mulberry tree, native to eastern and central China, is considered a cold-hardy survivor, tolerant of drought, pollution and poor soil. It can grow to eighty feet in height. They're also quite wind-resistant, used as windbreaks in the Great Plains. But that's not all. According to myth, as the abode of the Sunbird, it's considered to be a link between heaven and earth."

"Okay, okay...so *why* is he coming again? Paper said it was planned months ago. I have my doubts."

"Well...*I* can answer that!"

They both turned, at once. It was Jack.

"Sorry!" he said. "Couldn't help tagging along."

The general's eyes suddenly lit up. "Reporter? OKAY. Right now...*get him outta here*!"

Two officers came over, on the double.

"You're not authorized to be here!"

But Una stayed his hand. "It's...okay. He's with me. He won't cause a fuss, I *promise*."

Ashcroft sighed. "Very well. As you were!"

His men slowly backed away.

Jack loosened his collar, trying to breathe. "Anyway, if you believe the press, local Chamber of Commerce hopes to 'boost the region's economic ties to China'. The Ambassador's scheduled to meet with business leaders from the tech industry, places like Apple, Google and IBM, attend a private reception, the *works*. But first, he'll briefly address the public, here in the hotel courtyard. It's all for the benefit of Chinese investors with an eye on New York real estate."

"I guess you know about the APB?"

Ashcroft nodded. "Just came through. Good work, by the way. We're finally beginning to connect the dots."

"I couldn't have done it without Jianyu. He says people in town are pretty upset."

"Can't say that I blame them. Immigrants naturally fear China. *They* say the growing economic clout wielded here by China is leading to an erosion of their freedom to speak openly about human rights abuses. And they don't trust big business. Why *should* they?"

Madelyn shook her head. "But the Chamber says they're against 'any attempt to muzzle public opinion'."

Jack cleared his throat out loud.

"Reporters say *otherwise*," he said. "I know a woman from Canada who claims that she fled from China to pursue free speech, but *still* fears the long arm of the Chinese government. When she asked at a news conference about human rights, she was ignored. Later, in a crowded elevator, someone whispered to her from behind, 'Be careful when you step outside!' China's influence has been growing stronger. They want to control *everything*."

"Like the train station," said Una. "Any results from the autopsy?"

Ashcroft abruptly pulled her aside.

"Yes and No," he whispered. "The hair and beard were *false*, apparently to help him 'blend in'. Once removed, there was no facial hair, poor muscle tone and severe malnutrition--all self-inflicted. Coroner also found an anomalous mass; small, but organic in appearance. Its configuration and position lead us to believe it affords some sort of neural manipulation, apparently shielded with a membrane, to prevent an inflammatory response."

Her face went blank. "I don't understand."

"Neither do I. But in retrospect, studying surveillance video, it appears that the 'subject' displayed an uncanny ability to anticipate our every move, as if he had some kind of 'psychic' ability to know what our security team was thinking-- yet at the same time, the expression on his face was almost fearful--as if he did not understand his own actions. Right before his suicide, he apparently muttered something in Chinese. But his voice was so low, it took an expert to recover the audio, then an interpreter to decipher. In was in an obscure dialect spoken in a remote China province, far to the north, near Mongolia. Apparently, right before slicing his own throat, he said, "I don't...belong here!"

"Why would he *say* that?"

"We think it's tied to the...anomaly. We have reason to believe that this individual's actions were being directed--or at least influenced--by some force beyond his control."

She could not believe her ears.

"I spoke with some people upstate about that...who call themselves 'Experiencers'. You *can't* mean--"

"*Aliens?* Hey, don't look at me! I'm just the messenger. This assessment comes straight from FBI Headquarters. An expert there claims that *implants* have been detected in some UFO abduction cases high up in the nasal passage, as deep as the optic nerve, or pituitary gland. Subjects *reportedly* suffer from lifelong nasal problems, bloody noses, sinus congestion, and more. No matter how you look at it, that's pretty damn close to the brain."

Una stared at him in disbelief.

No *wonder* people were afraid. This whole scenario was beginning to sound like *Invasion of the Body Snatchers.*

He paused, then looked her straight in the eye. "And if *that's* true, a very real danger exists, that *all* the agents of SAN-TOU-LONG--no matter where they are, the world over--may contain a 'switch' that can be activated...at *any time.*"

22

ARRIVAL

The Chinese Ambassador, Xiong Woo, and his wife, Nuan, arrived at John F. Kennedy International Airport in New York by special plane from Beijing, on Friday, February 23rd, just after 10 PM. Though apparently fatigued from their fourteen hour flight, he graciously accepted a warm welcome from city officials, including the Mayor and a small circle of executives representing the *New York Chamber of Commerce*.

Balding, with short black hair, large wire-rimmed glasses and a gray-tinted moustache, Woo smiled pleasantly, stepping up to a microphone. His beautiful wife, in an elegant, dark coat with a designer leather handbag and matching shoes, stood quietly at his side.

"It is my great honor to serve as the Chinese Ambassador to America at this vital moment, as both countries move toward economic transformation. I am ready to serve as a bridge and work together with you to improve relations between China and the U.S. I feel the great responsibility entrusted to me from my government and its people. I will spare no effort in fulfilling my mission."

They responded with generous applause.

There was no time allotted for questions, due to the lateness of the hour. His ambitious trade agenda would include a slate of meetings with business leaders, both public and private, to begin the next day and stretch for a total of nine before returning to his homeland.

While everyone seemed content to adhere to this formality, an attractive young woman reporter, blonde in high heels and a red dress, apparently concealed beneath a plain-looking overcoat up to now, raised her hand.

"Excuse me," she said, boldly, "*Mrs.* Ambassador, please, my readers at *Vogue* are just dying to know. Can we count on your appearance at the upcoming *Fashion Hong Kong Show* of New York Fashion Week? All the hottest designers will be there!"

Airport security came rushing forward, to silence her, while Secret Service turned Woo and his wife abruptly away, toward a private limousine.

But Nuan had a flare for the spotlight.

According to many, she had broken the mold of Chinese envoys' frumpy wives by becoming a beauty and fashion icon. Her style had sparked a stampede of followers in China with her simple but glamorous look.

She turned gracefully, making eye contact with the woman from *Vogue*. For a moment, everyone froze to see what would happen.

Now, *this* was a far cry from her roots, born into abject poverty. When she was four, Red guards arrived at her house to denounce her family. Her mother was labeled a spy for having relatives in Taiwan. Her father was made to clean public lavatories for promoting 'culture' considered absurdly outdated, a vestige of *old* China. She joined the People's Liberation Army as a civilian at the age of 18.

These days, thanks to good looks and a sense for fashion, she was known as a 'power player' in her own country and *some* said she wore the trousers in the Ambassador household. When her husband once remarked that he didn't like her lipstick, she told him to "stick to politics".

Accompanying him now on his first trip abroad, according to the *New York Times*, she came as a "welcome gift" to help boost China's international image. In elite social circles long before her arrival, she was described by copy editors as "modern...outgoing...a sheer delight."

Some considered her a diplomatic idol.

Nuan smiled thoughtfully, and said, "It is our task to make the voice and story of China more engaging. With my husband's permission, I would be *honored*!"

***

The next day, no force on Earth could keep Una away from the Mulberry Hotel. She could not shake the image of hidden icons, from her dream, a few nights before. There'd been no time to discuss it with Rufus as they touched base briefly at the Precinct.

She could not take it literally, of course, but could not dismiss the notion of what it was *saying* to her. What if there *was* a connection beneath *all of it*: Chinese-American corporations, mysterious attacks in Chinatown, and now, the Ambassador's visit, supposedly aimed at the betterment of trade relations? And who was *really* pulling the strings behind SAN-TOU-LONG?

The Ambassador was scheduled to speak to well-wishers from a balcony in the hotel courtyard around 3 PM. Ashcroft would not object to her presence because they were in this together. Madelyn had agreed to monitor events from a security vantage point outside the hotel. While it made sense in theory, the *real* reason was far simpler--to keep her out of harm's way. Her best friend had risked far too much already by commuting back and forth to D.C., and Una would never forgive herself if something went wrong.

And Jack? She could not leave him out of the loop. Fortunately, Ashcroft had granted him clearance to accompany a chopper pilot making routine sweeps over the hotel grounds. Any press reports would require Homeland Security approval before publication. But Jack didn't mind. He was even permitted to carry a camera.

By noon, they were forced to close hotel doors to all visitors.

Slowly, she surveyed the courtyard. Largely sheltered from high winds, it held surprisingly little snow. Landscaped stone walkways around its edge gave way to a large grass-covered lawn in the center. Here, over 500 people were already gathered for the event, a broad mix of Asian-Americans, including many young business entrepeneurs and women--all properly screened and searched by Security personnel.

General Ashcroft waved to her briefly from an observation point higher up, to one side of the balcony. No one expected any *real* violence, but they could not afford a diplomatic *incident* either, such as an outburst from an angry protestor or the slightest act of sabotage, like disrupting the hotel's electronic communications. Even a simple thing, such as the loss of Wi-Fi could throw people into a panic. It was *his* job to maintain order no matter what, ensure the safety of the Ambassador and his wife, and see to it that everyone exited the grounds peacefully when it was over.

He eyed a number of positions around the courtyard where high-tech listening devices had been secretly installed.

Beyond the obvious, there was a *second* level of security work being done, the kind no one talks about because it points to an inherent lack of trust regarding foreign governments, no matter how 'diplomatic' everyone pretends to be. All communications between the Ambassador and his staff, including any and all sources outside the hotel, were constantly monitored. On the outside chance that any espionage might be involved--especially pertaining to trade secrets held by U.S. corporate participants, it was Homeland's responsibility to 'nip it in the bud' whenever possible.

The same team of terror experts would also be monitoring the Ambassador's speech live, to analyze it for potential phrases or 'key words' that might translate into some kind of 'activation code' to foreign agents, like the followers of SAN-TOU-LONG.

For Ashcroft, it was all par for the course.

***

Greeted by cheers and whistles from the crowd, Ambassador Woo made his appearance at the appointed time, following a magnanimous introduction from the New York Chamber of Commerce.

"Thank you," he said, "As Chinese Ambassador, I am proud to stand here today, in a city where Chinese work closely with Americans in harmony. China is willing to work with all sides to address global challenges, promote world peace and development. It is our goal to follow the principles of sincerity and good faith, building on three strengths:

mutual political trust, shared economic benefit, and friendship."

As he spoke, members of the Police Auxiliary--including Jianyu--moved slowly among the crowd, distributing moon cakes, in honor of the recent New Year's Festival. Round pastries with a rich, thick filling made from lotus seed paste surrounded by thin crust, each contained one or more salted egg yolks as a symbol of the full moon. Imprints on top consisted of the Chinese character for 'harmony', with flowers and vines. It was considered a precursor to the modern day fortune cookie.

"In recent days," he sighed, "unfortunate *rumors* have surfaced regarding our intentions toward America. The Chinese government is opposed to any sort of terrorism, and has always practiced non-interference in another state's internal affairs. Only a fool would 'poison the pool from which both sides drink' and hope to survive. It will be sad if the peaceful environment here today is disrupted by 'trouble-makers'. I am certain the police will ensure public order."

At this point, TV cameras, seeking a distraction from his somber tone, focused on the Ambassador's wife in her trademark look: a single string of pearls with a mandarin-collared jacket. Viewers at home enjoyed commentary from fashion experts.

All in all, events went according to plan. His speech was followed by enthusiastic applause. Woo and his wife were safely escorted from the balcony.

People filed out through the hotel lobby and cleanup crews proceeded to canvas the courtyard for moon cake wrappers, left on the ground.

Una breathed a sigh of relief, exchanging nods. It was another success for East-West diplomacy.

Then, suddenly, her phone rang.

It was Jack.

"Look, I don't know how to tell you this--but something weird's going on. We're in the air. From up here, we just witnessed a light show that was out of this world. Keep everyone off the grass!"

"What do you mean?" she asked.

"Somehow, they must've bypassed security, to leave their mark."

"You're not making any sense!"

"Okay, just listen. Twirling lights appeared, for less than a minute. Then suddenly, it was *there*, on the ground below--"

"What? Jack, is this some kind of joke?"

"I'm dead serious. There's a *message* of some kind, on the ground. Looks like the snow's melted. But I bet it's more than that...like something killed the vegetation. I've seen it before."

"What? How? I don't get your--"

"Crop circles...you know, like they get in the UK--or the American Midwest, for that matter--but also the world over, in places like the former Soviet Union, Japan, and Canada. Huge, flattened geometric patterns in cereal crops, like wheat and barley, most prevalent since the 70's, increasing in number and complexity every year, often associated with UFOs. Genuine formations exhibit plant stems that are bent, but not broken, and cellular alterations within plants, caused by an intense, burst of heat that defies scientific explanation. They're also known to manifest *electromagnetic* changes, frequencies that alter brainwave patterns and bio-rhythms. Research now indicates that they've also been encountered in China, near Mongolia, dating back thousands of years."

"But this--"

"Is on a much smaller scale, I know, but I can't compare it to anything else. The *icon* is there...the three headed dragon, perfectly symmetrical, encircled by a string of words...I've never encountered before. It reads like...*prophecy*."

Una could stand it no more. She texted Ashcroft:

SEAL OFF THE COURTYARD

Racing inside, she hopped an elevator to the top floor, banged a hotel door until it opened and flashed her Official ID, rushing to the nearest balcony. Looking down, to her astonishment, she read the words out loud:

THE DRAGON WILL COME
FROM BEYOND * BREATHING FIRE *
GATHER THE CHOSEN * AND
DESTROY THE WORLD

PART FOUR

BREATHING FIRE

*"When the Dragon comes,
it looks like everything you feared, but behaves
like nothing you expected."*

--Anonymous

23

VIGILANCE

Within hours, three new Homeland Security vans appeared outside the service entrance to the Mulberry Hotel. They brought medical teams specially trained to deal with chemical and biological warfare, environmental experts and equipment to decontaminate the premises. No one knew for sure if the courtyard 'incident' posed any threat to human life--but they weren't taking any chances.

Una spied a crew in red Hazmat uniforms, slowly making their way from one end of the enclosure, though she could not tell precisely what they were doing. Tensions were running high in the small guest lounge where she waited with others, to see a Medic.

"How long's this gonna take?" a woman said. "I just came to hear the speech. Can't we speed this up?"

An officer in black fatigues came forward.

"Sorry, ma'am. The hotel's under *quarantine*, bound by CDC protocols. No one leaves until it's officially lifted. Rules are rules."

Each of them received a temporary ID bracelet and info sheet on "warning signs" after giving up a small blood sample.

A young, red-headed athlete had to cover his eyes. "Sorry. The sight of blood makes me *weak*."

A nurse tried to smile.

"It's just routine," she said. "We'll screen for toxins and let you know by morning."

He sighed. "Provided we don't have a *zombie apocalypse*!"

Nobody laughed.

Since everyone was in the same boat, it made no sense to isolate people from one another. Ashcroft needed to contain the situation, keep everyone as comfortable as possible, and monitor all those potentially exposed.

Beyond that, he had to investigate the *cause* of this event. This meant reviewing the surveillance feed from all security cams aimed at the courtyard as well as any images picked up by helicopters in the air.

Eyewitness accounts were spotty at best, describing two bright, fluorescent "balls of light", sized somewhere between an egg and a football, moving quickly from one side to another, then circling over the center, where the icon appeared, before a third came zipping around it--all in a matter of seconds.

Their source? Impossible to say.

But not according to Jack.

"Give me a chance," he said. "I have a field investigator from MUFON, waiting outside. He can run a few tests, on the spot. *True* circles are not exactly toxic, but they *do* have definite effects upon plants and animals. Horses get nervous, dogs flee, and I once heard of a cat turning vicious."

"What about...*people?*" the general asked.

"The strongest effects occur within 2-3 hours of the actual formation. Some observers report feelings of uneasiness, like 'being watched', a peculiar 'metallic' taste, or even panic attacks. But there have also been cases of severe dizziness, nausea, and headaches."

Jack held up his cell with a photo of his bearded friend wearing a MUFON logoed baseball cap and t-shirt.

Ashcroft weighed it briefly in his mind.

"Okay...tell him to lose the hat. I'll see what I can do."

The sooner they got to the bottom of this, the better. Despite their best efforts to keep it quiet, reporters began showing up outside.

Then suddenly, a call came in, on his two-way.

"General? Sorry to trouble you, sir. The hotel manager *insisted* I contact you, directly. We seem to have...a 'situation' here in the Ambassador suite. It's... his wife, sir. She seems to be having...a *meltdown.*"

***

On the ninth floor, staff members stood by helplessly, as Nuan pranced around in a designer dress and high heels, leaving a trail of thick smoke from her elegant cigarette holder.

"Who do you think we are?" she said, "Simple tourists? What do you *mean*, we can't have visitors? You expect the Ambassador to conduct all his meetings by *remote*? We Chinese are no fools! These trade matters are highly sensitive. It's an outrage! I won't stand for it. Do you hear me? I won't--"

"It's all right," said Mr. Woo, trying to calm her down.

"You...be quiet," she said, "I'm trying to--"

"Do whatever it takes, of *course*," said Una, abruptly stepping through a line of security personnel.

"*Exactly*," the woman replied. "And who, may I ask, are you?"

"Una Waters, Ma'am...Special Agent, U.S. Department of Interior, on assignment with NYPD. How can I be of service?"

She held up a copy of *Vogue* Magazine. "Well, for one thing--"

"The *Hong Kong Fashion Show*? Marvelous! Where East meets West...in *style*. I wouldn't miss it for the world--and neither will you. The catwalk's at Moynihan Station, one block from Madison Square Garden. My friend Madelyn's from Brooklyn, and she's been *dying* to take me for years. Looks like she'll finally get the chance. We should make a night of it--

with you and your entourage, of course! What d'you say?"

Nuan placed her cigarette aside, rushing to embrace Una.

"You speak my language," she said. "At last! Where on Earth have you been? Something tells me...we'll have such a good time! But the quarantine! What about all these *rules*? I know what it means to abide by authority. In China, education is very strict, because it is the key to the upper class. I learned very young the importance of performing well in tests. To fail in education means to fail in life. So, all this commotion we're seeing--is it just another test?"

"Not *exactly*, Mrs. Ambassador."

Inwardly, she cringed, but vowed not to let it show. Something did not feel right, though she could not put her finger on it. As official representatives of the Chinese government, the Woos would be opposed to all acts of defiance from present or former inhabitants of Tibet--*especially* the Dalai Lama.

"General Ashcroft is very tough. I do not wish to cross him. Will he agree to this? Do you feel his heart?"

Una grinned. *More than you'll ever know.*

***

Until it *was* lifted of course, lockdown meant living in a vacuum of sorts, at least until morning. What was *really* happening outside? If only--

Her phone rang, playing *Uptown Girl.*

"Una? My god! How are you?" said Madelyn.

"Okay, for now. Feeling trapped, is all."

"Is it *true?* About the message, I mean. In the grass?"

"Apparently. I didn't see it happen."

"So what does it mean?"

"Well, it's a prophecy, from SAN-TOU-LONG. I heard it once before, from Mr. Lao. *He* thinks they actually believe it."

"About the 'end of the world'?"

"Not as *we'd* think of course, not destruction of the planet...more like the end of our World System, you know...political control."

Madelyn paused, to let it sink in. In spite of all her 'star knowledge' and talk about karma and cosmic destiny, she never really considered the concept of alien invasion. The closest she ever came was attending an all night B-Movie marathon with an old boyfriend, with titles like *Slave Girls from Mars.*

"So we're doomed...to become sex slaves?"

"Not *exactly,*" Una sighed. "What about the ABP? Any hits?"

"Nada. They're taking a different tack."

"What do you mean?"

"The new recruit. Ming's brother."

"Jianyu?"

"Right. Anyway, he's on the case, trying to help track him down."

"But it's been *years* since they even spoke. I mean, what are the chances? Does anyone believe it'll work?"

"Detective Stone. It doesn't take much, according to him. Just one tip can make all the difference. Like the lucky break they got with Chong."

"*What!!!??*" Una replied. "Harry Chong? But I thought he was in hiding."

"Not anymore. They brought him for questioning."

"When? When did *this* happen?"

"I dunno. Two, maybe three days ago."

"Why didn't you tell me?"

Maddie paused again. "Why? Maybe because we've been kinda *preoccupied*...with this whole 'Ambassador' thing? It wasn't on purpose. Just... slipped my mind. Anyway, they couldn't make him talk."

"What do you mean, *make* him? I don't like the sound of that."

"*You* know what I mean. They couldn't *trick* him. Most people get tripped up, if they repeat their story too many times. Not Chong. He was too smart for that. So, they had to try something else."

"Such as?"

"Allowing him to think you were *dead*--just briefly--enough to get him riled up. I felt kinda bad about that."

"*Then* what? Where is he now?"

"Still in custody."

Una wanted to scream. "But they can't *do* that, not without formal charges. He's no criminal. That does it! Stone has gone too far."

Then another thought occurred: *What if he's waiting...for me?*

***

Quarantine on the Mulberry Hotel was finally lifted by 6 AM the next morning. Except for a few reported headaches and other minor complaints, there were no signs of serious illness. Toxicology results came back negative.

Officially, the entire incident was chalked up to 'mischief' by the hotel staff, who declined further comment.

Through a spokesman, Ambassador Woo denied all knowledge of SAN-TOU-LONG, and blamed the affair on "radicals" trying to sabotage U.S.-China trade. "Diplomacy will continue," he said.

"What a relief!" said Una to Madelyn, at last in the hotel lobby. "By the way, any luck with--"

"Right here!" she replied, waving V.I.P. passes to the upcoming Hong Kong Fashion Show.

"*That* was fast. From *Vogue*?"

She nodded. "Funny thing about that. After seeing the airport reception on TV, I sought out the reporter--you know, blonde hair and red dress? Well, they never heard of her. It's like she doesn't exist."

Una froze. "You mean...she was a...*plant*?"

"Probably," said Madelyn. "Reminds me of something I learned in D.C., long ago. I once asked an old Congressman the secret to getting re-elected. He winked at me and said, 'Leave nothing to chance!'"

In that moment, Una realized why the Ambassador's wife made her feel so ill at ease. Behind that beautiful exterior was a conniving woman of enviable strength, undaunted by obstacles. Perhaps it was the secret to her *husband's* success, without him ever knowing it.

Her natural beauty inspired *devotion* and *obedience*. Throughout life, she'd learned to *exploit* it, making others "feel" the rapture of her delight--*or the heat of her wrath!*

Nuan was a woman *in control*...who didn't fret about whether fate would deal her a good hand.

Because she'd already *stacked the deck*--in her favor.

24

SHADOWS

Una *insisted* they accept a ride with Officer Shen from the Mulberry Hotel, so Madelyn rode along. Decent showers and a good night's sleep would have to wait. With Sunday staffing reduced at the 5th Precinct, it seemed like her best chance to speak with Harry Chong.

"Detective Stone won't like it," Maddie said.

"I don't care," she replied. "You don't have to do this. *I* do. I can't leave that poor man behind bars. All he wants is to be left alone."

Dark, wispy clouds stretched over the city like winged behemoths. Where scattered beams of sunlight managed to peek through, they forged dark shadows everywhere, shadows that seemed to move with a mind of their own. Una imagined that one of them was trailing the squad car. It gave her the creeps. Madelyn was probably right. They weren't in their best state of mind, running on empty.

But this was too important.

They found Harry Chong rolled up in a ball of blankets on the cold cement floor in one corner of his cell.

"Harry? It's Una. I've come to help."

At first, he did not move.

"Harry," she said. "I'm sorry. I didn't know you were here. No one told me. But I'm here now, and I'm going to get you out. But we have to speak first. It's part of police protocol."

"No one else," he said.

"Fair enough. But Harry, we haven't much time. Detective Stone is on his way. We've got to do this, right *now*!"

Sipping hot coffee, they sat across from one another at a small table in Interrogation Room A. As a favor to Una, Madelyn switched the cameras off, and locked adjacent doors, in case Stone showed up early.

"What happened?" said Una. "I thought you were in hiding. Impossible to locate. Like an alley cat. How did they ever *find* you?"

Harry grinned, slicking back his gray hair and beard with grime-covered fingers. "I had to put up a fight, make them think I wanted to...get away." Then his voice changed, as if he was trying to sound like a cowboy:

'*...some things a man just
can't run away from.*'"

Una's eyes opened wide. He *allowed* it to happen.

"But why?" she asked. "Why now?"

"I had to see you. Had to give them a reason to hold me, until your return. Something I should've told you sooner. But I was afraid to speak out. Afraid you might...turn me in. But, then I realized, it's not about me. It's about the people of Chinatown. What's happening to them is part of a pattern that was set into motion...long ago. Before any of us were born."

Her head shook. "I don't--"

"What I told them was *true*, of course--from a certain point of view. They asked me about my research, if it was connected with SAN-TOU-LONG. It was *not*--at least, not directly, but I had to leave *something* out, save it for you. They were not satisfied, so I gave them...a theory."

"For what?"

"To explain the danger to New York. The threat grows day by day, but not in the way I described. I asked them to think about...*water.*"

She thought of Brighton Beach. "On the coast?"

He nodded. "FBI already knows. These 'people' originate far north, near the border of Mongolia. This symbol, they call 'Three-Headed-Dragon'. So I told them *this*: In Chinese mythology, there is a deity known as the Dragon King, regarded as the divine ruler of an ocean. In fact, there are *four* Kings of the Four Seas, that rule different parts of the world.

"The greatest threat to New York *may* arise from the sea. Hurricanes of the past have *already* caused the city to shut down its subway, forcing evacuation of as many as 300,000. For years, storm surge advocates have called for construction of massive Seagates...to block an ocean surge from Long Island Sound and the Atlantic, into the East River and New York Harbor."

He lowered his voice. "Strange lights were reported at the Mulberry--were they *not*?"

She sighed. *How did he know that?*

"Well, *strange lights* are nothing new. Reports near water describe many events, like 'elevated turmoil', 'swelling', or 'surface rising, like an enormous ball'--all associated with light. One encounter in the Gulfstream recorded 'great sheets of water flung over the deck' and 'great thrashing from the sea', caused by an 'underwater glow'. The ability of *Unidentified Submerged Objects*--also called *USOs*, to manipulate water is truly frightening. They've been known to move at incredible speed."

"What are you saying?"

"I'm *saying* the threat to cities like New York is very real. Military knows all about it. In fact, we have reason to believe that *alien bases* may exist, deep underwater, near coastal regions around the world--in places like California, Malibu, Wales, New Zealand, and Puerto Rico.

"So, I *told* them to check water level indicators, noting that SAN-TOU-LONG's dragon mythology *could* parallel Chinese belief in Dragon Kings--thus manipulation of water levels *might* be used to inundate the city and render it...*helpless*!"

Una stared at him in utter amazement.

Suddenly, a commotion arose, somewhere in the Station.

Lights flickered.

She got up from the table, walking over to bang on a mirrored wall, with her fist. "Maddie? Can you hear me? Give us a sign."

The doors automatically unlocked.

"Time to go!" She said, grabbing Harry by the arm.

They slipped out into the hallway. Shouts came from her right, toward the Station lobby. Turning left, they raced for the nearest exit.

They found a number of doors locked, leaving them no choice but to duck into the only one open: the Ladies Room.

Una took his hand.

"N-nooo!" said Chong.

"Sorry! You'll just have to trust me."

Inside, she ran to the nearest window, flipping it open. Street traffic flowed by nonstop, two stories below.

"Wait for a truck," she said, "Then, *jump*!"

"Okay! Okay! But first, one more thing. *Most important*. In my work, as a government scientist, it was part of my job to review any and all descriptions of advanced technology spotted in foreign countries.

I've seen "S-T-L" abbreviated in Top Secret Air Force documents for unknown craft spotted by high-flying U.S. reconnaissance planes over Northern China. The S-T-L diagram *I* saw was unmistakable: a *triangular-shaped* UFO."

She understood.

Finally, a truck appeared, coming up the road.

"By the way," she said. 'How did you know I was still *alive?*"

"Simple," he grinned. "You would not abandon Chinatown!" Then his cowboy voice returned before leaping away:

"Take'er easy there, pilgrim."

And it dawned on her as an open flat bed full of gravel broke his fall and carried Harry Chong away, out of sight. The voice he was trying to imitate seemed familiar, for a reason. It had played in her mind, over and over, since the day she first saw that old movie poster in the general's Command Center for that Deep Underground Military Base in Arizona. The voice of a hero to young boys in America for generations.

It was the voice of *John Wayne.*

Detective Stone came barging in, with no apologies.

"Okay, hold it right there. Where's Chong?" Two police officers flagged him, to either side, weapons drawn.

"Too late!" she said. "He's...gone."

Ten minutes later, she rejoined Madelyn, in the lobby.

"What happened?" she said, as the two of them embraced. "One minute you were there, the next...I thought I'd *lost* you!"

"Harry's safe," she whispered, "Let's...get outta here."

***

Flashing their ID's to a special pane of black security glass, a door opened, to let them into CATBRIER. The high-tech elevator's soft hum was like music to their ears. Moments later, they both sighed, stepping into the comfort and tranquility of their private suite.

"*That's* odd," said Madelyn, as they turned on the lights. "Your statue. It's over there, by the window. Wasn't it further down, on the table, when we left?"

"I guess," Una replied. "What's it matter?"

"Well, it *doesn't*, except, I've moved it back twice already."

"Okay, so there's a logical explanation. Maybe the room's not level--"

"Or the table's slanted--"

"Or...," she stopped in mid-sentence, moving closer. Shiny silver beams gleamed in contrast to the antique bronze finish on the Duke's ten gallon hat and bandana scarf, not to mention his prominent facial features. "Paperclips...stuck all over, like it's...*magnetized!* What would--"

Then she answered her own question. After speaking to Chong, this actually made *sense*. The *pattern* was repeating itself. Jack once told her that UFO sightings occasionally produced effects in metal objects, like a compass that went haywire, or a stopped wristwatch.

She'd felt it the moment they stepped inside, but tried to shrug it off, that same peculiar feeling of "being watched"--*just like the Mulberry*. The same alien craft must have been *here*.

But she wasn't about to tell Madelyn.

The CATBRIER was more secure than Fort Knox. Even *if* electromagnetic fields could be altered through its walls, they had no reason to fear intruders coming for the statue, with the Hopi Rattle tucked inside.

And yet, that's *exactly* what she feared.

The moment of truth with this ancient artifact was fast approaching. At some point, she'd *have* to turn it over to Ashcroft, whether she *wanted* to or not--just to keep it from the wrong hands.

But *when*? When would that moment arrive?

She suddenly vowed to keep it with her at all times--which meant attaching it to her physical body somehow, or finding a subtle way to carry it--*without* the bulk of its bronze exterior.

A few wisps of cloud clung to the darkening sky as the sun began to set over Manhattan, with its grid pointing not exactly north, rotated by thirty degrees. If only she could be here in May or July, when sunset was perfectly aligned with that grid, producing a remarkable sight. People came to see it from all over. According to one brochure, they called it "Manhattanhenge".

She wondered what shadows might be lurking *then*.

While Madelyn took a hot shower, she went to the kitchenette. It contained plenty of ordinary things like yogurt, bottled water and fresh fruit. But it *also* displayed a few advanced foodstuffs, like protein bars developed for long tours of duty in hostile terrains without refrigeration. These were packaged in elastic covers like none she'd ever seen, with strange logos from defense contractors she did not recognize.

One peeled away clean, with no odors or residue.

With a little effort, she retrieved the *Hopi Rattle* from its hiding place and covered it with elastic.

With luck, no one would ever know.

Concealing it on her person would be a challenge, but she could usually find vest coats or utility pants with plenty of pockets. Minor application of sewing skills would provide just the right-sized carrying place.

She could do *that* once Maddie was asleep.

25

IMMORTAL

Monday arrived. And everyone who was anyone connected with fashion in the city of New York had a million things to do. Not just those being watched-- by industry leaders and retailers and paparazzi, but also the watchers, responsible for things like transportation, security and runway protection.

This year's participants in the Fashion Hong Kong Show had to contend with a few new security measures, thanks to the presence of Nuan Woo, wife to the Chinese Ambassador, and by all rights (according to some social circles), a bit of a fashion icon herself.

Una eyed the glass door entrance to *Moynihan Station*, waiting for Nuan's VIP arrival. The magnificent, light-filled facility, decades in the making and costing nearly 2 billion dollars, had been completed only 3 months before. Designed to accommodate both Long Island Railroad and Amtrak passengers, onlookers could look down from its retail balcony to the train floor below. Full service was still months away. Late New York senator Daniel Patrick Moynihan, for whom it was named, would have been proud.

Ashcroft had coordinated with FBI and show officials to make sure all measures were in place: suit and tie security guards, undercover escorts, interior and exterior 24-hour patrols, and on-site medical care--just in case.

She glanced for a moment at the neon pink ID band attached to her wrist--mandatory for all personnel in direct contact with Nuan. Without it, no one could accompany her through a series of invisible security check points, along the way.

A shiver went through her spine.

Appearances could be deceiving. Though she knew in her mind it was already past sundown, bright lights reflecting off fallen snow made it *feel* like the middle of the day.

Una sighed. Madelyn was *somewhere* beyond those doors, attending to last minute details. Their *one* chance to enjoy the glamour of an exclusive New York fashion show--with VIP extras like prime front row seating, backstage tours, red carpet photo ops, and admission to an after-party with a scrumptious dinner buffet, music and dancing--would *have* to be on duty, kept completely apart.

She couldn't *wait* to compare notes afterward.

***

From the rooftop of *Lao-Chi*, in Chinatown, Jianyu contemplated a different city view altogether. Facing his first official night on patrol with the Police Auxiliary, he wrestled with self-doubt.

NYPD supervisors all seemed preoccupied with the Fashion Hong Kong Show. He could not even carry a gun. *What if he encountered a life-threatening situation? Would anyone come if he called for backup?*

He did not want his first night on patrol to be his last.

"What are you waiting for?" said Grandfather Lao, appearing suddenly, out of nowhere, in traditional robes.

Jianyu did not sense his approach. Since early childhood, he often wondered if the old man had ever trained to become a Buddhist monk in his youth, learning the secrets of the universe, before starting a family. It was hard to imagine him ever being young enough to earn a nickname like "grasshopper". His unnerving ability to appear and disappear without sound, like a ghost, was sometimes hard to take.

"My first shift on patrol. I don't start for another hour. Just a little nervous, I guess. It's something I never...planned."

Grandfather grinned. "The 'plan' is not up to you. It goes far beyond either one of us. Do not fear what will happen. We are all in the Master's hands."

"And what about Ming?" he asked. "All the time he was gone, I wondered if he was dead or alive. I still don't know if he was taken, or he abandoned us. Now it feels like he's returned from the grave."

"You must *face* him. It is the only way for you to find peace. Perhaps it is no coincidence that you stand on opposite sides of the law. Two sides of one whole, like yin and yang, darkness and light. He succumbed to forces long ago bent on human destruction. But deep in his heart, he believes it is the *right* thing to do. You must discover why."

Jianyu nodded. "But...I'm afraid that we'll be like strangers, with nothing in common."

Grandfather sighed. "Your blood is a bond that cannot be broken. No matter what has taken over his mind, *that* will never change. His departure from the family left a wound in your mother's heart--a wound that must be healed. All things work together, toward the inevitable future of mankind. It is coming, like the opening of a gate that cannot be closed, unleashing our fate, whether we wish it or not."

"But how will I know what to do?"

"Let love be your guide. The loving thing and the *right* thing are usually one and the same. It is the key to our survival."

***

Sleek, black limousines of every shape and size began to arrive at last, outside the VIP entrance to *Moynihan*. Celebrities flashed well-rehearsed smiles to a chorus of clicking cameras. Reporters lined the red carpet with microphones, hoping to share a photo-op. Black light reactive jewelry, in luminescent shades from hot pink to yellow to green to indigo, lit up as they stepped inside.

Una could not shake one thought from her mind: *No sign of Ashcroft.*

Surely, he planned to be there. It was not like the general to be 'fashionably late'. Of course, he might prefer to keep his presence concealed from the public. *Especially* the paparazzi. The Ambassador's wife could not be upstaged.

Still, she *had* hoped for more.

Their task this evening was basically two-fold: to keep Nuan safe and reasonably happy in the midst of chaos without any mishaps, *and* return her safely to her husband when it was over.

As a red limo appeared, Una moved to the curb. Opening the rear door, she greeted Nuan, along with her private entourage, including a personal assistant, bodyguard and social media specialist--to ghost-tweet her comings and goings.

Never one to shy from the spotlight, Nuan paused to wave at the crowd, as if the entire event was staged in her honor.

Together, they marched toward the entrance, shielded by security.

Once inside, they enjoyed a pre-show champagne toast at a private reception with Fashion and Accessories editors from *Vogue* Magazine. Nuan did not seem to notice that the blonde reporter from JFK

International was missing--thus Una's suspicions were confirmed.

***

Jianyu began his patrol on an upbeat note, reminiscing with his new partner, Kai, about the struggles they both faced growing up in Chinatown.

"My parents worked in a factory," he said, "We shared a small apartment with my grandmother. My brother, sister and I all slept on one mattress for two years. Kids at school called me 'slanty eyes' and 'rice cakes'."

Jianyu sighed. "Most New Yorkers have no idea what it's like to be Asian in America. With the restaurant, at least we had food. But I felt bad for some of my friends, who were Korean. Everyone simply called us *Chinese.*"

Soon they encountered trouble, in the form of a liquor store robbery gone bad. The owner lay tied up, with a bullet wound to the chest. Covered in sweat but still breathing, he was unable to speak.

"He seems stable," said Kai. "But I'm not taking any chances. He may be in shock. I'll radio for help. You--"

But Jianyu did not hear another word. A door slammed, in the back, and suddenly, he was gone-- racing in hot pursuit.

They ran for three city blocks. Then the perp made a smart move, veering toward *Paradise Park.*

Situated in one of the oldest residential areas in Chinatown, it was the perfect place to *disappear*. From its crowded basketball courts at one end, to its newly renovated playgrounds, to open ground, where, during warmer weather, one could always find a softball game, it was the answer to every city kid's dream.

It was *also* a place filled with memories.

Flashbacks came to mind: shooting hoops with his brother Ming at the age of nine. At the park's far end, they once joined groups of fellow Asians playing cards, in the dead of winter.

In fact, he could see people playing, even now.

Then suddenly, a stranger shot toward him, peddling a ten speed, waving. Jianyu instinctively raised his own hand. The rider's palm slapped into his, riding by, nearly causing him to slip on the snow.

When he turned, the rider was gone.

In his hand, he discovered a folded piece of paper, with a note in familiar handwriting:

Beyond the fence--10 minutes.

And then, he remembered.

Glancing over one shoulder, as he turned, there was a mystery structure, fenced off, once used as a Recreational Center long, long ago, before his time-- or at least, so he thought.

With nothing to lose, and everything to gain, he approached the old snow-covered brick building, its roof now partially collapsed.

Pulling at a rusted section that appeared to be cut, he stooped gracefully, slipping under, without a scratch.

Just like the old days.

Entering an abandoned doorway, he detected light and warmth. A small fire burned in one corner, sheltered from the elements, beneath a broken window.

It was only then that he sensed the cold surface of a gun's barrel touching the back of his scalp--and realized it was a *trap*.

"Don't turn around," said Ming.

"I only came to--"

"Gloat, no doubt. The way you always did. Even though--"

"Don't be a fool. Do you *really* think no one knows where I am? They don't have to track *me* at all, of course, just my badge. Right now, someone is sitting in front of a computer, sounding an alarm. You've got five to seven minutes, tops, before--"

"Silence! Listen *up*--if you want to live!"

Jianyu fell silent. It seemed odd for his brother to hide. Part of his Auxiliary training dealt with *keen observation*. He needed to *see* his adversary.

Near the floor, against a wall, lay pieces of a broken mirror. The fire's glow gave off just enough light. *If he could just move a little--*

"Be *still*!" said Ming. "Don't make me shoot. The reign of man...is ending. SAN-TOU-LONG is already *here*...and powerful beyond belief. It comes down to a choice. Accept one truth: the world is about to *change*! Nothing will be the same. Those who reject it will be...plunged into darkness!"

Focused on one reflective corner, he saw...NO...*my god, what's happened to him?* The gun clicked. Jianyu feared the worst.

Then, suddenly, the fire went out, the room turned cold, and he was alone, once more.

***

While being escorted with her entourage toward the Fashion Show runway, Nuan surprised everyone by insisting they go backstage.

"Of *course* I want to see the catwalk," she said, "But that's only a small part of what goes on."

Suddenly, they entered a scene of organized chaos. It was much smaller, more crowded, and less plush than Una imagined. Mirror-lined tables surrounded the space, where makeup artists and hairstylists strived to bring the designer's vision to life on each model. Frantic dressers had to ensure just the right look, without garment mishaps.

Nuan seemed giddy. "What did I tell you? Pure adrenaline!"

Secretly, Una feared the worst. With no time to shift assignments, the Ambassador's wife could be at risk.

"Fruit parfait, anyone?" said a young server with a tray full of red and white mason jars. A videographer, documenting the event for HBO, turned suddenly, knocking the tray from her hands.

One jar flipped high, colliding with neon lights where it shattered, releasing Greek yogurt, fresh strawberries and broken glass onto everyone below.

"Noooo!" screamed Nuan.

All eyes turned. Tiny shards protruded from her face, glistening with trickles of red blood. Horrified attendants backed away.

Una's heart leaped.

Suddenly, Nuan seized the server's young throat, squeezing with such fervor that she nearly died, on the spot.

It took three people to tear her away.

Desperately gasping, the girl sensed deep scratches from long, sharp, claw-like fingernails...then collapsed to the floor.

"*Do* something!" they all shouted.

Emergency medics soon arrived. While men lifted the server onto a gurney for transport to an ambulance, Una fought her way through a tight-knit circle of strangers, to reach the Ambassador's wife. They remained eerily silent.

My god, she thought, *Don't tell me--*

"Alive and well!" beamed Nuan, with wicked delight.

Una could not believe her eyes.

Somehow, miraculously, as EMT's wiped her face, everything--glass, blood clots and all--apparently fell away, as if a layer of skin came off, shedding itself, to reveal her features, perfectly renewed.

At least two people fainted.

Slowly, fashion chaos resumed, as the circle strangers dispersed. One of them picked up a fallen parfait jar, inadvertently passing his hand beneath a decorative black light.

That's when she saw it--the Three-Headed-Dragon--tattooed in luminescent ink. She looked up, and the stranger was gone.

A call came from her two-way.

"Ashcroft here," he said. "Heard about your little 'mishap' with our VIP. Is everything...all right?"

Una could barely stop shaking as she held the radio to her lips.

"VIP's fine, so far as I can tell. But I can't explain it. I'm not sure anyone can. All right? No sir, I'm afraid *not*. In fact...*far from it*!"

26

INSIGHT

General Ashcroft considered himself a man with an open mind. He trusted Una's instincts...and her judgement. So when *she* described the Ambassador wife's recovery as *paranormal*, he took it to heart.

But he wasn't exactly sure how to respond.

"So, she's a quick healer," he said. "What of it?"

The security breach was one thing. Knowing that a number of SAN-TOU-LONG cult members had wormed their way into the Fashion Hong Kong Show-- despite everyone's best efforts--did not make him happy.

"I'm *not* exaggerating," she said. "Anyone else would've died. Yet somehow, Nuan walked away...without a scratch. What does it *mean?*"

"Don't know," he replied, "But I sure as hell plan to find out!"

As Una returned to her Qwik-Ride, waiting outside, somewhere deep in the back of her mind, she heard a small voice: *Jack would know.*

***

In the Ambassador's suite at the Mulberry Hotel, Mr. Woo shook his head and turned off the TV News.

"You must be more careful," he said. "These Americans love to stir up trouble. It's my job to smooth things over. Beijing is watching us. We cannot afford to fail!"

Nuan looked down from their balcony to the giant symbol in the courtyard below. "I can *still* see it from here. These ground keepers are so lame. They should've removed it by now. In China we would not stand for it."

He sighed. "Are you even *listening* to me? This is serious! I need your help. If you persist--"

He froze suddenly, as their eyes met:

> *You'll what? Curtail my freedom?*
> *Embarrass me before my fans? No,*
> *you won't. Why? Because I own you.*
> *You wouldn't be here without me!*

Every word came directly to his mind, though her lips never moved. He was used to it, by now. Sometimes, she would interrupt him in the middle of an important meeting, with timely advice. And she was always right. Though often praised in diplomatic circles for his keen ability to outwit even the fiercest opponent, in *truth*, he owed it all to Nuan. Without her, his career would have faltered long ago.

"So...what now?" he said, humbly.

"We press on," she said. "Three days, until our return to the Mainland. Your task is far from over. Be patient, my dear. I sense...an opportunity is about to come our way."

He did not ask how she knew. That would be pointless, and foolish. She would not answer him, anyway.

***

Jianyu felt more than a little nervous, waiting in the Precinct squad room. His preliminary report on Ming apparently got kicked up from Stone directly to the FBI. Gazing at an Investigation Board constructed so far from clues gathered in the SAN-TOU-LONG case, he half expected a reprimand.

Suddenly a door closed in the back as several men approached, He could hear their boots coming down the hall. The first to appear, in Black Ops uniform and red beret, was General Ashcroft.

Jianyu leaped from his seat, awkwardly attempting to salute.

The general grinned. "At ease, son. I'm here to get it from the horse's mouth. I believe you're onto something. Let's...have a seat."

For the next few minutes, he tried his best to explain the chain of events that led him to Paradise Park. It all happened so fast. Technically, it was *not* considered part of his 'beat', and the fenced-off building *was* clearly marked with KEEP OUT signs. But there was no time to alert Park Officials. His meeting with Ming came as a total surprise.

"Slow down, son. *Think.* What did you see?"

"Nothing, at first," he replied. "It was too dark. But then...there was his reflection, in the fire's glow. But I...can't be sure."

"What do you mean?"

"Well, he wasn't himself, exactly. At least, not the way I remember him. He's changed. The voice is the same, but his face...pale and thin, emaciated, with no facial hair, wearing dark glasses to cover his eyes."

"Drugs, maybe--or severe lack of vitamin D. Maybe ritualized starvation. Not unheard of with cults. Anything else?"

"He seemed...jittery, anxious, and...extra talkative."

Ashcroft nodded. "Lack of sleep, another form of control."

And it dawned on him that this set of characteristics was eerily familiar, reminiscent not only of the suspect from the train station, but also his *own* bizarre encounter a while back...with the mystery man in gray uniform he mistook for an *albino*, who ordered his withdrawal from Alpha Bravo in Arizona.

At the time, he gave no name, simply displaying a peculiar blank, white I.D. card with a three-sided holographic pyramid.

He could not help but think there *must* be a connection--the kind most, true blue Americans could not accept, spawning theories of collusion between government leaders and aliens. Ordinarily, he would not even consider such thoughts, but it was getting *easier* by the minute.

"And another thing. He said the world's about to *change*...and those who reject it will be...plunged into *darkness*."

The general's eyes lit up. A threat like that *could* be supernatural, referring to evil, unhappiness, or gloom. It might infer a state of ignorance, suggesting loss of knowledge. But he was inclined to take it more literally. In the middle of winter, only one threat could produce all of the above: loss of power, or light...from *the electrical grid!*

"Good work," he said finally, "You may earn high marks from the Auxiliary --but don't count on it. Some people just can't handle the truth. And *don't* try to leave Chinatown."

Like most major cities, New York's power came from a variety of sources, including coal, nuclear, gas, and petroleum, not to mention hydroelectric and wind farms--impossible to threaten all at once. But how to narrow it down?

Maybe it was time for another "face-to-face"...with the "Albino".

Ashcroft well knew that conspiracy buffs on talk radio often postulated the existence of a secret or Shadow Government, wielding true power over the people. Proponents of this theory believed its members to be agents for mysterious entities like the Council on Foreign Relations, Trilateral Commission, Illuminati or the Bilderberg group. A few claimed that it was also collaborating with aliens.

Secrecy at the highest levels was an unfortunate necessity in the modern world. The general could not do his job without it. When President Dwight D. Eisenhower warned the American public in his 1961 farewell address about the dangers of the so-called "military-industrial complex", he couldn't have been closer to the mark.

C'est la vie, according to the French. *That's life.*

So when it came to tracking down a 'mystery man' somewhere deep in the middle of that, one might expect it to be a damn-near impossible task.

Not for Ashcroft.

His first "official inquiry" might even be stonewalled--but that did not bother him. He knew ways around it.

Since their *last* meeting, his star had risen considerably within the intelligence community. He'd been very selective about those he admitted to his 'inner circle", and these contacts knew how to pass information without leaving a trace.

The biggest problem was time. No one knew when or where this "change" alluded to by Ming would actually occur.

Haunted by Una's pleas, it was time to take the next step. And so, he waited until Jianyu was gone, then boarded his Hummer, escorted by two MP's in black uniform.

"Where to, sir?" his driver asked.

"The Mulberry Hotel," he replied. "And *step* on it!"

***

When seeking private audience with the Ambassador, it was customary to phone ahead. But in cases of diplomatic urgency, one could chance a surprise visit, provided the hotel concierge was properly notified.

Ashcroft stood by, hands folded behind his back as an attendant from Room Service rapped gently on the door.

At first, there was no response. Then, just as the hand was about to rap a second time, the brass knob abruptly turned and gave way--not to a member of her entourage, but Nuan herself, all smiles with hypnotic green eyes.

"General!" she said, "What a pleasure to finally meet the man responsible for our safety. Without your efforts, I am certain my little 'mishap' at the Fashion Show would've ended far worse. As you can see, I am unharmed. Please, do come in. We've been...*expecting* you!"

He sensed a *dig* in there somewhere, but resolved not to let it show.

How she was able to anticipate his arrival, and every question, it seemed, before it could even escape his lips, he did not know. But it caught him off guard, like confronting an enemy who knows all your battle plans.

Finally, he realized there was no need for small talk. This woman clearly sensed the reason for his visit.

"Please, do not take offense," he said, "But I *am* here on official business. We've been working round the clock to neutralize any threat posed to you or the people of new York by this mystery cult, known as SAN-TOU-LONG. In fact, we now believe the danger they represent may go far beyond the borders of Chinatown. But I suspect you already--"

Nuan sighed. "*How* far, I wonder? To your nation's capital?"

"Be careful," said Mr. Woo. "To not say things you may regret. Beijing does not respond well to accusations."

Ashcroft nodded, signaling to his men. "We're fine, now. Please...wait for me, outside."

As the door closed behind them, he sensed...a sudden, severe, undirected form of anxiety--even though, at first glance, everything remained the same.

But then, he looked more closely at his two companions.

The Ambassador's facial expression and bodily position appeared to be frozen. In fact, his eyes did not blink, his chest did not rise, and his gaze remained fixed, straight ahead. He was apparently "turned off", as lifeless as a department store mannequin.

His wife, on the other hand, continued to breathe and blink normally.

Meaning to inquire about this bizarre turn of events, the general found himself unable to speak. Though he sensed the passage of air into and out of his lungs and the familiar rhythm of his own heart, in fact, he could not move a muscle. All external sounds fell away, as if he could no longer perceive them. Perhaps strangest of all--in spite of all this, he felt unusually *calm*.

Nuan smiled at him, speaking *into* his mind:

> *You are not so clever as you imagine.*
> *I know all about you. The terror you*
> *suffered as a child on Flight 564...*
> *the recovery mission that failed in an*
> *Arizona cave three years ago...and*
> *the prize that got away. Would it*
> *surprise you to learn...that prize is*
> *here...even now... nearby?*

And suddenly, it occurred to him that Una was right. Mental telepathy did not conform to any expected mode of behavior.

Paranormal *indeed*.

27

AWAKENING

Ashcroft sat in complete silence as his driver coursed city streets, en route to the CATBRIER. He could clearly recall everything that transpired in the Ambassador's Suite, despite Nuan's attempt to conduct a *memory wipe*--thanks to P.O.W. survival training.

Inserting a special key from his neck chain, he took the 'service elevator' down a mile underground. As it opened, he traversed an extended, ramped tunnel, eight-foot in diameter, with non-skid surfacing and two-foot thick reinforced concrete walls. After scanning his ID, sliding panels admitted him into an automated decontamination area, followed by heavy, blast-proof steel doors into the Strategic Command Post.

Ashcroft grinned, looking up.

Its Big Board contained a series of real-time maps and postings showing military conditions worldwide, including updates on weather, force movements, aircraft, missiles and defense satellites.

Slowly he moved through an array of workstations and computer consoles, with state-of-the-art voice communications and information displays, all manned 24/7 by nearly three hundred military personnel.

This nerve center was designed to transmit Command Authority directives to all strategic forces. In time of war, it could be completely sealed off from the outside world, with its own emergency power supply, water source and rations. Electromagnetic Pulse (EMP) protection ensured that the Post would continue to operate, even in the disturbed EM environment which would follow a high altitude nuclear burst.

"General," said a woman in uniform, rushing forward, "We just received word. Your official inquiry--it's been *denied*."

He nodded. So much for round one. If only he could speak to Una right now. But of course, *that* was impossible.

Climbing two open flights of stairs, he entered a glassed-in office, from which he could still see the Big Board. Sitting at his desk, he glanced at a "Red Phone", connected to well over 200 operating locations around the world, including missile launch control centers, Washington, D.C., and other command headquarters. Hopefully, he would not need to use it.

Oddly enough, though originally built in the 1950's, this entire complex had been redesigned in the mid 80's to reflect Hollywood versions of a military War Room--after officials decided that they looked better in movies than real life.

Placing his fingers to a keyboard, he opened a secure program for Satellite Communications, and typed in a single Keyword command:

EVERSOR

***

Una woke in the middle of the night, distressed by a peculiar glow. Though at first she thought it might be from the living room or kitchenette, it was actually coming from the bedroom closet.

She opened it, shielding her eyes...from the Hopi Rattle.

Why now? she thought. *What did it mean?* She raced to the nearest window, thinking there must be a UFO nearby. She could see nothing, but also realized, it might be invisible.

***

At the very same moment, Mr. Lao stood alone on his snow-covered rooftop, gazing up at the stars. A rare, easterly wind came over Chinatown, persisting to heights of 3 kilometers or more. Pressure was generally high to the north of this region and low in the south, but this was no ordinary storm.

Let it blow, he thought.

Within it, he sensed an ancient presence from a very far corner of the world, all the way from Tibet. He could not tell his family because they would not understand.

He could tell no one.

And so he chose to accept it, to *merge* with it, the only way to find peace in the light of renewal that came over New York.

Few people would speak of it the next day. Fewer would comprehend its meaning. In the eyes of the majority, life would continue the same as always-- until the moment it abruptly stopped.

Feeling a chill, he finally turned away from the sky, trusting this would *not* be the end...but a bright, new beginning.

Only time would tell.

***

General Ashcroft assembled his Satellite Communications Team for an office briefing. A 16-foot wall display carried all the essential data from the Big Board, with a few special modifications. Smaller images across the bottom displayed video conference participants from Command Posts in D.C., Rhode Island, Massachusetts, Connecticut and New Jersey.

There was no apparent sign of the 'Albino'.

"My source is classified," he said. "But I have reason to believe the NYPD cyber-attack was the first move in a game of chess, so-to-speak. A game we dare not lose. Therefore, I have ordered a change in satellite defense readiness. Everyone in this room is cleared to receive the following directive: EVERSOR Satellite code-named: DS-1769, placed in orbit nearly two decades ago, is hereby declared to be a nuclear weapons platform, with warheads pointed at Beijing."

A young Systems Engineer raised her hand. "I don't understand. That seems a bit...extreme, sir."

"The security breach at the Fashion Hong Kong Show has brought...new evidence to light. We *need* an effective counter strike, ready to go. Beijing's population, roughly equivalent to New York State, fits the bill."

"*A valid point*," said an eerily familiar voice from his speaker phone, apparently listening in the whole time. *"But China is not to be trifled with. Their war machine may be greater than our own."*

Ashcroft cringed.

So *this* was it then, the intrusion he'd been waiting for, playing devil's advocate with his command--just like he did three years ago, in Arizona. The 'Albino' even managed it without revealing his face.

The general would not back down. "The Pentagon's had contingency plans for decades. It was only a matter of time. We *have* to act."

"But we don't know--"

"Enough? Sure we do. At this point, it's all about defense readiness. Like moving from DEFCON 4 to 3."

And then, just as suddenly, the speaker phone went silent.

But it was no sign of retreat. Ashcroft knew better than to claim victory. This conflict had yet to play itself out. The 'Albino' would no doubt rear his ugly head again, sometime soon.

Moments later, as team members filed out of his office, one by one, the Systems Engineer paused before him. "Just one more thing, sir."

"Yes?"

"The satellite code name. It's a bit out of my time frame. I was born too late to appreciate the meaning of 'DS'. It doesn't appear in any of our manuals. Could you--"

"*Dragon Slayer*," he replied.

***

Madelyn didn't like the idea of Una going out alone.

"I'll be with Jack," she said. "We're meeting at the American Museum of Natural History. What could be safer?"

"*This* early? They're not even open. Can't this wait until daylight?"

Una laughed. "I'll be fine. We'll have coffee first. Give me until noon...and don't *worry*!"

The Qwik-Ride driver didn't seem surprised to find her waiting once more on an empty street corner in the middle of nowhere.

"Thanks," she said, climbing into the back.

"Where to?"

"*Life at the Limits*," she said.

"Excuse me?"

"*You know*, the Museum Exhibit. Incredible stories of survival? It's going on right now!"

"Right. Of course. Except--"

"I know," she said, rolling her eyes. "Too early. So...nearest coffee shop, *what's* it called?"

"*JAVA-Culture*?"

"*That's* it," she said, texting the name to Jack on her cell phone.

Maybe it was just nerves. But she could've sworn a figure in the shadows was matching her pace on the sidewalk.

It's okay, she told herself. *It's a public place.*

Minutes later, she stepped inside. The long and narrow space was already lined with people eyeing books or laptops. She could feel her tummy grumbling for an egg and cheese burrito.

"Pssst. Over *here*," said Jack, waving a hand.

For the next forty minutes, she poured out details of Nuan's death-defying recovery, and her strange ability to control others.

Jack listened thoughtfully to every word.

Finally, she paused, waiting for his response.

"You won't like it," he said.

"What do you mean?"

"I *have* heard of this before, but not exactly the way you describe. Sometimes, 'Experiencers' report healing from conditions like TB and cancer through contact with an alien rod of 'light'. Others report a bizarre capacity for *one* type of alien to heal itself-- much like the lizard that grows back its own tail."

Una froze at first, trying to process it.

"Okay," she said, finally. "What does that *mean* exactly?"

"Well, it *means* that we've crossed into new territory. Up to now, all our discussions have dealt with either humans or aliens, but never--"

"The two of them *combined?* I remember that meeting in upstate New York. A few spoke of breeding, but--"

He nodded. "It's been touched upon, by a number of researchers, who study abduction. The point I want to make: this woman, Nuan, seems to exhibit abilities that go *beyond* the human norm. What if she's--"

"An alien-human *hybrid?*"

Together, they sighed--as if a cloud had been lifted. All this time, they'd apparently shared the same suspicion, afraid to say it out loud.

Una raised her coffee cup. Ironically, a brochure for the Museum Exhibit on the table touted questions about key factors which enable one species to outlive another:

Suits of armor?
Defense against predators?
Longer lifespans?

And she could not help but wonder if a new era had already begun to unfold for humanity, secretly, without fanfare or acknowledgement. If Jack's theory regarding Nuan and her 'super abilities' was true, how many 'others' of her kind might be out there, at this minute, walking the face of the Earth?

While most Americans seemed to make a habit of assigning value to every new discovery, rating it good or bad, right or wrong, one thing she had learned from her newfound friends in Chinatown: *inner peace* came more from *acceptance of what is* rather than trying to conform the world to a set of personal expectations. Outwardly, living in the white man's world, Una tried to understand resistance to change caused by *fear* of 'newcomers' to any social order. But inwardly, she felt that acceptance was always the better course.

Everything happened for a reason.

And this "follower" she glimpsed from the corner of her eye was no figment of her imagination. Though tempted to ask Ashcroft more than once whether his 'friends' at the FBI had placed a "tail" on her, she already knew the answer.

And although logic would simply say it was an agent of SAN-TOU-LONG, she did not believe that.

Maybe *fear* was holding her back.

There was only one way to 'awaken' from this state of limbo and discover this "follower's" *agenda*: turn around and *meet* him, face-to-face.

28

CATASTROPHE

Snow fell steadily as Una and Jack walked from *JAVA-Culture* to the American Museum of Natural History. Glancing from side to side, she could not help but wonder if the hooded "follower" might be lurking somewhere nearby.

Next time, I'll turn the tables, she thought, Get some answers.

Colorful banners for Life at the Limits showed breathtaking images of the Mimic Octopus, Giant Dragon Lizard, and Immortal Jellyfish as they climbed steps to reach the museum entrance.

"It's awfully dark for this time of day," she said.

"That's winter in New York," said Jack. "A maze of narrow streets between skyscrapers. Some places get less than an hour of sunlight per day."

Once inside, they explored displays of Dinosaurs, Pacific Peoples, and Mummies, got lost more than once (even with a map) and finally found their way to the Limits exhibit.

A narrator's voice could be heard as they took their seats:

> "*Some insects live only a few hours,*
> *while a tortoise might last for centuries.*
> *Humans rarely make it past 100 but*
> *there are some trees older than the*
> *Great Pyramid. A few creatures even*
> *gain years through suspended*
> *animation, a sort of reversible death.*
> *How is it that lifespans can vary so*
> *wildly? Is death truly inevitable?*"

Suddenly, all light and sound ceased as the auditorium went dark. A few gasps were followed by bits of nervous laughter. After about two minutes of uneasy silence, cell phones began to ring.

Una's call came from Madelyn.

"My *god*! It's everywhere! What's happening?"

"The power?" she replied, "Y-You...too? Impossible. When?"

"Just now. It's creepy. No lights for miles. Is it *true*?"

"What? I don't get your--"

"They're saying it's an *attack*."

"*They*? C'mon...get a grip! If this was terror-related, I'd *know* about it. So far, not a word. You're at the CATBRIER?"

"Uh-huh. Pisces always have the strangest bad luck. Today my 'scope said, '*Beware of secrets, they can lead to disaster.'* Could this have anything to do with your *artifact* from Arizona?"

Una cringed. "What? No! Definitely--"

Then her phone died.

"No power, no signal," said Jack.

"You *know* how rumors spread. Is it possible?"

They shuffled along, aided by emergency lights, toward the nearest exit. No one really believed it was true. The entire city? All at once?

He sighed. "*If* someone knew enough about our system *and* succeeded in hacking it, they *could* engineer a series of seemingly unrelated events, to turn lights out. But it's never been done."

Stepping outside, they faced an impossible sight: the entire New York City skyline, gone *dark*. Except for the headlights of street cars, everything else--every window and doorway, every electronic billboard, every street lamp and traffic light--appeared lifeless and cold.

Instinctively, Jack hailed a Qwik-Ride.

"Parking decks'll be jammed," he said. "I don't want to get trapped right now."

She shook her head. "Suppose it's true. What's the *plan*?"

His eyes rolled. "For a city with eight million? Well, I did some checking the moment I got here. In a few secret locations, they've stored food and water-- but not enough for everyone. Most people *think* there's a contingency plan, but no one can actually point to it.

"I've searched the archives. Beyond a few guidelines for weathering the first 72 hours, the people of New York are on their own. Winter, with no heat, can take its toll. Filled with hungry, freezing people, each passing day only increases the potential for violence. *There is no plan*!"

Their Qwik-Ride appeared.

"Mr. Hou!" said Una, "Long time no see! Can you get us to *New Heights*?"

The Chinese cabbie grinned. "Hello, my friend. You are in luck. I know a few tricks from the old days, in Manila. Hope you're up for it!"

They zoomed away from the curb.

Without stoplights, most intersections reverted to four-ways, while major freeways, overwhelmed mid-day with commuters abruptly forsaking the workplace to rejoin their families, slowed to a crawl.

"In the Philippines, driving's more dangerous," Hou said. "We change lanes, three at a time with no signal, slow down but never stop at red lights, and ignore speed limits. It makes the day go faster!"

Jack looked like he was going to be sick.

***

The Command Post never lost power. Its massive communications array maintained links to every power plant and military base in the region.

"Okay," said Ashcroft, facing the Big Board, "What do we know so far?"

"It's not good, sir," the com officer replied. "A 3,500 megawatt power surge affected the transmission grid, approximately 29 minutes ago. *First Wave* outages have been reported in the Canadian province of Ontario, Ohio, New York, Michigan and New Jersey. Early estimates say 30 million without power, but that could go much higher. All trains running into and out of New York City are shut down. Airports, banks and businesses are closed. Police and Fire departments are scrambling. Broadcasters have resorted to emergency radio. The mayor has announced a city-wide curfew after dark."

"What about cause?" he asked.

"Unknown, sir...except, we've ruled out EMP. Cars are still running. Massive gridlock. All streets, highways, bridges and tunnels appear to be jammed."

"Source?"

"The blackout originated from two Indian Point nuclear reactors on the Hudson River near Peekskill, spreading to Nine Mile Point, the Ginna plant near Rochester, and the Fitzpatrick reactor near Oswego-- all shut down."

"That *shouldn't* be possible."

As satellite images showed the blackout in real time, his mind grappled with the meaning of it all. He'd often wondered how long it took for those in charge to realize that the events of 9-1-1, two decades ago, were not random accidents, but well-planned attacks

Manhattan appeared, including Wall Street and United Nations headquarters --and suddenly, he felt a lump in his throat. Motorists stuck in traffic jams were the *lucky* ones. No doubt, at this very moment, there were many more; fighting for access to stairwells, stranded in subway cars or trapped in elevators.

And though it went against his military instincts, General Ashcroft found his heart *aching*--not for countless Americans struggling to survive in the midst of chaos, because it was his duty to protect them from all threats, foreign or domestic --but for a *single soul*, courageous and true, who changed his worldview forever through the light in her eyes.

How would he *ever* find Una?

"Sorry to interrupt, sir," spoke a uniformed aid. "The Governor wants to declare a state of emergency, but he's requesting an official update regarding the Chinese Ambassador and his wife. Can we comply?"

He nodded, with eyes opened wide. "Not to worry. Still at the Mulberry. We're watching them *very* closely."

***

In the Ambassador's Suite, Mr. Woo removed another silk shirt from its hanger and folded it neatly, before placing it into his leather suitcase. Two other bags, already full, stood against one wall, beside an oak wood dresser.

The hotel phone rang, but neither of them would pick it up.

"What's happened to New York?" he said. "How is it that we're the only ones who still have power?"

"We're not the *only* ones," Nuan replied, smoke drifting in from their balcony. "Generators supply the whole building."

"You *know* what I mean! Everyone is blaming China. But we know that's *impossible*. Beijing would not authorize such an act with us still here. This puts us at risk. The Americans will never let us go!"

She approached him, taking another puff.

"We're not *going* anywhere. We have nothing to fear. I intend to be right *here*...when the lights come on."

The Ambassador shivered. "Please...come in, already. Close the doors. You'll catch cold!"

Nuan's eyes flickered red as she tossed him a copy of *The Weekly World News*. "*Au contraire*, my dear. Haven't you heard? I'm invincible!"

He sighed. It was pointless to protest.

Besides, Mr. Woo did not really *believe* the Americans would hold them accountable. He just wanted to go home.

Finally zipping his bag, he placed it on the floor and wandered over to their hotel refrigerator.

Glancing inside briefly, he turned away.

"Why can't you eat like normal? I'm tired of steak and caviar. Some nice white rice and fresh Wonton would go good about now. Wish we could order some good *Chinese*!"

***

Without power at *Lao Chi*, Hongi had no choice but to send her customers home, locking the main entrance.

"First, we clean," she said. "Then, everyone upstairs!" Waving a flashlight, she came from the kitchen. "Where is Jianyu?"

By the look on her face, Mia knew, but seemed afraid to speak.

"It's all right," said Liling, facing her on one knee. "In troubled times, it is always best to tell the truth."

Mia's eyes welled up with tears.

"He was...in uniform. I *told* him not to go. But he said it was part of his duty, to help. That people were in trouble and they needed more police, to keep law and order. To make everyone...safe."

"It's okay," said Hongi. "Your father is very brave. Let's all make him very proud...by doing likewise, until his return!"

***

Mr. Hou's Qwik-Ride dodged orange cones and pedestrians like an obstacle course, running curbs to avoid traffic jams, before they came to a stop on a six-lane with no wiggle room.

"Here's where we part," said Jack, still shaking as he paid in cash. "Thanks for not...getting us killed!"

"No problem. Happy trails!"

Una recognized a few a landmarks. "We're more than half way," she said. "My hotel's not...far from here."

Jack gazed around, at empty buildings. "What? You're kiddin' me! This whole place looks abandoned."

"You'll just have to *trust* me...*compadre*!"

And he laughed.

"It's weird," he observed, minutes later. "That sound...high pitched, but low volume. I thought it might be a siren, coming from far away. But now, I'm not so sure. Can you hear it?"

Una sighed. She could *feel* it, coming from the Hopi Rattle.

Looking up, heavy clouds made it hard to see the sky. When they cleared, she noticed something else: due to the blackout, things like the Milky Way and orbiting satellites--normally hidden due to the effects of smog--were suddenly visible to the naked eye. There was a bright spot.

"Thank god for the moon," said Jack. "Like an old friend, watching over us. I remember as a kid, taking road trips at night, with my parents. I'd gaze out the windows of our old Chevy station wagon. The moon *followed* us, every time, all the way home."

She also sensed a *presence*, like a corresponding rhythm...*from* the sky...like she did the night of the parade. The light's perfect round silvery surface caught her eye, and she knew instantly--it was NOT the moon.

Suddenly a dark, narrow alley gave her goosebumps. Jack sensed nothing. She wanted to stop, and turn back.

But it was too late. They were surrounded.

"Welcome...to the *jungle*!" said a creepy voice. A gruesome, pale figure stepped forth from the shadows, in black leather, with a chain around his waist, flashing a switchblade.

It *had* to be Ming.

"You tried to fool us," he said, "Removing your *prize* from the Smithsonian. We stayed with your 'envoy' on the train--until she gave us the slip. But now, we *have* you. The Dragon Lady sees all. She placed us *here*...in your path!"

Then, out of nowhere, came an overwhelming voice:

OH--ICHI--CHIO--OH--AY--IO

Hands up to his ears, Ming *collapsed*, with his gang to the ground.

The hooded stranger appeared, revealing his half-human face with dark eyes, no brows, small nose and chin. All this time, he'd been following her, not as a stalker, but a *guardian*.

They won't be out long, she sensed, in her mind. *Go, while you can.*

Jack and Una turned, to abruptly face military Humvee headlights. An officer in Black Ops uniform hopped out to greet them.

"General Ashcroft sends his regards. Come with us, if you want to live!"

She glanced back. The stranger was gone.

***

A revised image came up on the Command Post Big Board. All eyes turned with a renewed sense of horror.

"*Now* what?" the general said, chomping an unlit cigar.

"New reports...of a *Second Wave*. As you can see, with all affected areas marked in red, the blackout now covers a large, triangular area bounded by Lansing Michigan, Ontario, the shore of James Bay, Ottawa, New York and Toledo. That *includes* D.C.!"

"All right. Team coordinators in my office. NOW."

Like trained dogs, people formed a line to the open stairs, huffing two flights on the double, to enter his private glass enclosure. Within two minutes, all stood assembled before him, ready to be briefed.

"First, the particulars," he said. "Any confirmation on source?"

"Early signs indicate the cyber attack originated from a Chinese IP address in Shanghai, but we can't confirm who was behind it. It may have been launched from another country, altogether. It's impossible to know whether such an attack is government sponsored. Officials in Beijing deny all charges, challenging U.S. authorities to provide evidence."

His eyes narrowed. "We can't *do* that--and they know it. Producing evidence would reveal classified sources and methods."

Through the glass, he could see two M.P.'s arriving below, with Jack and Una. His heart leaped for joy, but he dared not let it show.

Thank god she's safe.

His office door opened unexpectedly, as a staff sergeant came bursting in. "Sorry General! Excuse me, sir...but this couldn't be helped. A large network of defense satellites has apparently been compromised. But it's even more serious than that."

Reaching up, he changed settings on the 16-foot wall display. A sequence of red dots appeared, all overlapping, with military insignias:

Fort Drum in Jefferson, NY
Fort Hamilton in Brooklyn, NY
U.S. Military Academy in West Point
Watervilet Arsenal in Watervilet, NY
Picatinny Arsenal in Morris County
Fort Dix in Burlington, NJ

"Okay, so we're looking at *Defense Readiness* for the region. Fine. Give it to me straight. Where do we stand?

"That's just it, sir. We're...*shut down*."

"What do you *mean*, Sergeant? I don't have time for games. Which base *is* it? I can't tell from the display."

"ALL of them, sir."

Ashcroft pressed a button for Emergency Intercom to the entire Command Post. Jack and Una looked up with everyone else to see him standing before the glass. Flashing lights everywhere preceded the sound of his voice:

"LADIES AND GENTLEMEN,
THIS IS AN ACT OF WAR!"

29

NEED-TO-KNOW

In the depths of space, cruising at about 1,038 miles per hour, and exactly 42,164 kilometers from the center of our planet, Department of Defense (DOD) Satellite DS-1769 occupied a sort of "sweet spot" matching the Earth's rotation, known as geosynchronous orbit.

Its geostationary position, directly over the equator, meant that it was always over a single location. It could "see" environmental features like clouds, bodies of water, snow, fire and pollution, and also take high quality photos, which allowed U.S. intelligence analysts to count numbers of troops, tanks, aircraft and missiles--vital to U.S. military operations worldwide.

In Earth orbit since 1995, its "mission" covered most of East Asia, including parts of China, Vietnam, Malaysia and the Philippines.

Within hours of the Blackout, in line with strict military protocols established after 9-1-1, a series of classified codes reached the *Dragon Slayer* from U.S. Cyber Command--and the COUNTDOWN began.

General Ashcroft paced slowly within his glass enclosure like a caged animal, contemplating the "failsafe" point of no return, 24 hours away. Beyond it, orders for a retaliatory strike could NOT be rescinded.

He never *wanted* this to happen.

Part of his "peace of mind" regarding the threat of WW-3 had always come from the fact that decisions to *go* to war came from higher ranks. He would not *need* to fret about whether his superiors were right or wrong. That was above his pay grade. But now, with communications down and no way to reach the Pentagon or D.C., survival meant paying the price.

***

The official communique came delivered by special envoy directly to the Ambassador's Suite, after clearance from security personnel. Mr. Woo found his hands trembling as he opened the sealed carrier, and eyed its red letterhead, from the Ministry of Foreign Affairs of the People's Republic of China:

> Attention Ambassador Woo:
> The Chinese government finds
> this situation extremely
> regrettable. High-level
> economic talks with all parties

in New York are hereby
suspended. Your diplomatic
mission is now cancelled and
you have been recalled. All
arrangements have been made
for departure. You must leave
the United States at once.

He knew that the meaning of this message went far beyond words. Returning to Beijing under these circumstances, in disgrace, would mark the end of his 10-year career as China's leading diplomat to the U.S..

"I won't go," said Nuan.

"What? Of *course* you will. We have no--"

"Choice? But we *do*, my husband. And *I* choose not to be humiliated! We shall turn this around, and when it is done, we'll return...*victorious*."

He sighed. "How can you be so sure?"

"Because I know what men fear most, what keeps them awake at night, and I've seen the future of mankind. One day, the world as we know it shall be transformed. All this strife between nations and peoples will fade away. And when that day comes, *we* shall rule over them."

"China? Over the world? Is *that* what you mean?"

Nuan grinned the way only a woman can, with the light of eternal mystery in her eyes, the mystery that stirs men's souls, fills them with desire and makes them desperate to win a woman's favor.

"Not...exactly," she replied.

***

Una raced up the open metal staircase, before Jack--or anyone else--could stop her. With all the commotion created by the general's announcement, the entire Command Post went into 'crisis' mode.

She fought her way through an avalanche of team coordinators streaming from his glass enclosure, and reached his door just as it was about to close.

"General! Plleeeaase! I have vital information!!!"

Not until that very moment, as they came face-to-face through the glass did he realize it was her voice.

"Una!" he said, as they finally embraced. "My god. What a relief! To hold you, at last. I thought--"

And her lips met his in a passionate *kiss*--each of them drinking up the other as if nothing else could ever satisfy their thirst for life and love and purpose, as if they'd been waiting a lifetime to find this one-and-only answer to all the questions that ever really mattered.

Then a red flashing light caught his eye, and he stepped away.

"S-s-sorry!" he said, "I didn't mean to...well, you know!"

"Yes...of course, absolutely...me, too," she said, with a sigh.

"So, you were...saying?"

"I had a run-in...with Ming."

"What!!! Are you all right? Why wasn't I--"

"Relax! There was no time. Your men came."

"And? What happened? Is he...*dead*?"

"No, no. Nothing *like* that."

She could hardly blame him. Death was on everyone's mind. All she could picture was Kuwanyauma's "many columns of smoke and fire" from their meeting in Hopiland. One key question came to mind:

Could this be the start of WW III
by one of those peoples who
"first revealed the light of wisdom"?

"You're making a mistake," she said, with the door closed.

Ashcroft drew a deep breath. "What do you mean?"

"It *sounds* incredible I know, but...I think we've been...*misled*."

The general folded his arms, slowly circling her, eyes fixed on every aspect from head to toe, searching for clues. Ordinarily, he was quite adept at reading body language. It came from years of sizing up opponents on the battlefield.

He cautiously grinned, "You'll have to do better than that."

"All right, but first, what have you learned about the Blackout? About its *source*, I mean. Did you find a specific cause?"

He hesitated. "That information is considered classified. We're talking U.S. Defenses. Sharing it's based strictly on a *need-to-know*."

"Bullshit!" she replied.

His eyes narrowed. "Cyber-attack. Surprised? Don't be. For years, Chinese hackers have been very active, targeting U.S. government and industry. They've been conducting a massive assault on our economy. The entire Northeast Corridor from Washington to Boston has been hit hard--with Chinese attempts to steal corporate and military secrets. It was only a matter of time."

"Okay, logically one might be persuaded that--"

"*Might* be? I suppose you know better!"

"Just listen! In the Blackout, Jack and I were trying to cross town, to reach the CATBRIER. Traffic jams forced us to travel on foot. We entered a dark alley--and there was Ming, with his goons, waiting."

"So? Bad luck."

"No--it was more than that. He said, 'Welcome to the jungle.' *Then* he said, 'You tried to fool us...But now, we *have* you. The Dragon Lady sees all. She placed us *here*...in your path!'"

He nodded. "Same thing happened to me...face-to-face. She's *dangerous*. Psychic. I get that. She knows all about us and our past. She's after something, here in New York. A prize, supposedly from that cave in Arizona. Do you--?"

"Yes! Yes, that's what I'm trying to tell you! The whole time, tracking down this cult, SAN-TOU-LONG. The *Dragon Lady*. I think she's their leader!"

"And?"

"Somehow, they're behind this--"

"No," he said, "That's impossible. No cult could ever harness the resources to pull this whole thing off. A power outage is one thing--but we've lost contact with D.C. and the Pentagon, and every base in the region."

"What if they had help?"

"China's military--"

"No! *Another* kind. One we can't spy on. Colin, I *know* what she's after!"

She reached inside her vest coat, and retrieved the Hopi Rattle, still wrapped to prevent it from touching her skin.

"What *is* it?" he asked.

"The prize. An ancient Hopi artifact...from the cave. A source of great power. Somehow it explains what happened to me, that night at the parade. I was afraid to tell you before, afraid you might--"

"Not here," he said, pushing her hand back. "Not now. Too many ears and eyes." For a moment, he glanced up, and she knew he was thinking of the stars, and otherworldly visitors.

"But I--"

"Let's just say I *believe* you. Keep it for now. Your friends, the Sky People. Something tells me...they mean us no harm."

And immediately she felt haunted by an image of her pale *guardian*, in the alley, peering into her with huge, dark eyes. Skin tingled on her forearm, where he touched her, once Ming had collapsed to the ground. She noticed tiny hairs, standing straight up, from static electricity. And she could *hear* him, speaking to her mind:

> *MAKE CONTACT.*
> *HEAR THE ANCIENT VOICES.*

***

Acting on an "anonymous tip", Jianyu left his assigned patrol route to enter the New Heights Industrial Park, on his Harley Softail Deluxe. Though it seemed lifeless at first, he found signs of recent activity: tire tracks that slowed to a stop near one particular street corner, again and again.

He *thought* it might be a joke, until he spotted footprints. Apparently from a single female, they circled a city block. He traced them, until he spied a lone figure, in fashion boots and fur coat, with a cigarette in her hand.

Three familiar hoods appeared, like winter wolves, moving in for the kill. It was Ming with two members of his gang.

The woman apparently flipped them off.

Bad move, Jianyu thought.

Then Ming pulled out a switchblade.

Moving closer, he suddenly realized it was *Maddie*, the woman from Brooklyn, now working with NYPD.

Why would she be out here?

Before he could intervene, they nabbed her, climbing into the Jag.

They'll use Maddie to get to Una, he thought. *I can't let her out of my sight. I can't let them get away with this. Ming's got to answer to the law!*

Jianyu revved up his Harley. There was no one to call for back-up.

He had no choice...but to follow.

***

Suddenly there was a commotion outside the enclosure as a wild moving figure appeared. MP's tried to pull him away, but he fought them, pressing his face to the glass. Una could not believe her eyes.

It was Jack.

"What's he *doing*?" said Ashcroft.

"He knows more about this than I do," she said, "Please, I know it's a lot to ask, but I trust him and he's only trying to help. Just hear him out!"

Ashcroft opened the door.

"Apologies, sir," an officer said. "We won't let this happen again. Do you want us to lock him up?"

"Not...just yet. Release him...to me, for now."

Jack shook them off, smiling as he stepped inside.

The general crossed his arms. "You've got three minutes, before I toss you in the brig."

"Okay. You already know the Blackout began with two reactors at Indian Point. But you may *not* know that just before it hit, a woman in Peekskill reported a red-lit triangular object hovering near the facility, firing a beam of light, then shooting away. Five other witnesses reported the same thing, at Nine Mile and Fitzpatrick."

"Cell service is down. How'd you get this information?"

"Directly from MUFON," he said, waving his satellite phone.

"What? Hey! That's military issue. How'd you get that?"

Jack ignored him. "With nuclear power offline, fluctuations in the grid forced remaining plants automatically into 'safe mode' to prevent overloads-- except it didn't work. Am I *right?*"

Ashcroft reluctantly nodded. By the look on his face, wheels were starting to turn. "Same thing happened at Pease Strategic Air Command, a year ago. It was officially closed in '91, but not underground. Nuclear weapons test. Missiles went down, one after the other, into a 'no-go' position. They were unlaunchable. UFO reports were dismissed. Well, *something* shut them down!"

Una smiled, as their eyes met.

***

Minutes later, a new set of computer codes reached Satellite DS-1769, to stop the COUNTDOWN. Unlike its previous response to instructions from Cyber Command, for some reason, these codes were *not* accepted.

The satellite had turned *off* its communication link, going "silent".

30

FLOODGATE

A sleek black limousine arrived at the Mulberry Hotel early, just before 6 AM. Its driver, impeccably dressed, entered the quiet lobby. Powered by state-of-the-art generators, a few solemn-looking guests enjoyed hot coffee and pastries from the continental breakfast. TV screens remained blank. Ordinarily, the lobby would be buzzing with activity.

Knocking politely on the door to the Ambassador's Suite, he stood in the hall with hands folded, waiting for a response.

At first, there was none.

Ordinarily, a member of the Ambassador's entourage would appear, making apologies for the delay. Diplomats rarely seemed to be on time, expecting flexibility from others, as if schedules did not apply to them.

He could hear muffled voices, from behind the door.

"What shall I say?" inquired Mr. Woo.

"Tell him to come back later," Nuan replied, "We're...not ready."

There was a pause.

"This is *no* ordinary flight. They've reopened the terminal just for us. Don't you understand?"

On the balcony, she stood with arms wrapped around her shoulders. "The clouds are getting dark, like a storm's coming."

"Why does it matter?"

"I know all the signs. You laughed when I first told you that I am the 'dragon-king's daughter'. In 2012, a *super storm* devastated New York. Did you know that? The ocean surged, destroying thousands of homes and businesses along the coast."

"So?"

"These Americans never learn. It's been nearly a decade since civil engineers proposed storm surge barriers--four different designs--to protect the city, but nothing has been done. Each focused mainly on lower Manhattan--incidentally, the location of Chinatown. They even proposed building a 'great wall' around New York harbor, but the cost was considered too great. I cannot help but wonder how it compares to the cost of *not* building one."

***

General Ashcroft eyed the COUNTDOWN clock in his office. The satellite's failure to respond did not seem to affect it in any way. In eighteen hours and three minutes, the *Dragon Slayer* would execute its previous set of commands, launching a retaliatory strike on Beijing--and there was no way for him to stop it.

Computers could be *damned unreliable.*

It was impossible to detonate, or launch a space-bound intercept. No way to warn millions in East Asia of the devastation coming towards them.

Except, of course, for the "red phone".

He considered using it to contact the Chinese leadership, in an attempt to prevent a full scale attack from the other side. But since this had never happened, there was no way of knowing how the other side might respond.

Ashcroft poured himself a drink. Old Kentucky Whiskey. Sometimes it was the only thing strong enough to ease his pain.

Seventeen hours and fifty-nine minutes.

The clock was still counting.

***

Jianyu held back, trying to maintain a discreet distance on his Harley from the black Jaguar winding its way north, beyond city limits. Surprisingly, it did not take long to leave all familiar landmarks behind.

Where are they going? he thought.

In the back of his mind, he tried to prepare himself for what might happen. Police Auxiliary training included self-defense, traffic control, security and patrol techniques--but not much about firearms or detective work.

He'd never stand a chance taking them head on, outnumbered three-to-one. If only he could split them up.

As a youth, his grandfather once taught him the "way of the short staff" using a 40" hickory combat cane. And although he had not practiced in years, he kept one at home. Out here, he'd have to improvise.

Soon they approached a blighted industrial waste site, once the location of an open-pit iron mine. Here the Jag veered off road, through a frozen, wooded marsh and nearly disappeared.

Jianyu slowed, concealing his bike behind trees to proceed on foot.

He could not believe his eyes.

Around a huge pile of crushed rock, hidden from view, lay a sophisticated camp, with pole-buildings, power generators and mobile satellite communications.

The frozen terrain reminded him of tales from his grandfather. According to Buddhist tradition, the sea-dragon was "chief of three hundred and sixty scary reptiles". Its power of transformation enabled it to become *invisible*, but when it rose to the surface, one could still see the ocean surge, with waterspouts and raging typhoons. When it flew, winds howled, sweeping away everything in its path, roaring like a hurricane.

If only he could call upon one now, to help rescue Madelyn.

***

Like it or not, Una was trapped for the time being, underground, in the Cyber Command Post. But she needed privacy to unwrap the Hopi Rattle, to keep it hidden from others. After some careful thought, she could only come up with a single place to go: the Women's Bathroom.

Selecting the farthest stall from the door--labeled "Out of Order" just in case--she stood with her back against one wall, eyes closed--to block any sudden burst of light. Though its vibrations had ceased, she thought they might start again any moment.

As its glistening metal surface came in contact with room air, kinetic energy exploded all around her. Water flowed from every faucet, all at once. Toilets all began to flush. The combined rush of sound reminded her of Niagara Falls. She could barely hear her own thoughts.

Then, she touched it with bare skin.

Blinding, white light gave way to completely different surroundings, as if she were in a familiar dream, from the night of the parade. Somewhere, far away, she could hear the music of gongs, lutes and mandolins, and cardboard "poppers" releasing confetti.

Slowly, her eyes came into focus, and there seated before her, on a bench between two attendants, was the *spirit woman*: Kuwanyauma, with a smile of greeting on her face. She spoke without moving her lips:

"You are in New York
to keep our PROMISE to the Creator.

World War III is coming,
to TEST all who walk upon the Earth.
Ambitious minds must decrease,
while people of good hearts must increase.

The NEW ERA is at hand, when
WOMEN must bring wisdom and healing,
to bring Earth back into BALANCE.

Star Warriors must again FIGHT
Children of the Serpent,
As a Dragon awakens, Alerting an Armada
to INVADE from Beyond.

This POWER to Destroy men hold
in their hands is real, But
their freedom to use it? An ILLUSION.

Ask yourself : WHY has
No Atomic Bomb been used since WW II?
Why has NO ONE landed on the Moon
since the Eagle?

The ANSWER is one and the same:

IT IS NOT ALLOWED."

***

In the Ambassador's Suite, a small alarm-clock-radio, which had delivered nothing but static overnight, began to whisper with human voices as power came back slowly, in isolated parts of the city.

A local reporter for WNYC, New York Public Radio, stationed at JFK International Airport, gave the following Emergency Weather update:

> "To *anyone* who can hear the sound of my voice: A sudden, unexpected winter *storm surge* has caused flight cancellations and delays.
>
> As of this morning, all Friday departures from JFK are *cancelled*. No aircraft will remain overnight. Normal operations are not expected to resume until Sunday. Government-issued storm and flood warnings are in effect for the East Coast and parts of New York.
>
> Please, this storm is *not* to be taken lightly. It has already claimed one life. A doorman slipped and crashed through a glass window while shoveling snow on New York City's Upper East Side, cutting him severely, according to police.

Get to a place where you and your
family feel safe, and stay put. At this
point, no one knows exactly how
long *any* of this will last."

Nuan's eyes lit up with satisfaction. Somehow it seemed as if her predictions *always* came true.

Mr. Woo shook his head. This had happened before, too many times to count. By now, he had learned to accept the fact that strange happenstance-- working in their favor--would often strike within minutes, hours or days of when they needed it most.

PART FIVE

BUT LIFE ITSELF

*"Self-sacrifice can point the way
out of prevailing darkness."*

--Dalai Lama

31

MISSION

Jack found Una quietly sipping coffee, watching the sunrise on a digital screen in the staff break room. This simple link to the outside world enabled Command Post personnel to keep their sanity, pretending they were not so far underground.

"Where have you been?" he asked. "I couldn't--"

"It all came back to me," she said.

"What? I don't--"

"You were right. About the UFO. About everything."

He sat across from her. She had a distant look in her eyes.

"Your 'missing time'? But how?"

She opened her vest coat, to show him the Rattle.

His face turned white as a ghost.

"You brought it *here*? My *god*! We're surrounded by feds! The *military- industrial complex*. Ashcroft! He'll try to--"

"He knows," she said.

"He *knows*?"

Jack hopped out of his seat, in a panic, scanning the room for unwanted listeners. They were completely alone. Grasping a fresh cup of coffee with both hands, still shaking, he returned to the table.

"Look, I don't understand. You'll have to--"

"Your friends in upstate New York...the 'Experiencers'. Well, I can finally relate! You even suggested 'regressive hypnosis' to recover my memory. I didn't *have* to, because last night, the Hopi Rattle brought it all back. I saw a *light* in the sky, above the parade. The Kuchinas. They *came* for me. After all this time, it's such a relief!"

Jack's face was still blank. "*And?*"

"We're here for a *reason*. All of us. You, me, Ashcroft. To fight SAN-TOU-LONG."

"*How?*"

"By joining...with others."

***

Neither Jack or Una could have possibly known, but at *that* very moment, Grandfather Lao rushed along a snow-covered path on Broome Street toward the *Zen Temple*, with its gilded lions, shrouded in clouds of incense.

He could not do otherwise.

There, monks of all ages were already gathered in a large circle from at least a dozen temples, monasteries and meditation centers, in the sacred shrine, before a 16-foot golden Buddha, in silent prayer.

They held his spot open.

***

Jianyu faced a real quandary. Ming had already taken Madelyn inside the compound. There appeared to be only one way in or out. It was impossible to know the odds. If he took the plunge and failed, they could both wind up dead.

But he could never forgive himself for not trying.

Among the debris piled up outside were left-over construction materials, including sections of metal pipe. He found one very close to 40" in length. It would be his only weapon.

Apparently Ming did not anticipate being followed. A single lookout, with an M-16 slowly paced the compound perimeter, rubbing his hands for warmth.

Every minute lost *increased* the danger to Maddie. She might be tortured for information on Una's wherabouts--or worse.

Jianyu cringed. It was now or never.

The lookout jumped as a piece of ice, roughly the size of a golf ball, bounced off a heap of crushed rock nearby to knock him on the shoulder.

He looked up, to his right, anticipating more.

Jianyu's staff attack came from the *left*.

Employing a swift series of moves in close quarter combat, he struck using the butt of his weapon, employing elbow, knee and head blows to not only disarm his opponent but disable him in a matter of seconds. Having no use for it, he tossed the M-16 aside.

In lookout's attire, he entered the compound's main entrance moments later, offering a silent prayer to his ancestors.

He could not believe his eyes.

No one paid him attention. They were far too busy.

Followers of all ages and races, from every walk of life, apparently labored here. Huge wall maps detailed the locations of designated "landing sites" just outside New York City. One assembly line created thousands of backpacks filled with "human essentials" for those ready to depart the Earth "at a moment's notice" on ships "from beyond". Another put together "assimilation kits" to welcome and ease the transition to life here for new "Overlords".

Signs everywhere proclaimed "Prepare for the CHANGE" in black around the huge, red SAN-TOU-LONG symbol of a Three-Headed Dragon.

The entire "complex" stretched into the mountain, a maze of passageways like the internal workings of an anthill he had seen once as a child.

Other diagrams displayed NYC as "ground zero" for a massive infiltration of human society, with giant red arrows pointing North, South, East and West across the globe, targeting major population centers to be "absorbed"--including D.C.

Jianyu trembled with fear.

But where was Madelyn? He did not have to look far. A row of transparent "holding cells" lined one wall like some kind of futuristic "zoo" with people and animals combined.

While most workers meandered on foot, a few of higher rank buzzed about in miniature, armored transports resembling high-tech golf carts that seemed to "float" above the ground.

As one of them slowed to a stop nearby, Jianyu reached forth his hand, yanked out its driver and hopped aboard, racing toward Maddie's cell.

The transport easily *crashed* its clear barrier, causing it to "vaporize".

"No time to explain," he said. "Come with me!"

Smiling, she complied without a word.

An alarm sounded as they zoomed toward the entrance.

Ming was right *on* it, zooming up behind them.

Jianyu frowned in dismay. *What'll I do?* he thought.

"Red button," said Maddie. "Trust me."

As he pressed it, they were suddenly *outside*, zipping over frozen terrain.

So was Ming.

Blinded by bright snow at first, Jianyu slowed, enabling Ming to overtake him. Both driverless transports stopped as the two embattled brothers rolled together across the frozen swamp.

As they came apart, Jianyu held forth his improvised "short staff".

Ming laughed. "You are a fool! In a matter of hours, the prophecy will be fulfilled. *We* shall be part of the ruling elite, while you and yours shall become our servants."

But then, he collapsed under the weight of Maddie's *Coach* purse, slamming him upside the head.

"Not according to my *horoscope*!" she cried.

Struggling to get up, Ming pulled out a small explosive device like a hand grenade, but it slipped from his grip, dropping a few feet away. His efforts to reach it proved useless, with one foot trapped in broken ice.

As Jianyu and Madelyn boarded his Harley, they heard a horrific explosion from the swamp.

Neither could bare to look as they rode away.

***

In the Ambassador's Suite, although his wife did not seem at all troubled by recent events or even affected by the winter cold, blowing smoke on their balcony, Mr. Woo found it increasingly difficult to relax as storm surge radio reports seemed to grow worse by the minute:

"The storm tide at Battery Park, at the very tip of Manhattan, now twelve feet according to the National Hurricane Center, and still rising, could top the previous record. This high storm tide has been created by a 9.1 foot storm surge and evening high tide during a full moon, when tides are higher than normal.

This surge, which has already overflowed the city's historic waterfront, apparently developed from a *mystery wave* somewhere off the East coast. Unlike previous Storm Sandy in 2010, which affected the entire eastern seaboard from Florida to Maine, baffled experts are calling this one a 'fluke', which does not conform to any previous Weather Forecast Models—aimed squarely at New York. They've named it: *Mongol* for its fierce, sudden attack, without warning.

The extreme rise in water level has sent Harbor flooding into the streets of the Financial District and other parts of Manhattan. Countless homes are currently at risk, including potential damage to the city's subway systems, from flooding.

The Governor has declared a state of emergency. In addition to cancellation

of all flights into and out of JFK,
LaGuardia and Newark-Liberty
airports, Metro North and Long
Island Rail Roads have
suspended service. The Tappan
Zee Bridge, Brooklyn Battery
Tunnel and Holland Tunnel
have all been closed.

The Mayor has called for
mandatory evacuation of Zone
A, which comprises areas near
coastlines or waterways. Two
hundred National Guard troops
have already been deployed..."

Haunted to this day by his own callous acts as a
Chinese border patrol guard, over the years
Ambassador Woo had tried to convince himself that
meritorious diplomatic service would *somehow* erase
his guilt.

It did not.

As he sat all alone, wringing his hands, a quiet
resolution took shape in his mind. Perhaps better
than anyone, he understood the formidable powers
harnessed by Nuan. Her wrath knew no bounds. And
although he never quite understood their source, their
capacity to do harm was undeniable.

Perhaps it was time to let go of his personal
ambition, surrender the Ambassadorship to someone
younger, less riddled with guilt from past mistakes--or

less troubled by conscience to do whatever *must* be done to ensure China's emerging role of leadership in the world.

In countless speeches, he had often referred to himself as a *humanitarian*. Stopping this surge was the *least* he could do.

Dispensing a tiny bottle of sleep tonic that he carried for just such an emergency into her glass of red wine, he approached his wife now with a gentle smile on the balcony.

"You seem tense, my dear. Perhaps this will help you...*relax*."

32

OF SPACE & TIME

The turnaround time between Madelyn's safe return to the Fifth Precinct and the arrival of NYPD Swat Teams with FBI support could not have been more than three hours. As two black armored vans entered the industrial waste site in upstate New York, one thing became abundantly clear--it was *empty*.

"Impossible!" cried Jianyu rushing inside the main entrance.

He stood alone, scanning the cavernous hideout with his flashlight. There was plenty of discarded equipment, including one lifeless "transport" with its power source removed, a few tattered banners, and long tables--apparently used for backpack "assembly lines"--but no documents, no weapons, and no people.

Detective Stone arrived, chomping an unlit cigar. "*Another dead end!* In spite of its apparent size and sophistication, this 'facility' was never meant to be permanent. We're facing an enemy with the capacity to move quickly. Where the *hell* did they all go?"

An FBI agent wearing a headset rushed over to him. "We don't know their exact location--but suspect they may not be far. Choppers have identified a widespread array of exit routes, across the snow, at least a mile in all directions, but ending abruptly--as if those making them...*vanished* somehow."

"Or got *beamed up*, I suppose!" Stone was not amused. "Your people will have to do better. I can't take *that* back to headquarters!"

Jianyu raced over to inspect the long row of empty "holding cells" along one wall. Their high-tech "transparent barriers" were completely gone, with no signs of a struggle, and no bodies.

"Either they escaped, or were taken in tow," he sighed.

Stone shook his head. He'd tracked plenty of jail breakers from detention centers in Brooklyn, Lincoln and Manhattan. They all seemed to flee north, as if the untamed wilderness represented some kind of "promised land" for crooks. Lacking survival skills, most became weak after a few days without food or water.

"The long arm of the Law will find them," he said. "They can't run forever."

But secretly, something *else* bothered him. Ever since this whole crime spree began with SAN-TOU-LONG, incredible *signs* kept popping up. Signs he could not explain. Stone didn't believe in magic or little green men from Mars. He was a *realist*. Every perp he'd ever arrested was made of flesh and bone.

Crime Scene Investigation was fine. It had become the crux of modern police work. They'd gather bits and pieces for analysis, like always. And sooner or later, clues would point them in the right direction.

Even Ming's bloody remains in the frozen swamp outside would yield *something* of value.

But that wasn't the problem. Difficulty arose when all the clues in the world didn't "add up" enough to "explain" what really happened. One might uncover the "what" without ever getting to the "why".

He didn't like *unsolved* mysteries.

But then, he had a thought. *What if the mystery here's not supernatural at all--but more like an old-fashioned trick?*

Either this cult possessed some 'magical' ability to disappear, or the trails were simply intended to throw police off track.

Impulsively, he ran again outside to one of the black armored vans. Its dashboard intercom was equipped with loudspeakers for riot control. Flipping a switch, he leaned toward the in-dash microphone:

"ATTENTION: MEMBERS
OF SAN-TOU-LONG. I KNOW
THAT SOME OF YOU MAY BE
IN HIDING, BUT CAN STILL
HEAR THE SOUND
OF MY VOICE.

IT GETS MIGHTY COLD

OUT HERE AT NIGHT.
PEOPLE FREEZE TO DEATH.
IS THAT WHAT YOU
REALLY WANT?

I URGE ANY OF YOU
FACING A 'CRISIS OF
CONSCIENCE'. COME OUT
INTO THE OPEN.
SURRENDER FOR THE SAKE
OF YOUR FAMILIES. IT'S
NOT TOO LATE. REJOIN
THE HUMAN RACE!"

After a few moments of silence, Jianyu approached Detective Stone, almost afraid to look him in the eye.

"Excuse me sir, I am sorry to--"

"*Name*?" said Stone.

"Lao...Jianyu. I am member of Police Auxiliary. They were *here*, sir, I swear it. Where do we go from here?"

Head down, striking a match, Stone lit his cigar.

"Beats the *hell* outta me. I'm just an old-fashioned cop. I go with my gut. As far as I'm concerned, the only peaceful out for these *Chinks* is to give themselves up--otherwise, we'll have no choice but to hunt 'em down, one by one!"

Jianyu cringed.

Looking up, Stone seemed to suddenly feel a pang of conscience eyeing the young Chinese officer. "Er...you know what I mean...*no offense*!"

"None taken," he replied.

***

Grandfather Lao quietly entered the temple gathering, taking his place among the other Buddhist monks, to complete the Prayer Circle. With clasped hands and bent heads, in silence together they sought *guidance.*

In their ancient homelands of the East, each of these venerated spiritual masters would be more properly referred to as *Lama,* an honorary title for teachers of the *Dharma* in Tibetan Buddhism.

On his wrinkled face, a smile began to form.

Standing there, flesh-to-flesh, he sensed their combined energy flowing *through* him, growing stronger by the minute. Its healing power invigorated every cell in his body, increasing blood flow, restoring internal balance, making him *feel* younger than he had in years, like "an arrow ready for flight".

It was said that Lamas could travel hundreds of miles in seconds, and that they possessed magical powers of telepathy. Through *Qi,* a biological signal carried by electromagnetic waves, they knew enhanced psychic powers like clairvoyance and healing. *Qigong,* a holistic system of coordinated body posture, movement, breathing and meditation, dissolved barriers of relative perception, revealing the "true nature" of existence.

He remembered it now.

How it all originated with ancient societies high in the Himalayas, kept secret from the outside world. How mystics became "one with the Absolute" through an altered state of consciousness, attaining *insight* into ultimate truth that led to human *transformation*.

One example, recalled from his youth: a power known as *Empty Force*; the ability to move another person or object, even from several meters away, without laying a finger on them. Emitted from the palms, it could penetrate not only wooden boards, but also walls, bricks and even iron. Its existence was known continuously through the Chinese people, although there was a mysterious gap in the historical record for several centuries. The Ancients used it for fighting and killing as well as healing.

All at once, they began to pray, and the words came instantly to mind, so that he knew just what to say:

May we
be a Guardian for
those who need protection,
A Guide for
those on the Path

May we
embrace You, the Earth,
our Home, and acknowledge
the harm we've done to your
waters, your lands, your air

*May we
be bringers of Peace
and accept our role as Star
Warriors to defeat
Children of the Serpent*

Until All are Awakened.

A pure light came into the temple from outside, through a small round window far above. It was too high to be a from a street lamp, too low for reflections from city traffic.

It came from a mighty "pearl" in the sky, the same that first appeared over Chinatown the night of the parade.

Mr. Lao did not fear it.

He remembered it as a child, growing up many years ago, standing all alone, on a mountain peak--in the Himalayas.

***

With the Dragon Lady asleep, Mr. Woo poured himself a glass of red wine, listening to the radio news:

> "Surge waters from *Mongol*—
> along with the high tide that
> resulted in historic water levels
> in New York Harbor--have
> started to recede, according to
> the National Weather Service.

As officials cope with cleaning up
and accounting for those missing,
the death toll continues to climb,
reaching a total of 38 so far.

Recovery efforts have now moved
to center stage, moving people,
bringing food, water, gasoline and
power to badly damaged areas.

Subways, railroads and busses are
starting to roll again. Cars are once
again clogging roads, despite long
lines for fuel. JFK Airport has
reopened and flights are resuming.

With communications finally
restored between major cities,
Washington officials from FEMA
are participating in conference calls
with the Mayor's office and the
NYPD. The federal government
will pay 100% of the costs to help
get power and transportation
restored to New York."

He held up the small bottle of sleep tonic, eyeing
its golden liquid. With any luck, he'd have *just enough*
to keep her subdued--until they were on the return
flight to Beijing.

***

General Ashcroft wiped sweat from his brow, eyeing the Big Board from his glass-enclosed office.

Three U.S. Navy ships, the cruiser *USS Lake Erie* and the destroyers *USS Decatur* and *USS Russell* were posted in the Pacific Ocean waiting for an optimal time to launch.

They would get one ten-second window within the next few hours to fire one of their SM-3 missiles, before the armed satellite tumbled to Earth.

He couldn't let that happen.

If DS-1769 fell through the atmosphere with no missile interference, its warheads could survive the fiery descent to reach Earth's surface intact, causing devastation that would be *unthinkable.*

He recalled a dinner party conversation with a member of the Joint Chiefs--not six months before-- who'd had too much to drink.

"I'd like to *poke* the Chinese," he said, "To show them not only that we can shoot down a satellite without creating lots of debris, but we can do it anyplace in the *world*, because we're doing it from the ocean. See how they react to *that*!"

Ashcroft cringed at the thought.

In spite of everything, there was still a chance of *missing* the satellite all together, because it'd be moving so fast. And hitting the bus-sized target was only *half* the battle. To be completely successful, the missile would have to destroy the satellite's fuel tank, which held about 1,000 pounds of toxic hydrazine.

Either way, there would be consequences.

A failed U.S. attempt to destroy the satellite could send the wrong message. China and the rest of the world *might* take it as evidence that our technological lead in space had declined.

The Big Board showed *9 hours, 11 minutes*.

It could mark the end of this whole nightmare-- or the start of World War III.

***

Jianyu joined the rest of his family, dressed in black. There was no time for the traditional overnight vigil. They had decided to skip the wake for Ming, due to the disembodied nature of his remains.

He'd left them no final wishes. He hadn't expected to leave the world so soon. Not like *this*, anyway.

His funeral had elements of East and West. There were floral arrangements of white roses, lilies and carnations. An altar bore Buddha offerings: a cooked hog's head and chicken, three cups of rice liquor, three cups of tea, and three sets of chopsticks. Incense and paper "passports", for travel to the afterlife, were folded in the shape of a fan.

A white-edged burial blanket, draped over his simple, closed wooden casket, displayed a golden center embroidered with lotus blossoms. A cheerful photo of Ming, in his youth, appeared to one side.

Jianyu fought back tears.

What happened to him? Why would he abandon his family, to help bring about the "end of the world"?

Grandfather Lao chanted "*Ah Mi Tuo Fo*", meaning "Infinite of Space and Time". Perhaps in death, his brother would find peace, at last.

In Tibet, the body would have been placed in a fetal position and fed to vultures in a ritual known as "sky burial". Tibetans were encouraged to confront death openly and to feel the impermanence of life.

He sighed. Soon, after leaving the cemetery, they would share a last family meal, in honor of the deceased, at *Lao-Chi*.

Thank god they lived in America.

33

DEFIANCE

Maybe it was her last conversation, over coffee, with Jack. Una couldn't shake the thought of her *mission* here in New York. *Thank god* Madelyn was back, safe in Protective Custody. If only they had time to catch up.

Tension inside the Command Post was so thick she could barely breathe. They were ordered to stay put. But with everyone running around, it felt wrong to sit still. What else could she--

Suddenly, her chest began to *vibrate*.

She reached for the Hopi Rattle.

Images flashed through her mind...a nearby service elevator to the CATBRIER...its security code to access the rooftop...then a heavy-duty steel enforced exit door, marked AUTHORIZED PERSONNEL ONLY.

Moments later, she stood trembling, gripping a handrail, as the elevator shot up a mile, toward the surface.

This is crazy, she thought, *What am I doing?*

Minutes later, rising up through the hotel, she arrived at its heavy-duty door, which opened automatically with an instinctive tap from the Rattle.

A blast of cold air suddenly reminded her of winter's chill. She tugged her Hopi shawl a bit tighter around the neck.

Somewhere below, a police car arrived, lights flashing. Una tried leaning over the rooftop's edge to see, but the driver was already gone.

Through snow swirling down, she searched gray clouds for a patch of open sky. It was still dark, except for twinkles of starlight. Dawn would not arrive for at least another hour.

The satellite, DS-1769, came to mind, up there somewhere in space, with its deadly weapons pointed at Beijing. All those lives at risk. She knew it was too *far*, in orbit half way around the world. If only...

Wiping a tear from her eye, she pulled out the wondrous Hopi Rattle, glowing faintly in her trembling hands. In spite of the cold, it felt warm to the touch, pulsating gently. It almost seemed *alive*.

Why can't you do something? she thought. *Please! Make it STOP!!!*

She pictured *E.T. the Extraterrestrial* with his jury-rigged device, alone in the forest, waiting for wind to kick up the trees, trying to "phone home".

Except for one thing: *he wasn't alone.*

"HEY UUNAAA!" a voice cried from somewhere nearby.

She turned, and could not believe her eyes.

301

There, on an adjacent rooftop.

It was *Rufus!*

"What are you *doing* here?" she asked.

"Wait! Step back!"

Holding rope attached to his waist, he swung around a heavy metal grappling hook and let it fly high, attaching itself to a rooftop antenna tower. Running, he leaped into the air, swinging across the gap, like Indiana Jones, to plop down beside her.

She gasped. "Where'd you learn how to do that?"

"Didn't I ever tell you?" he grinned. "I used to be in *Explorer's Club!*"

***

With the ten-second "launch window" for intercept missiles from U.S. Navy Ships fast approaching, Ashcroft sought estimates of "collateral damage" that might result from destruction of DS-1769.

According to NASA, the number of man-made satellites operating in Earth orbit numbered around 3,000. A high-altitude nuclear explosion of sufficient yield could potentially disable all Low Earth Orbit (LEO) satellites within a matter of weeks that were not specifically shielded or "hardened" to withstand the radiation. "Hot bands" of space with higher peak radiation could persist up to two years, placing all satellites passing through them at risk.

Defense systems dependent on LEO's could be among the first to suffer, followed by telecommunications, weather forecasting, mapping capabilities, and manned spaceflight--not to mention the threat of nuclear retaliation.

"I need to see what's happening up there," he said.

By overriding a strict set of computer protocols designed to protect the privacy of satellite "feeds", his crack team accessed the combined camera strength of perhaps a dozen "eyes in the sky" to generate a three-dimensional image of the *Dragon Slayer's* orbital position.

"What the hell is...*that*?" he said pointing to the only object on screen that did not conform to any known LEO design. Its bright, smooth silver-like swirling surface reminded him of a giant pearl.

"An...'unknown', sir," came a com-tech's nervous reply.

A series of tiny red lights on DS-1769 began to flash, repeating every three seconds. Restraint brackets began to pop one-by-one along its base, emitting streams of argon gas.

"Now what?" said Ashcroft.

His tech swallowed hard. "The missile pre-launch sequence, sir. Apparently, it has begun."

"How much time?"

"Approximately twenty-nine minutes."

"Good god!" he replied.

Suddenly a buzz came into his ear, breaking the general's concentration.

He abruptly turned away from the screen.

"Whoever this is, you'd better have a damned good--"

"*Command Post Security,*" a voice replied, "*Sorry to interrupt, sir, but there's been a breach.*"

"What?!!! Of all the...explain!"

"*Someone has utilized an Emergency Exit to vacate the Post, sir, without authorization.*"

"And? Details, dammit! I don't have time to chat. How many?"

"*We...don't know.*"

His face became flushed. "All right, listen up! I need a head count. This entire facility. You hear me?"

"*Copy that, sir. Right away.*"

Turning back, the general gasped as his computer screen, and a number of lights surrounding it, all went dark.

"*Now* what?"

He received no immediate reply.

"Report!"

"It's the satellite, sir, DS-1769...it's not... responding."

"What? What do you mean?'

"I'm...sorry, sir. We've...lost contact."

***

"What's up?" asked Una.

Rufus grinned. "Exactly! Funny you should say that!"

She wasn't smiling.

"Okay...it's like this: something *weird's* happening over Central Park. Some kind of cloudlike formation. People thought it was just an incoming storm at first, but it's not moving. It's been 'fixed' in the sky, hovering over a single spot, for over an hour."

"What do you *mean*?"

"It's not natural, is all. Sure, they put some weather guy on TV to tell everyone it's a 'fallstreak cloud'."

"What's *that*?"

"According to *him*, a 'rare atmospheric phenomenon' that forms when 'part of the cloud layer forms ice crystals which are large enough to drop as a *fallstreak*'--but nobody's buying it."

Una tried to process it all in her mind.

Somehow, intuitively, through the Rattle, she sensed what was happening in the Command Post, far below. First their wayward satellite began its launch sequence to dump nukes on Beijing...*then* contact was lost...and *now*, Rufus shows up, out of the blue on the rooftop of CATBRIER--a secret government hotel that supposedly doesn't exist?

"Wait a minute," she said. "How'd you *find* me?"

Rufus tried to look away, searching for an answer, as if he didn't know what to say--but Una could read it in his eyes.

"*Jack!*" she blurted out loud.

He nodded. "He's waiting for us...in the car."

Suddenly, the idea of stealing a police car didn't seem so bad, knowing he at least had adult supervision.

"Okay, but lose the gear--we're taking the elevator."

Glancing upward, he instinctively ducked at the sight of a huge metallic object soaring through the sky.

"You guys. *Relax*!" said Una, rolling her eyes. "It's *just* an airplane!"

***

Meanwhile, at JFK, Ambassador Woo buckled Nuan into the passenger seat beside him. It had taken a few extra drops of sleep tonic on her tongue to keep her subdued all the way from their hotel to the airport.

Unfortunately, their departure was delayed by dramatic events taking place in Manhattan, over Central Park.

According to their stewardess, the threat of a new potential storm made Air Traffic Controllers uneasy about giving the go ahead.

Nuan seemed restless, not quite aware, but still talkative.

"Where is my entourage? Where's my--"

"I'm *here*," he replied, taking her hand. "Right beside you, my dear, as always...you've had a rough night, and need to rest. Don't worry. Everything will be fine. I...promise!"

But she squirmed, pulling at her seat belt.

"My mouth is so dry. Water!" she cried. "Get me water!"

Instinctively, Woo jumped up, racing toward the bathroom, with a glass in his hand.

He could sense the commotion behind him, followed by a flash of light.

By the time he returned, she was *gone*.

"What happened?" he said, searching in vain. "Wh-where is she? I don't understand!"

A stewardess tried to console him.

"I'm very sorry, Mr. Ambassador. We can't find her...anywhere."

"The light!" he said, shaking, "What was the light?"

But he knew in his mind she'd been *taken*--by whom or what he dared not say. Nuan's unexplained disappearances, often in the middle of the night, were something he'd learned to live with--even though she never gave an explanation.

Maybe because the truth frightened him.

And he didn't *really* want to know.

***

Their police car arrived at Central Park, lights flashing. Jack hopped out first, with his camera in hand.

And there it was: a massive, dark formation, just hanging in the sky, about 2000 feet overhead, so huge that it was difficult to comprehend its size, blotting out the moon and the stars, casting a shadow that crawled over the park. Within it were strange flashes of colored light. Portions, at the very center, almost appeared to be moving down.

The air smelled brassy, and damp with electricity.

Una climbed out to stand directly beside him.

"It's very intriguing," he said, "Because these same *type* of formations have turned up in Russia and South America, and every time some 'expert' appears to tell people it's a 'rare natural phenomenon'. Somehow, I don't *think* so."

Rufus tipped his head. "What's that *sound*? Hear it?"

They both paused, to listen.

"Like bees," said Una, "Swarming."

"There," said Jack, pointing, "Can you see it? Three distinct points of red light, equidistant from the center."

The entire cloud appeared to be lit up from within.

Then, bursting out of its center appeared a pointed object, in a slow-moving, gravity-defying maneuver, like an upside-down pyramid, to reveal a triangular-shaped UFO.

"My god!" said Rufus. "There it *is*. What we've been trying to understand all this time. *SAN-TOU-LONG...the Three-Headed Dragon!*"

All around them, people oohed and aahed.

Others emerged, suddenly from all sides, wearing backpacks, joining to form a circle below...S-T-L cult members, ready to be 'taken'.

A huge explosion of light arced out around the UFO, separating into countless, flaming red sparks-- swarming down to 'touch' each of them, and one-by-one, they disappeared, in a fiery 'flash'.

Una sensed vibration, as the Hopi Rattle suddenly came to *life*.

***

In the Command Post, General Ashcroft jumped as his satellite link to DS-1769 came back on line. It showed the missiles launched from U.S. Navy Ships approaching, then *missing* their target.

Nevertheless, a sudden burst of white light enveloped the *Dragon Slayer*, obliterating it from his computer screen.

"What *happened?*" he said.

It took a few moments to access other satellite feeds, as com-tech officers tried to determine its status.

"*Report,* dammit! What do you see?"

"It's...gone, sir! No shrapnel, no debris. Just...completely *gone!*"

The general sighed with relief.

***

Before anyone else, Una sensed *another* circle, much wider, on the ground, forming slowly from every corner of Central Park.

Buddhist monks had arrived, with Mr. Lao, in the white robes of *Star Warriors*, heads bowed. Closing in, with hands raised, they combined the power of "Empty Force" to create an invisible shield-like Dome, rising upward and outward to encompass the Park and all its inhabitants, to *defeat* the Dragon.

And, in spite of its best efforts, the UFO was unable to land.

Suddenly, red flaming sparks seemed to turn in mid-air, like angry bees, all swarming together, in one direction.

They were coming for Una.

"Oh no you don't!" said Rufus, leaping out in front of her.

All at once, they shot *into* him, a thousand red sparks, causing him to light up with a burst of flame from head to toe.

Then, he was *gone*.

The Three-Headed-Dragon ascended once more into the massive cloud, as *Children of the Serpent* were repelled. Flashes of colored light within it went out and the cloud began to dissipate.

Finally, darkness gave way to dawn--as daylight returned.

34

SPIN CONTROL

The next morning, Una heard voices of a local TV Newscast coming from the other room as she and Madelyn got dressed to leave for the Precinct Station House. The more she listened, the more she felt her blood beginning to boil:

> "Here's live footage yesterday in Central Park, as firefighters and EMS workers responded to a group of stressed out New Yorkers, all trying to cope with a bizarre event that experts today are calling a case of *mass hysteria*. Here to help us unravel the mystery is Dr. David Floyd, a certified clinical psychologist."

> "That's right, Katie. Mass hysteria can strike anywhere, anytime. When stressed out, the mind can make the body sick. Outbreaks most often affect women more than men, with

fainting and hyper-ventilation the most common symptoms. Once the affected crowd disperses, symptoms tend to disappear. Physical symptoms are experienced as *real*, and when they strike, the victim, swept up by the anxiety of the crowd, may also feel nausea and stomach pains."

"So, what was the 'trigger' in this case?"

"According to the *National Weather Service*, a rarely seen atmospheric disturbance, known as a '*fallstreak cloud*'. When part of the cloud layer forms large ice crystals under just the right set of conditions in extreme cold, they can drop, creating a bizarre shape in the sky, an optical illusion, that resembles--"

"A *UFO*?"

"Yes, that's right."

"Here to help us gain some perspective is our historical correspondent from the *New York Public Library*, Tanya Bowman."

"Thanks, Katie. Historically, people's mistrust of the government, combined with cold war fears of nuclear attack have

fueled previous waves of hysteria.
A recent string of gang related
threats in New York's Chinatown,
for example, have ignited fears
that China may be to blame.
No wonder.

"Well, In the early 1950s, when
people in the state of Washington
were nervous about nuclear
testing, many believed that cosmic
rays or shifts in the Earth's
magnetic field were causing
windshield pits or dings in their
cars. Some even blamed it on '
super-natural gremlins'. While this
is actually an example of *collective
delusion*, it shows how a worried
group can over-interpret physical
phenomena. *Doctor*?"

"Yes, Tanya, you've hit the nail on
the head. Whenever we face
uncertainty, our minds crave
explanations. If we have no way
to account for symptoms, we feel
out of control and our fear
escalates. The result can be
psychosomatic: people hyperventilate,
thus exhaling too much carbon
dioxide, causing muscles to spasm,
which can explain the numbness,
tingling and muscle twitching that
some victims experience."

"Turn it OFF!" said Una, trembling, with tears. "I can't believe it. Anyone who was there can tell you it was no *delusion*. I didn't *imagine* what happened to Rufus!"

"Of c-course not," said Madelyn, rushing to her side.

The two women embraced in silence.

"Y-you must be devastated. He was such a bright kid!"

"He still is."

"*What?* What do you *mean?* I thought he was--"

"Oh, he's *not* dead."

"But how do you--"

"It's...hard to explain. I just...*feel* it."

By the time they boarded a *Qwik-Ride*, Madelyn had picked up two papers from the hotel lobby.

"Listen to *this*," she said, reading from *The New York Times*:

> When asked for official comment,
> a spokesman for the Mayor's Office
> issued this public statement :
> "Recovery from the recent storm
> surge and power outages is still
> underway. By and large, New
> Yorkers are resilient and level-
> headed. At this point, we're
> thankful to all those who
> responded quickly, reaching out

to the people of this great city,
and we're happy to put another
unfortunate event behind us."

"What a bunch of *B.S.!!!*" she laughed. "Didn't you say Jack was there? I was hoping for some front page news!"

"So was I," sighed Una.

"I believe you totally. Hey check this out," she said, holding up a copy of *The Weekly World News*.

Una could not believe her eyes.

There it *was*, plain as day, albeit in black and white: a crystal clear photograph of the giant UFO they all witnessed in Central Park. According to its lead story, the craft first appeared around 1:11 PM.

Just like the "glitches" from New York to D.C.-- "1", the number of *creation*.

Madelyn shrugged. "Of course, some asshole from the NYPD has already gone on record, calling it a fake."

Their eyes met: *Detective Stone*.

***

Una's visit to the Fifth Precinct was short and sweet.

Exiting their Qwik-Ride, she left Madelyn struggling to catch up as she marched through its main entrance, across the station lobby, oblivious to its ordinary chaos, ascended its beautifully-carved oaken staircase to the second floor, opened the unlocked door to its DETECTIVES OFFICE, and approached Stone, standing with a newly-poured cup of hot coffee in rolled up sleeves, wearing his faded blue tie.

Winding up with all of her might, making a fist, she eyed him directly, and socked him right in the nose.

He stumbled back and collapsed on the floor.

"*That* was for Rufus!" she said.

Before he could get up, she was gone.

***

Her phone rang as she stepped again outside, for a breath of fresh air.

It was Jack.

"It's about time!" she said. "Where the hell are you? What's happening? They're trying to pass this all off as some kind of *delusion*. How can they *do* that? What about all of us who were there? Jack! *Talk* to me!"

"Put down your phone. Look straight ahead."

There he was, in front of the Station, waving to her from his blue Corvette.

She frowned. "Why didn't you--"

"You never gave me a chance!" he replied.

"I saw the *Times*," she said, sliding in the booth across from him at *JAVA-Culture*. "Where's your story?"

"I wrote one. But they won't print it. *Go figure*! I did manage to get *this* off the wire, before they let me go."

He held up an *Official Press Release* from NASA:

SATELLITE LOST

According to NASA tracking data Acquired within the past 24 hours, a U.S. weather satellite, DS-1769, has been lost. Agency records show it was the 13th to be launched as part of a Defense Meteorological Satellite Program which the U.S. military developed in the 1990s to help plan reconnaissance and surveillance missions. U.S. Cyber Command confirms that the "catastrophic event" came after a "sudden spike in temperature" was detected, followed by "an unrecoverable loss of altitude control". While operators were deciding how to "render the object safe" they detected that the satellite had been destroyed. There is speculation that the power system failed, causing an explosion. Due to the age of DS-1769, it was no longer a critical part of the network. The government expects that its loss will cause only a "slight reduction" in real-time U.S. Defense data.

"But Jack," she said, grasping his arm. "They killed your story. How will people ever know the *truth* about what happened?"

He grinned. "By word of mouth. The same way it's always been. They can keep it out of print, but they can't keep it out of our hearts and minds. So, it looks like I'm off to Winslow."

Una sighed.

"Just tell me you won't give up," she said.

"Never! Like my father before me. He told me a few stories I'll never forget. Did I ever tell you about *Walter Cronkite*?"

She shook her head.

"My father met him in the early 70's. CBS was making a special documentary about UFOs. Since my father had been in the Air Force and was considered a prominent newspaper man, he was asked to contribute, and had lunch with Walter one day while working on the project.

"After a few minutes of small talk, Mr. Cronkite looked him straight in the eye and said, 'Let me tell you my UFO story.'

"In the 1950's, he was part of a pool of News Reporters brought out to a small South Pacific island to watch the test of a new Air Force missile. After a brief inspection, reporters were led to an area that was considered a safe distance from the launch site.

"Reporters had been warned that photography of the missile test and any audio transmissions or recordings by the press were forbidden. Just as the test was ready to proceed, with everyone writing as fast as they could, Air Force Security personnel walked around the perimeter of the site with guard dogs. News reporters watched as the missile was fired up, about to be released.

"Then, suddenly, a large disc-type *UFO* appeared.

"Cronkite guessed it to be about 50 feet in diameter, a dull gray color with no visible means of propulsion. Because the missile was so loud, he couldn't tell if the disc made any actual sound.

"As Air Force guards ran toward the UFO with their dogs, the disc hovered about 30 feet off the ground, and sent out a blue beam of light which struck the missile, a guard and a dog, all at once. The missile was frozen in mid-air. This all happened with a space of five minutes.

"Suddenly, the missile *exploded*, and the disc vanished. The guard and his dog were quickly taken away for medical testing. At the same time, guards ushered the reporters into a concrete observation bunker. After thirty minutes, they were brought out into the air again and addressed by an Air Force Colonel.

"He told them 'it was all part of a test', saying that the event was 'staged' to test media reaction to UFOs, stressing that when people saw Flying Saucers, they were actually seeing secret Air Force technology.

Well, Walter didn't believe that. He was certain that this 'new technology' was *not* of Earthly origin.

"After the event, newsmen were told that they could not report on it. *Needless to say, this story was NOT covered or even mentioned in the UFO Special.*

"My father learned an important lesson that day from Walter Cronkite, 'the most trusted man in America', about the art of conversation: knowing when to talk and when to *listen*!"

35

FAR FROM OVER

As they left the aromas of fresh-brewed coffee behind at *JAVA-Culture*, Jack and Una stood together outside, amid snowflakes drifting downward.

With all the commotion in Central Park, there had been no time to think. He did not blame her for "breaking their vow" regarding the Hopi Rattle. Rufus had sacrificed himself to keep it from SAN-TOU-LONG. They couldn't keep it a secret forever. At least Ashcroft was a survivor of Flight 564. This gave them all a *common bond*.

But he still felt reluctant to name it out loud.

"I'd keep the *you-know-what* close, if I were you. The threat of war never goes away. Besides, the Dragon may return."

She nodded.

"Well, I've got a flight to catch. Maybe the *Arizona Journal* will cut me some slack, print my story under 'Strange News from the Big Apple'."

"Send me a copy," she said.

"I will. What about you?"

She held up a text message from Madelyn on her phone. "I have a lunch date."

Jack hailed her a cab. As it pulled up to the curb they embraced. Una wiped a tear from her eye.

"Until next time, *Compadre*."

"Adios," he replied.

***

As she climbed out a few minutes later, near *Lao-Chi*, Una could not shake the feeling that she was being watched. Sub-consciously, she sensed the subtle movements of an observer, somewhere on the street, nearby.

This ability to *feel* another's eye contact seemed like a form of ESP, because she couldn't point him out, exactly...she just *knew* he was there.

But how could *he* know? How could he anticipate her arrival just *now*?

Or had he been waiting *all day*?

The weird part about it: Una felt no fear.

Not like with Ming. From the moment she'd first spotted him in chains at the New Year's parade, fear of ambush had plagued her--right up to the moment she and Jack almost died in that alley following the blackout.

But what she felt now was more akin to *curiosity*.

Because even though she did not know his name, she sensed, in his eyes, an abiding sense of good will.

This was not the hungry gaze of a predator.

More like the watchful eye of a doting parent or guardian angel...or secret, invisible friend, watching from afar.

It was the half-human stranger who *saved* them-- then abruptly disappeared in the glare of Humvee headlights.

And without meaning to, in the back of her mind, she'd given him a name, to describe what he meant to her...watching over her at all times, yet eerily mysterious and otherworldly, up until the moment Una first glimpsed his pale face with dark eyes but no brows in that alley and did not know what to make of it.

He was like *Casper*, the friendly ghost.

She must find a way for them to meet again.

As she opened the red entrance to *Lao-Chi*, she knew he would not follow her inside. Delightful aromas of chicken dumplings, hand-pulled noodle soup and rice-flour donuts made her mouth water.

No sense in telling Maddie, just yet.

***

Jianyu greeted both women at the small table they shared, offering a platter of Tibetan Momo appetizers to whet their appetites. Flour dough rolls, filled with a mixture of mashed potatoes, onions, mushrooms, olive oil, cheese, paprika and tomatoes, Una could not resist.

"We haven't seen you at the Precinct," said Maddie.

He nodded. "My role with the Police Auxiliary is complete. I now divide my time between *Lao-Chi* and the Temple. Grandfather is teaching me to read *The Divine Incantations*."

Hongi appeared, to pat him on the back.

And it occurred to Una that the prophecies of Hopiland and Tibet might be coming closing together. Kuwanyauma once told her how the four races with four sacred stone tablets, Red, Yellow, Black and White, were given Guardianship over the Earth, Wind, Water, and Fire. She said,

> "...peace will not come until
> the circle of humanity is complete,
> until all four races sit together
> and share their teachings."

During her stay in Chinatown, she had learned so much more than she ever expected from this ancient people. Perhaps Hongi was right in her greeting the day they first met:

> "We are like sisters, long lost,
> from far sides of the globe."

And she also wondered if recent events involving the Hopi Rattle, the Three-Headed-Dragon, and Star Warriors might be taken as a sign that the completion of humanity's "Circle" was close at hand.

Pondering the wrap-around mural of *Lhasa*, the capital of Tibet, with its palaces, temple, and monasteries, she noticed that every creature within it, including the Imperial eagle, giant panda, snow-leopard and golden monkey, had its head turned in one direction.

Tilting her head likewise, she found a familiar face, approaching.

"Greetings!" said Mr. Lao.

Rising from her seat, Una bowed to him, respectfully.

He motioned for her to come forward.

"I was hoping to see you," she whispered. "I'm a little confused about this whole 'prophecy' thing. The *dragon* came, but there were no *bombs*, and the world was not destroyed. What does it mean?"

He grinned.

"Not all prophecies are fulfilled. They serve as 'warning signs', pointing the way to disaster--*unless* we return to the Sacred Path. It is our task to follow...to the ends of the Earth."

***

Departing *Lao-Chi*, Madelyn hailed a Qwik-Ride. "Tomorrow, it's back to D.C.," she said, "I almost wish we could stay."

"That gives me an idea," said Una, eyes darting all around. 'Casper' was still somewhere nearby. She could *feel* it.

"What? You're not--"

"Sure, sure...I'll...catch up with you later. But first, there's something I have to do. It's hard to--"

"Ashcroft?" said Maddie, with big brown eyes.

"Well, in a way, *yes*, that's part of it."

"I *thought* so, girl. Don't be too late!"

The Qwik-Ride pulled up. She waved at its driver, Mr. Hou.

And suddenly, she knew what to do.

As Madelyn rode away, Una straightened up. Moving down the sidewalk, she spotted the small sign for *Bennie Lee's* Chinese laundry.

Stepping inside, she was greeted by the Asian woman in charge.

"I'm sorry to impose, but do you...remember me?"

"*Sure* I do! You crazy lady, woke up in our dumpster. What can I--"

"I'm with the police and need a small favor. Could I just slip out the back? Someone's tailing me, and I--"

"Go already! Want no trouble. Have nice day!"

In a wall mirror, Una thought she spied 'Casper' hanging out with others at a Bus Stop across the street. Exiting *Bennie Lee's*, she cut through an alley, looped back inside a crowd using a busy cross-walk, and approached the Stop, minutes later, from behind--only to find it *empty*.

Curiously, there was a folded note taped on the seat marked *UNA*. She opened it and read:

You've missed me. My
foresight allows me to
anticipate your moves.

Tonight.
Hayden Planetarium,
11:00 P.M.

Una sighed. Not exactly what she had in mind. She pulled out her cell, dialing the number on the back of her Corn Maiden amulet.

***

Dinner at the *Moonlight Cafe* seemed like the perfect way to spend her final evening in New York. A star-filled sky twinkled over the Atlantic Ocean. Sipping from her wine glass, she smiled at Colin Ashcroft, as their eyes met. In many ways it reminded Una of the bizarre set of circumstances surrounding Flight 564 that first brought them together, so many years ago.

"You've got something on your mind," she said.

He grinned. "As a matter of fact, I do--but first, I must warn you, this information is *Classified*. Tell another living soul, and I'll have to--"

"Shoot me. I *get* it. So?"

He drew a long sip. "I just read a report, from the Pentagon. It turns out, the Chinese were watching us the whole time, to see how things would play out.

They knew all about DS-1769. Their official denials at the State Department regarding cyber breaches in New York did not change one important fact: they've got a few spy satellites of their *own*--big ones, too."

"And?"

"Apparently, officials in Beijing were huddled in deep shelters, aware of the missile countdown, ready to retaliate--with their finger on the button. We came *this* close to all-out war."

"Thank god, you found a way to stop it."

He silently raised a finger to his lips.

"That's just the thing," he whispered. "It wasn't *us*. A mysterious white craft, resembling a giant pearl appeared in orbit, just before the satellite was destroyed."

The Kachinas, she thought.

***

In spite of all her fears regarding crime in New York, Una could not resist the chance to meet 'Casper' face-to-face.

The Hayden Planetarium was part of *The American Museum of Natural History*. At precisely 11:00 PM she stood alone, waiting outside its well-lit entrance, even though a sign clearly read:

OPEN DAILY
10 AM - 5:45 PM

Mr. Hou had agreed to wait curbside, with his motor running.

After several minutes, 'Casper' appeared at the window, pointing to a side entrance. She followed him around to a smaller wooden door.

She found it unlocked, and stepped inside.

This way, he seemed to say, although she did not actually hear his voice. It was more of a thought in her mind, like that night in the alley.

Turning to her right, she climbed an old set of stairs. Everything around her seemed old; the doorknobs, the railings, the floors and walls. The Planetarium was apparently housed in a grandiose old building, and somehow, this gave Una comfort.

On the landing, she sensed dim light to her left and followed it through glass doors to a circular display room with exhibits containing things like moon rocks and antique telescopes and photos of distant galaxies, though it was too dark to read any of the signs that accompanied them.

She heard shuffles ahead from a winding staircase and sensed 'Casper' beckoning her to follow, up to the second floor.

A curved hallway with many doors reminded her of ancient *Palatkwapi*, in the Hopi cave, with its chambered design. Light flowed from a single open door. Stepping through it, she gazed upward in awe at the huge domed interior of a spherical theater.

Overhead, the "Hayden sphere" appeared to float in a 95-foot high glass box, a kind of "cosmic cathedral".

"It's designed to help people forget the presence of walls," she heard a voice, echoing all around her. "To help you imagine you're out in the open air, with only the sky overhead."

"Works for me!" she replied.

He approached, stepping softly, with a minimal smile.

She detected no eyebrows or lashes, over-sized black pupils in huge, almond-shaped blue eyes, a small nose, thin lips, light skin and blondish, short fuzzy hair. He seemed almost Scandinavian, dressed in gray janitorial overalls, which sagged as if they were too big for his narrow frame.

"I've been watching you," he said. "I...came to see you."

"Yes," she replied. "But I don't even--"

"Sure you do," he said, pointing to his CASPER nametag.

"But *how*?"

"It's a gift. Like I wrote in the note."

Something about his mannerisms, the way he looked at her so intensely, his gaze felt familiar, like that of a *brother*.

He seemed to be 'reading' her thoughts.

"Our fates are like...two paths in the wood, that merge into one. This world has so many problems. But the future will be better...for everyone."

"I don't understand," she said.

"There's...a *CHANGE* coming...difficult, but inevitable. You and I are part of it. Everything you've learned is all part...of...a process that leads to the future. At some point, in the future, it will end."

"When?" she asked.

"When the goal is achieved," he replied.

Una blinked, and he was gone.

36

BEYOND

Una had trouble sleeping over night. Although her exit from the Planetarium and return to the CATBRIER had been uneventful, she kept imagining otherwise in her dreams. There she found all the "Experiencers" from upstate New York gathered in the snow, waiting to confront her outside the secret hotel, wide-eyed and weary, demanding to know all about Casper.

Where's he from? they all asked. Why now? Why you? Are you part of the plan? To help us...or enslave us?

And she felt overwhelmed. So many lives had been disrupted, apparently turned upside down by alien abduction, and yet she, like so many of her cohorts in D.C. had completely ignored their accounts, dismissing it all as the product of delusion.

No more.

Una felt as if she'd taken another step away from childhood, away from the comfort of familiar surroundings, into the unknown.

As a child, she'd always believed in Sky People. But now, it seemed as if her view of life in the universe was suddenly expanding, from Kachinas to SAN-TOU-LONG to Casper's mysterious place of origin, all from somewhere out there--beyond the Earth.

Jack would understand.

But what about Maddie? Could she make the leap from "stars controlling our destiny" to forces at work beyond our comprehension, bringing people here from other planets--maybe not just now but for centuries, spanning the history of mankind, with various agendas--some to help us, some to harm us, and some to help themselves to Earthly resources without any regard for us whatsoever?

Una wasn't so sure.

It would take time to make sense of everything that had happened to her in Chinatown. What exactly did Casper mean about the future? What goal was he talking about? And what about Rufus? Would they ever see him again?

Somehow, she knew that the Hopi Rattle was the key. It had opened her eyes to another dimension. When she cried out for help, it made her voice heard...on the other side. It was like a compass, leading her toward Truth that could only be found on the Sacred Path.

She dared not part with it again.

LaGuardia Airport's "third world appearance" from ongoing construction efforts that had been dragging on for years reminded Madelyn of all the reasons why she dreaded a return trip to D.C.

"Hardly any place to sit or food to grab. It feels cramped, crowded, filthy and damp. Did you see the Ladies Room? Broken tiles and rusted sinks. What a disaster! They *claim* this'll all be complete by next year," she sighed. "I find that hard to believe!"

Una held up a copy of the *New York Times* with its latest headline:

AMBASSADOR'S WIFE MISSING

"She disappeared in plain sight. They're calling it a mystery. No details," she said, scanning the page. It would have to be part of her Field Report.

Maddie perked up.

"Nuan *did* have a real sense of style: clothes, hair and makeup. She seemed to love it here. Maybe she defected."

It's no mystery to me, Una thought, *Or anyone who was in Central Park!*

Just below it, a smaller headline appeared from the Beltway:

HEARINGS TO INVESTIGATE
GRID FAILURE

Madelyn rolled her eyes. "As if *that'll* do any good! No one has the fortitude to do what it takes.

All they want is someone to blame. In the end, nothing will come of it, and the truth will be obscured. We've seen it too many times!"

"You sound jaded," said Una.

"I guess coming home to New York made me realize what I left behind. I used to have so many hopes and dreams about living in a better world. I thought I could make a *difference*, but now..."

She paused to look up at *Departure Times*, then whipped out her cell phone, almost trembling.

"What is it?" asked Una.

Madelyn tried to catch her breath. "Well, my 'scope hasn't *exactly* been so good lately. No luck or romance of any kind. What's a girl to do?

"I'm not sure--"

"Well, I *just* realized...I forgot to check it today."
"So?"

"Our flight's been moved *up*. Well that's pretty much unheard of around here. Most people face delays of at *least* an hour. It's as if someone has *intervened* on our behalf, like a higher power. I just *have* to see what it says..."

Una paused to gaze around LaGuardia, patting the Hopi Rattle beneath her vest coat. She could not help but wonder about Casper, the alien-human hybrid, his purpose here on Earth, and when she might see him again. Then, glancing at her reflection in an airport mirror, she spied an amazing sight:

Casper stood,
behind her--as if he'd been there,
all along. In a matter of seconds, more
ghostly hybrids appeared, one by one,
materializing out of thin air, scattered
everywhere inside the airport, smiling
with thin lips, pale skin and
big almond eyes.

When she turned around to check, they were *gone.*

"Found it!" said Madelyn, holding up the screen of her cell phone:

> "PISCES : March may be
> demanding, making you feel
> stressed. Delays could make
> you anxious and annoyed.
> Manage yourself first. Stay
> level headed, have patience."

"I don't get it," she said. "What's *that* supposed to mean? Back to the same old routine?"

Una seemed distracted, reaching out, as Ashcroft emerged from an Airport Men's Room, wearing civvies, with his carry-on bag.

They held hands.

"Not *exactly*," she replied.

Her mind was filled with so many questions.

She did not know where to begin. But with Colin at her side, at least she would not have to face them...*alone*.

THE END

ABOUT THE AUTHORS

T.J. & **M.L. Wolf** joined forces in the field of Healthcare, exploring mutual interest in the work of UFO researchers like Budd Hopkins and movie directors like Steven Spielberg. The History Channel's *Ancient Aliens* became a focal point of their quest to uncover the truth regarding humanity's purpose and how it pertains to our future. Married over twenty years, they write speculative fiction and live in Boardman, Ohio with their six-pound Yorkie, who keeps the family in line.

Be sure to look for:

BEYOND THE WORLD

BOOK THREE

THE SURVIVAL TRILOGY

Coming to AMAZON in 2018

Made in the USA
Middletown, DE
10 January 2019